ONCE A MAN

Rick Moss

ONCE A MAN

A novel in three parts

RARE BIRD
LOS ANGELES, CALIF.

Other novels by Rick Moss:

Ebocloud
Tellers
Impossible Figures

To learn more:
rickmoss.art

THIS IS A GENUINE RARE BIRD BOOK

Rare Bird Books
6044 North Figueroa Street
Los Angeles, California 90042
rarebirdbooks.com

FIRST HARDCOVER EDITION

For more information, address:
Rare Bird Books Subsidiary Rights Department
6044 North Figueroa Street
Los Angeles, California 90042

Set in Minion Pro
Printed in the United States

Book Design: Rick Moss

10 9 8 7 6 5 4 3 2 1

Library of Congress Cataloging-in-Publication Data available upon request

Contents

Prologue / 9

Part 1 / 11

Part 2 / 85

Part 3 / 217

Prologue

Yes, Luna, a letter. Smirk if you must. With email gone, what else can I do? But it's good. Aldrin sees me with pen and paper. He could pick up worse habits. Unless I'm mistaken, the last time I wrote to you by hand was my Peru trip sophomore year. I remember my longing, if not my words. I'm sure you could recite my promises. How many have I broken? I'll make none now.

And yes, Aldrin knows I'm writing to you. He asks about you less often now, but still. Just earlier: Arms, can we visit Luna's family in Mex-io someday? I corrected him, although I suspect he was teasing: There is no longer a Mexico, per se, and Luna lost touch with her folks. He looked dejected, but then said: So I can call it what I like. How about Ex-ico?

That reads cuter than he came off. He's become a cocky eight-year-old. Yes, eight. All parents say childhood years race past, but they have no idea. My boy is quite normal. My boy is quite special. What parent doesn't think these things? I take cues from Ride, who manages Aldrin's advancements in stride. She keeps pace without divulging amazement. That's perfect for a big sister, right? Never look impressed, that's our Ride.

Were you here, you'd share Ride's cool. She inherited it from you, after all, as did Aldrin—the way you measure with your looks, how you hover like the moon.

Sorry, I miss you. It comes out in bad similes. It's true, though, as unsettling as it may sound, Aldrin has your stillness. And yet, in recent months, I see my anxiety emerging, as well. In this way, he and I grow closer.

I note other developments. Yesterday, Aldrin woke early and headed straight to the brook. Ride and I found him using limbs and stones to block the water. He'd managed to divert the flow over the bank to create a pool, flooding a small glade. This, I assure you, was not our suggestion. He said he woke with the idea. Ride got on his case. You'll swamp the roots of those beautiful elms, she told him. It's not good to mess with the habitat. Aldrin was unperturbed. Beavers do it, he said. For a reason, Ride countered. It went on.

How should I take this behavior? He devised his own test, I suspect to gauge our reaction. Taking such initiative—the temerity—it's concerning, right? Don't answer.

I'm proud of Aldrin, I confess. I believe you when you say you want no part of him. Nevertheless, it feels wrong you're not here to share the parenting with me. I can't feel unmarried. I'm barely half what parents should be. But you're present, despite your disavowal. You carry through in Ride and me. Aldrin senses you. I'm sorry.

Hell, I'd have refused this role too, but the alternative, as you know, terrifies me in ways that make fatherly jitters trivial. And as he grows, he grows on me, and so mingled with my wonder, with my love, is fear of what he may mature into—what he needs to become. Does every father fear his son's potential? I'm thinking no, not until it's too late.

Much more to relate. I'll write again soon.

Love always, regardless,
Arms

Part 1

This let me crave, since near your grove the road
To hell lies open, and the dark abode
Which Acheron surrounds, th' innavigable flood;
Conduct me thro' the regions void of light,
And lead me longing to my father's sight.

—*The Aeneid*, **Book VI by Virgil Translated by John Dryden**

DAY 1

This morning, for the first time, I left Black Hornet. I climbed over Boise Ridge into the world and kept going until I hit the trailhead at Five Mile Gulch. I walked for some time longer, and now here I rest, writing while there's still light.

I need to find Arms. I hope to find Ride as well, but that may have to wait.

At the top of the ridge, I paused before getting on my way. I sat with Gordon and rested against his sunny-hot back, his north side that looks out into the world. I felt the shifting breeze on my face, the stone behind. Gordon is the grandest boulder I know. I call him Gordon because he's full and low and has upper lumps like a bull napping in a meadow. Gordon is a good name for big things. Clark and Lori called their bull Gordon. Clark and Lori were farmers who lived nearby and the other two people I knew, but they've now gone as well.

With my back against him, Gordon and I hummed our low-note song. We passed the notes back and forth, three notes descending in thirds, then one rising a half step. It's off-putting, that half step. It's discomforting, and so comforting when we return to the three whole notes. Unease and ease.

On that ridge looking out into the world, I felt a twinge under my ribs, like eagerness and unease at odds. I will not know the boulders or the trails I come upon. I will see trees I've never seen and, with each new turn, unfamiliar things. I will see new people. If I simmer the roots of meadow salsify to make a tea, it may help settle this feeling. Arms showed me pages about plant species that live in Idaho, many outside Black Hornet. I hope to see many species and make use of them, maybe elk thistle, maybe Oregon grape. One of the real songs Arms taught me is Heard It Through A Grapevine. I hope to see a railroad.

Such a pleasure, writing in this unused notebook. I found it years ago, hidden on a bookshelf. Arms acted surprised. He made like it was mine, mine to keep, though I think he'd been saving it for himself. I was young, but I could write and did write every day. I asked if it was new. He said, New is hard to come by. Make do.

Hard to come by and make do were expressions Arms used.

The notebook's covers are scuffed and the edges rough. Inside, the lower margins are water stained, but all the pages are blank, page after page. Before Arms left, I filled three other notebooks, first from front to back, then back to front between the lines, then forward again around the margins in tight square spirals. After Arms left, I filled another, but this one I saved for today. It's whole and blank, so making do is easy.

Arms told Ride and me, Write every day to learn about yourselves. To learn about the world, read every day. Hear what others have to say. We had no books written by people who live now, but as I go into the world, I am sure to meet them. They may offer me their stories, and I can offer them these pages.

So if you are reading this, welcome. I write to learn about me, but I also write for you. And maybe someday, I'll sing it too.

How I like to sing! I know four real songs from the world, and I sing many things. It's nice to hear a voice out loud.

ARMS and the man I sing.

This is Virgil's opening sentence from The Aeneid, and I include it to welcome you. I make use of it. I draw courage from it. It gives me pride. Thank you, Virgil.

Arms never needed to ask for The Aeneid by name because it was our special book from before I can recall. When Arms would read me Virgil's first line, how could I not think it was written just for me? And yet Aeneas, Arms explained, was a man of war—ARMS of war.

So, no, Virgil's ARMS is not my Arms, but The Aeneid is ours, always our book.

Did Virgil sing? To hear his words in that way, how sweet that would be.

I carry our copy of The Aeneid next to my notebook and, to trade, many tinctures I've brewed and herbals I've dried. These things are weighty, and these things are necessary.

The sixth new moon of the year rose six nights ago, and so I'm now living my sixteenth year.

After descending the ridge, I followed a deer trail well into the afternoon. I saw no new people. I caught the sound of a scurrying doe about the size of Molly, but if it was her, she didn't know me outside of Black Hornet because off she ran. Or maybe my feet sound different out here, not knowing the trails.

Once I reached the Five Mile Gulch human-made trail and walked it for some time, I thought for sure, but still no new people. I did find a candy wrapper. Gummy Fire Cats. It smelled like a fruit, but I don't know which.

DAY 2

For breakfast today, I ate one and a half serviceberry cakes, leaving me with four and a half in my pack. I brewed my tea from the wild strawberry leaves I found by the stream. There should be some camas nearby, so I'll gather bulbs for dinner and for tomorrow. I'll also check the next fence line. That's where meadow salsify grows. They look like big, fluffy dandelions.

Arms did not find me in my dreams last night, but Ride was there. She showed me a trick on her bike, one wheel aloft, spinning slowly. We pedaled up roads of soft pebbles, Ride running circles around me, and next up a steep hill. My wheels lost hold in the dry soil, and I slipped back while Ride went airborne, hair flaming orange, surrounded by brown-gray birds, maybe starlings, maybe cowbirds.

With this morning's chill and misty drops, I expect again I'll see no one, but the rain is bound to break. Maybe later people will come out to walk in the sun.

Off I go. Today I hope to find newspapers as well.

I now know three people in the world: Jordan Kolowitz, Mel Chan, and Zoomoo. Also, I know Alice, who is here tonight, lying with me. I'm so full of new things, it will be hard to sleep. Mel Chan's garage smells bad from his truck's oil and gas. He gave me two blankets for the floor. I'm thinking, as a guest, I should stay in here to be polite and not outside where it smells right. And there's a light, so I can write about my day.

The sun did not break through early today as I'd hoped. It rained steadily all afternoon. Still no people on the Five Mile Gulch trail. My rain parka is too tight. If I can find some fabric, I'll open the back seam and add room.

I entered pine-sheltered woods. The trees had been planted long ago in straight rows, tall, respectful, swaying Douglas firs, not the hemlocks and yews of Black Hornet. I sang their song as best I could. Creaky sorrow. Not much beneath their dark cover, yet, though early in the season, I found blue chanterelles. Arms loves the gold chanterelles we find in Black Hornet. Blues are hard to come by.

The trail opened out into a broad meadow, human-made as well, cleared for a line of electricity power towers that stretched to the north, up and over some foothills, and south, down through a cleft and around a bend into a vale. At the base of the nearest tower, set in a big concrete post, an old sign read HIGH VOLTAGE. It was rusted scrawled with paint: MY NAME IS AI OVERLORD. LOOK ON MY WORKS. Around the next post farther up the hill, I found plenty of meadow salsify and rosehips too. I climbed, but the metal was coarse from corrosion, and I only got so high before my legs shook. Looking out toward the south beyond the bend, I saw over the cottonwoods that there was a road. I watched until my fingers hurt. I saw no people or cars.

I continued to the other side of the meadow where the trail cut downward into birch and then into the cottonwoods. It was well past noon and hard not to think about eating. Then, the path dropped into a down-sloping meadow. I could see the road ahead. The rain fell heavier, fat and solid, but the wind calmed. I found a small thicket of cedar on a hillside by the road and sat beneath it with the small bit of camas mash I'd brought from home. I chewed some of the rosehips, but with all the hiking and climbing, I was still hungry. It may have been eagerness-hunger. I opened Lori's cheese.

I was considering a second small chunk when I heard a truck crunching on the gravel from the east beyond the curve, its engine moaning from the weight it hauled. I have only known one truck, Clark's flatbed. This one was heavier, with tires that looked too big, raising it way above the road humps. The body was painted a red hardly different from the rust it tried to cover. It had a bed like Clark's but also a wood frame built to support a canvas cover that rocked with the dips in the road, the cover bulging and swaying under the full load.

It stopped when it got to me, and I could smell all sorts of truck things. The driver slid over far enough to put his head by the passenger window and asked me, You Lost Boy?

I misunderstood it in that way, having not heard a person's voice in some time and never one of the world. It sounded like he was looking for Lost Boy. He waited while I thought.

I said, I'm heading north but walked south when I saw this road. Would this road take me somewhere to buy newspapers?

This road can't, but I can, he said. Come on.

Inside, the driver's smell hit me, much like the short-style onion paste Arms used to smear on my chigger bites. Also, there was a grease odor that could have been old, cooked meat or farts.

The truck rocked back and then grumbled its way up the incline. We were off.

He wore an orange cap set back on his head so the brim nearly touched the roof. It bore a symbol formed from two or three intertwined letters that I failed to decipher. He said, I'm Jordan Kolowitz, but in a way that made it sound like a question. He looked at me and then the road and then looked again at different parts of me. I opened my pack to stow the cheese and knife.

Then he said, Goat?

This time it was clearly a question, but he didn't wait for me to think. He said, I'm looking to know a new source. My source, whom we can call Toby, did a disservice to the Twenny Niners. In fact, Toby's brother and him got into it bad with the Niners, and since then, not Toby nor his brother, whom we can call Sandy, have appeared at our meeting spot. It's been weeks. People couldn't get enough of Toby's Humboat, which is goat, which people love. That goat?

I cut him off a chunk.

He smelled it. When he took a bite, his face did a variety of things, causing his beard to wiggle this way and that.

Yes, it's goat, I said. I felt confident with my reply.

He raised his eyebrows and kept chewing. Somewhere, he said, if Toby and Sandy are gone as I imagine them to be, there's lots of goats full of milk. But we don't know where their place was 'cause they were clever that way. Were you to consider revealing your source, I can make it worth your while.

The only answer I could have given would have been a lie. Arms and Clark, in particular, always spotted my lies. Lori I think, too, but she would just change the subject.

I grabbed a folded-up newspaper near my feet. Is it okay if I read this? I said.

He shrugged, which seemed like yes.

It was the Idaho Courier, but it looked old.

Is today May 12, 2045? I asked him. He said, It's more like the second week in June 2046, maybe the third.

I checked for ads on the last two pages anyway, and sure enough, there was one for Cumae Insurance. Cumae is an important place name in The Aeneid. The tiny type at the bottom of the ad warned about all the things Cumae Insurance was not responsible for. That went on for ten lines. Then the wording became jumbled and the last four lines contained strings of letters that weren't words. I'd found the code Arms taught me to look for, but of course it was a year out of date, so useless to me now.

Looking for work? Jordan said. I can maybe use help offloading. If you don't trust green, I got elk jerky. And then he said, And if you can see your way to revealing your goat source, I can keep you on for tomorrow and the next day 'cause I'm heading into Boise. I'll need someone to watch the truck and help me load. But I can't have an employee who won't trust me with his source 'cause trust is a bedrock of an employee-employer relationship.

I explained I don't eat animal meat. He offered grape raisins instead, which I've eaten once and truly enjoyed. I also said, We'll see about the employment.

We'll see was an expression Arms would use whenever Ride asked if she could pierce her nose.

Sure, we'll see, said Jordan, which gave me assurance that he too understood. Then, he said, We'll be offloading at Mel Chan's. He added, Which, yes, is a store. But you won't find a job out this way in a newspaper, unless you're looking to get conscripted into the Guard. And, by the way, you should watch out for them showing up at Chan's. And for that matter, the Twenny Niners of which I was speaking, might make an appearance, or the Final Standines and, God forbid, the Free-For-Three, unless you're of that ilk already.

He took his foot off the accelerator until we were nearly at a standstill and looked my way.

I made a mistake then. I think the prospect of losing out on the grape raisins loosened my tongue. No, I'm not one of them, I told him, and also quoted Arms who says guns, rifles, violence, and other forms of armed resistance are self-defeating because they only serve to trigger violent interactions.

Jordan scratched under his beard and then got the truck rolling again. Who's Arms now? he said.

I could see changing the subject wouldn't work. I said, Arms is my dad. Short for Armstrong.

Okay then, he said. And you're called what?

Aldrin, I told him.

And that's when Jordan Kolowitz told me he grew up in the city of Chicago when it was still functioning. He seemed to take pride in his memories of such things as his family's brick home, his uncle's motorcycles, and of accompanying his father to work installing floor tiles in huge buildings. He once rode an elevator to the top of one of the tallest buildings on Earth.

I wanted to know more, but Jordan began doling out each bit of information like Ride's game of Truth or Dare, expecting details about me in return. I thought it best to pretend Chicago wasn't interesting.

We were quiet for some time. The rain clouds finally broke and revealed the sun lower than I'd expected. The road took a steep upward jog, and we turned northwest onto a length mostly paved, but Jordan still had to swerve this way and that to skirt bad spots.

The motion lulled me. I found the blurring brush on the roadside calming.

At a point, he asked, Are you singing? I was.

Then, as we came to a mound in the road, I looked out my window onto railroad tracks. We hopped over quickly, but I was able to see old rail cars sitting a ways down. I asked Jordan if he'd ever ridden on a railroad train. He had. It ran through the city of Chicago and climbed above the streets high enough to see into people's windows, people who lived or worked up in tall buildings. He said the train would then plunge underground, like a roller coaster, something he'd never ridden but had once seen operational. I told Jordan that Arms once described a roller coaster after using it as a metaphor.

Jordan asked me if Arms made the cheese. I said no and tried not to talk anymore.

We passed someone's house. It was set back among thick red cedars, so I couldn't make out if it was lived in. Then, when we turned onto another road, I saw six houses, all close by the roadside, some with cars, many with intact glass windows. Two kids, boys, played in front of one house. They had a pushcart. One boy was inside, the other rocked the cart and tried to dump him out. That was their game, one they likely invented. For Ride and me, inventing was as fun as playing, often more so.

Two more turns along the lane, and we came to Mel Chan's. His placard was hard to read. I could only make out GEN AL STORE, being that it was obscured by a hearty clump of black hawthorn, the berries of which are still yellow, weeks away from ripeness. I've seen pictures of stores, so I was expecting dresses or food behind windows and boards that told you how much things cost. Mel Chan's windows were covered with metal gridwork and planks.

Propping open the door to Mel Chan's was a big cushion chair occupied by a very small old woman. She sat in the sun, mending a shirt with needle and thread. Jordan called out, Mel? The old woman nodded to her left without looking up from her work.

Jordan drove in that direction around to the far side of the store building, passing under two poles supporting what was left of a blue-and-red sign. Some words were still readable: DIESEL and FOOD MART.

He got out and kicked at a wide metal door. After a few minutes and clanking noises, the door opened from the bottom up. It slid on rails and, as it rose, divided into sections that tilted to the horizontal and tucked away inside. Mel Chan was doing the pushing. Since I was by far the tallest present, I helped with the final heave.

Jordan and Mel Chan exchanged remarks about items Jordan had failed to procure. Jordan unbound his canvas tarp, then waved for me. Together, we uncovered the cargo, which included crates and grain bags. Mel Chan walked me inside his storage area and pointed out where each item was to go. Nothing was too heavy for me to carry myself, so Jordan left the unloading to me.

Jordan talked in whispers to Mel Chan, who seemed aggravated. Soon, they were laughing. Jordan said to me, Any more like you at home? And they laughed more. I laughed too, although I didn't fully understand.

Their conversation continued in this joking manner, and I tried my best to contribute while I finished offloading, but then I asked Mel Chan about newspapers and the laughing stopped. He said that, in exchange for doing some chores, he could give me not only today's Idaho Courier but tomorrow's Boise Voice, once delivered.

I told Jordan I would not be able to be his employee tomorrow. I apologized. Jordan accused me of holding out to give Mel Chan my goat source. I assured Jordan that was not my intention.

As he tied down his tarps, Jordan told me I'd have to find my grape raisins elsewhere, which seemed hurtful, given I'd done the work I promised. Mel Chan said I could find grape raisins in his store. That's when Jordan hopped down from the truck and got very close to Mel Chan. He told him he was being cavalier about protections. Mel Chan stood firm, hands on his hips. Jordan got into his truck and turned it around but, before leaving, let Mel Chan know that trust is the bedrock of any supplier-vendor relationship. And lastly, he said, The Standines are right about you people.

Mel Chan kept his eyes on Jordan's truck until it was gone from sight, then turned to go inside. He said, I can feed you first or you can do your chores. I said food. He said, Smart choice. Zoomoo's making mapo.

Zoomoo is Mel Chan's mother. She cooks in a room behind the store that has a sink, a stove, a small bed in the corner, and an indoor toilet in a closet. Mel Chan said Zoomoo has a nice house nearby where his sons and daughter live, but he's at the store most of the time and needs to sleep within hearing distance of his stockroom. He left the kitchen to take care of a customer in the store.

Zoomoo's shelves held jars and tins filled with herbs, syrups, oils, and spices, all labeled in a Chinese language. She chuckled when I asked if I could watch how she cooked. She stirred an oily red sauce with a smell so pungent it stung my nose. She said she'd used quail in her mapo, but preferred pork when they could get it. I explained about eating meat, so she began a new batch without. I knew some of the ingredients she worked with, but by their Idaho names. Others came from farther out in the world, like the soybeans she'd fermented into cakes.

Her wrinkles up close are a wonder. They cross, forming tiny patterns, making perfect turns around her features. They looked like a language that would, were I to learn it, explain how her life had gone. I said, I've never met anyone as old as you, to which she said, You sure know how to charm a girl.

Zoomoo's soy cake was smooth like pudding, and her sauce hit with a tang, soon overtaken by a burn, spreading and tingling the skin on my neck and cheeks. She gave me seconds and added rice, which was more delicate on the tongue than any I'd eaten.

In the room was a green plastic radio box. Zoomoo was listening to music from China, but not the region her people were from. The musical scale was different from the songs I know. I had fun trying to sing along, and I made Zoomoo laugh. On the kitchen wall hung an old photo of Zoomoo's parents on the farm they owned in California. It was taken, in her memory, during a happy time. But I was a kid, she said. Kids don't understand.

I carried bags of grain and cases of canned goods from the stockroom into the store. Mel Chan taught me how to stack things in ways that make the shelves look fuller. The grain barrels had high bottoms for that same reason. The store was clean and smelled of fresh lavender, onions, and mint, all of which filled baskets near the front. The Idaho Courier was also stacked by the front. Mel Chan put one to the side and patted it. When you're done, he said.

After chores, I stood in the sunshine, my back to the front doorpost, imagining how I might greet a customer or joke with the next delivery driver. The air was still and interrupted only by the house finches filling a tall hemlock. Chip, chipridip.

I took my newspaper to the kitchen and found Mel Chan sitting there, listening to the radio. A black dog with tan spots stood and greeted me. That's Alice. The radio played a conversation between two men speaking in a Chinese language. They spoke forcefully, but with occasional laughs, so the topic must not have been all that serious.

Mel Chan said Alice comes by late each day to accompany Zoomoo back to the house, then back again to stay the night with him at the store. He pointed to his cot and said, I've got a shotgun under there.

I asked if it was the Standines who gave him trouble. He said, Not so much. They talk shit about me to others. Once they wrote INFILTRATOR on my wall. They're too cowardly to come at me, but they try to get people around here riled up. The Twenny Niners, they get personal pleasure from doing damage, but they need my goods. One day, they'll get it in their heads to break in and take what they want. So here I am, waiting, every night. And then there's the Free-For-Three. Thank God they aren't interested in the valley area for now. They're on a mission, so there's no reasoning.

What would you do? I asked him. He said it's pointless to plan for some types of disasters, and the Free-For-Three showing up would be in that category.

We sat listening to the discussion on the radio. My Chinese is sketchy, Mel Chan said, and I rarely hear them say anything consequential. I'm not sure why I bother.

I told him that Arms would sometimes argue with Clark and Lori about the Chinese. Clark and Lori were raised in a time when Americans pledged themselves to America. They would say, The Chinese think they could run this country better than we can. Arms didn't have anything good to say to Clark and Lori about either government but would tell me that every people want the best for their own.

Mel Chan nodded. You don't have to defend the Chinese on my account, he said. I'm American. My family stopped being Chinese when they came here three generations ago.

Alice brought me a ragged rabbit doll, so I sat on the floor and held on while she sunk her teeth in and shook her head. I asked Mel Chan if he thought the Chinese could run things better than the American government. He said, There is no American government, just pathetic men with a weak grip on the past. They wish they knew what the Chinese know about control. But the joke's on them because Americans never could handle being controlled. That's why we're Americans.

And Chinese people can? I said. Mel Chan laughed. Well, he said, they like it when the electricity works and water flows from their faucets. Americans would rather live like lawless pigs.

I surrendered the rabbit to Alice. She laid it back at my ankles, so I tossed it for her.

I asked if control is why Americans didn't like artificial intelligence, and he said, Maybe, but the Chinese understood control for thousands of years before AI. And only fools blame America's problems on AI.

I asked him about a story that carried the biggest title on the front of the Idaho Courier. It said, Logan Denies Chi Ties. Mel Chan explained that Logan is the regent governor of South Idaho, meaning the Feds gave him the job. It used to be that governors were elected. Logan is a huge landowner and bargained with the Feds for even more land. In exchange, he does whatever the Feds need.

The article made it sound like Logan was working for the Chinese, not the Feds. I felt like Arms's advice about not trusting governments applied. Mel Chan agreed but also warned me not to believe anything the Idaho Courier writes. He said, When AI wrote all the articles, it was harder to tell where the lies were coming from. Thank God that's over with, but now the Secessionists own the Courier and their message is clear. They want to replace Logan with a governor willing to join up with Oregon and form a country, like Texana did. They invent all kinds of discrediting bullshit about Logan.

I asked if he thinks the Secessionists will win. Mel Chan said, They'd love to take Logan out, but he's rich enough to build his own army. Plus, he has the Standines in his pocket. So the best the Secessionists can do is make Logan look like a Chinese puppet, which is ironic because he's a puppet of the Feds. People have an easier time hating the Chinese than the Feds.

I found it all puzzling. Mel Chan smiled and said, We all have trouble keeping the players straight.

What confused me weren't the players, but that none of them were worthy of Mel Chan's trust, someone with a family to care for. I also thought, somehow none of these problems feel threatening to me, Ride, and Arms. I guess I imagine that all will be well again once we're back together, as if returning to Black Hornet would render all harmless.

Mel Chan told me to bed down in the storeroom but to sleep light because he half-expects Jordan Kolowitz will be back to pull something.

I laid the Courier out on the garage floor and flipped through each wide page, enjoying the still-crisp feel and the woody smell. The printed rows were orderly but spottily inked and disrupted by awkward mis-spacings. I could feel the touch of the people who made it and could see why Mel Chan was glad AI was no longer in control.

I found the ad on the inside back page, this time for Actium, an accounting company. As before, I found a long string of nonsense letters buried in the tiny print. I had the code. I left the ad intact in the paper as Arms taught me and copied the coded parts into my notebook. With luck, I'd find the cipher tomorrow in the Boise Voice.

I read more stories. One was about a water control station torn apart with a construction machine. The mayor of the nearby town credited the

Twenny Niners, who claim they fight for the rights of people denied water due to rationing. I couldn't tell if the mayor was angry or happy about the destruction, which seemed like it would make it harder, not easier, for people to get the water they need. The article seemed to support an accusation that a big farmer named Whitford was responsible. He's in a water battle with Logan.

Then, there was a story about a mother who sold a bodily organ, they wouldn't say which, because her two sons owed so much in taxes that the Feds threatened to conscript them into the Guard. She was jailed, not for the organ, but for bribing a Fed officer. There was also a cartoon about a robot, but I couldn't figure out why it was funny.

Alice scratched at the door. Now, she's lying next to me, her back curled against my ribs. I'll rest my head next to her and smell her instead of the old oil.

DAY 3

I'm waiting for the delivery of the Boise Voice, which Mel Chan says arrives around noon on Thursdays. It's past that now. I'm using the time to write.

Alice nuzzled me up before dawn. We took a walk, and as the sun came up, I spotted some mature wild ginger in among the ladyfern of a cedar grove. I also pulled up quite a few short-style onions. Alice led me to those no doubt because she smelled the marmots who'd been digging at them.

Zoomoo was happy with what we brought her. She knew how to find ginger, but not onions. I suggested she ask Alice, which was a joke, I guess between Alice and me. Zoomoo cooked me oats and that's when I got my grape raisins along with some toasted pine nuts, which together in the porridge were so delicious I don't have words.

Mel Chan was out with his truck, picking up from Sue's Grains and Feed because Sue's guy couldn't deliver today. I wanted to be useful, so I found a wrench and climbed up on the roof to see if I could correct the wind turbine. It was clearly not oriented properly. I had trouble with a rusted bolt but found a short length of iron pipe to put on the end of the wrench for leverage. I turned the assembly about fifteen degrees west and locked it back down.

I remember now that I dreamed of a coyote last night. I was trying to dismantle a computer but became frustrated. I removed panels and pulled at wires, which became tangled roots that, as I pulled, drew out animal parts. The coyote circled around and observed. He asked me to follow him out of Black Hornet, but I couldn't locate my bug-out pack. In the end, I did follow him, but I've forgotten the rest.

Risha and Blaze. That makes five people I know in the world. I hope to know Blaze for a long time, but may have seen the last of Risha, which is probably for the best.

I'll describe what happened today while the fire's high enough to throw light.

Mel Chan returned from Sue's with his grain about an hour after noon. Once I'd offloaded and organized the bags in the storeroom, I found him out front, standing with his arms crossed, eyes on the road. He told me Jordan Kolowitz had been to Sue's.

He had a guy named Lancaster along with him, said Mel Chan, who is a Twenny's belonger. They leaned hard on Sue not to sell to me anymore.

I asked Mel if Jordan was still offended by what I did. He shrugged and said, Sue doesn't normally take orders from Jordan, but she's got plenty to worry about without pissing off the Twenny's. She gave me what I needed, but maybe for the last time. And I expect when Jordan comes by next, he'll have one of those morons with him, and his prices will be a lot steeper.

I was wondering how to apologize for what seemed like my doing. Mel Chan asked me if I could stay on. He said, I can probably give you ten dollars a week some weeks. At least seven, and meals. We'll find a bed.

I asked about the Boise Voice delivery. He said, No, not this week if they're not here by now. But likely next.

I said, If you want me for violence, I don't know if I'd be any good at it.

The idea, he said, is it wouldn't come to that if you're standing there with me and Alice, a big kid like you, holding a bat. These people are ignorant cowards, you understand.

I asked about the rest of his family. Truth is, they're gone, he said. We lost Paul to sepsis. Sammy got conscripted last spring, and Janice said she and her boyfriend would circle back this year, but I'm not sure.

I didn't know the right way to say no. If I wait a week for the Boise Voice, I might not have the Idaho Courier that matches, and then I'd need to wait another week.

Mel Chan could see me struggling. He said, Look, clear your head this afternoon. I could maybe make sure it was ten every week.

I said it wasn't that and I'd let him know.

I'd seen a loon overhead swooping down east, so Alice and I headed that way, following a muddy stream bed to a marshy glen. There, I found a nice spread of wild strawberry. I took three plants, roots and all, and gathered some field mint as well. I sat for a while as Alice rooted around by the water. The loon didn't land, probably due to her.

In the quiet, I thought about a part of The Aeneid, the opening of Book V, when Aeneas is sailing off from Carthage and turns back to see the funeral pyre burning for the woman he loved.

Then, casting back his eyes, with dire amaze,
Sees on the Punic shore the mounting blaze.
The cause unknown; yet his presaging mind
The fate of Dido from the fire divin'd.

Aeneas left when he realized his captivation with Dido had distracted him from his mission. Dido, in her grief, threw herself from a cliff.

I found Zoomoo and Mel Chan eating in the kitchen. Zoomoo stood to get me a plate. I said, I don't think I can stay on like you asked, so you don't have to feed me.

I laid out the foraging on her table and explained how I brew my favorite tea from two parts wild strawberry leaves and one part field mint. I also explained that the mint in a tincture concentrate is good for sore joints, which I know trouble her.

Zoomoo pushed me into a chair and gave me Choy Sum from her garden, cooked with the onion and ginger I'd given her earlier.

I would like to come back and help you out, I told Mel Chan, but I don't think I should promise. I left Black Hornet because I have something important to do for my family.

Mel Chan waved his hand.

I also left them a bottle, extract of yarrow, which I told them stops bleeding and is a good disinfectant. Zoomoo looked uneasy. Maybe she thought I expected violence to come their way, and yes, maybe that was in my thoughts, along with the sepsis that took her grandson.

Mel Chan gave me four dollars. On an old map hanging in the storeroom, he traced the way to Rosie Springs, where I'd find a pharmacy that sells newspapers.

If you're set on this, he said, you should get going while there's daylight.

Mel Chan held onto Alice, so she wouldn't follow. I took a shortcut over a wooded hill by way of an old logging trail and came to a southeast-bound paved lane winding along beside a creek. With all the twists and turns, I could see it would take most of tomorrow to walk to Rosie Springs. The newspapers could all be gone by then. I've been without Arms for so long, I'm not sure why waiting a week or two feels intolerable. Maybe it's that I'm seeing dangers in the world and, for the first time, fear for him.

A car and three trucks passed within the first hour, and the only one heading my way ignored my thumb. Then, Risha stopped. She had a big yellow car with a back cargo space stuffed with clothing. Most of the back seat was taken up by clothes, too, all hanging from a rack she'd rigged. Most were brightly colored dresses in flower patterns.

She is what people call a redhead. Her hair was gathered up in a bunch, but some had come loose, some of it gray. She wore a pink, checked shirt with no sleeves. Her upper arms had fat that wobbled when she turned the wheel, more fat than Lori, and she had a bigger chest too.

Risha smiled a lot and called me sweetie. She talked more and faster than anyone I knew. She talked about her thriving business selling clothes, which she did door-to-door and at market days in towns all over Southern Idaho. She got her supplies from stores in Boise, clothes the store had given up trying to sell. Once a year, she went all the way to Portland to get women's shoes. I could see she enjoyed talking about work, so I asked why she thought she could sell the same dress a store couldn't, and she said rural women had different tastes.

Risha asked if there were women in my life who might like a summer dress because she had some lovely calicos. I said, No, but thank you. She squinted at me and asked, Are you out here all on your own, sweetie? I said, Yes, but I've been on my own for quite some time.

To change the subject, I asked if she had a parka in my size, without considering how I might buy it. She said, No, but I do have some T-shirts that might fit you.

And then she asked, Are you on your way home? Where is it you're from exactly? Does your family know where you are?

Evading these questions would be hard. Arms always stressed that Black Hornet was our special place that could only stay that way if we kept it to ourselves. I thought it might be best to get out of the car but couldn't come up with a reason.

I told Risha I was on my way to see family, which was true enough. I also implied Clark and Lori were around if I needed them, which was no longer true. Regardless, it was a mistake to pique Risha's curiosity.

She chewed her lip. So, Lori, she said, would that be Lori Macomber up in Cascade by any chance? I can't recall her husband's name.

I asked if she had any spare fabric I could use to widen my parka, and we talked about sewing and mending, so that worked for a while. Then, she wanted to know if my mother taught me to sew, and I said, No, Lori, since I'd already mentioned her, even though it was really Arms. I couldn't safely talk about Arms. Ride could make a whole outfit for herself, but I didn't want her asking about Ride either.

By this time, we were out of the hills and into the broadest valley I had yet seen. The road ran right through the middle, so I could see far in all directions. Most was cultivated with cattle feed growing in rows that narrowed to nothing at the horizon. Far off, I could see poultry houses, like Clark's, but much longer.

With my clear view, I spotted the crossroads from a distance out. Someone was there. As we approached, I thought, here's a solution to Risha's questioning. It was an old man, very thin, leaning on a crooked STOP sign. He wore a floppy hat under the hard sun and a long-sleeve blue shirt.

Before we'd come to a full stop, I hopped out to give him a hand. I could hear Risha struggling to get her words out. I opened the backseat door and helped him with his pack. By compressing the dresses on the rack, I was able to clear enough room.

He said, Well, it's rare one meets with this quality of service. I laughed.

Risha scolded me. You should not take it upon yourself to handle my merchandise, she said. I apologized, then I told him that Risha sold clothes to women all over Southern Idaho. Maybe he had a woman in his life? I thought this would get their conversation off to a good start. It didn't.

Risha asked him what he was doing so far from town, to which he replied it was a lifestyle choice. Risha then asked him if he was in trouble with the law. He said, No law that I recognize. Risha said, We're not asking people like you to recognize laws, just to follow them. He laughed in an annoyed way and said, Who's we, and who do you imagine are my people? And Risha said, People like you who got what was coming to them down in Texana, and people like me who still believe in this country.

Things then happened rapidly. The old man's temper snapped. He screamed at Risha, stabbing at the air between them. Risha raised her voice to drown him out, twisting back, swatting at his pointer finger. A trucker approaching from ahead blew his horn because we'd veered out of our lane. That shocked Risha into yanking the car to the roadside. She braked so hard I felt the old man collapse against the back of my seat.

I reached over to Risha because she was having trouble breathing, but I guess she took it wrong and threw her arm out. I ducked, but she caught me solid in the ear, hard enough that my head rang. Behind me, I heard the door open. I turned to see the old man crawling out onto the ground, pulling his pack behind. When I turned back, Risha's pistol was in my face. Her hand shook, and she made a whiny, spluttery sound.

I grabbed my pack and was out of the car without a thought otherwise. Risha took off with my door still open, her tires slinging gravel. A second later, we heard her gun go off. Her car swerved and slowed, then returned to the proper side of the road and off she went.

The old man shook his head and laughed. I pulled out my canteen and gulped at it hard before remembering my manners. Just feeling his steady hand accept the bottle calmed me. Seconds earlier, he'd been furious, but standing there, he was like a windless day.

We got right to talking about our best options, as if we'd been partners all along. With only an hour left of daylight, we agreed the chances of getting a ride into town were slim. There was also his hip, which he said got aggravated when he'd rolled out of the car.

We walked south toward the closest stand of trees. I hung his pack from the front of me and led the way. He kept a hand on my backpack for support as we worked our way through shoulder-high barley, chatting all the while, I think, to keep his mind off his pain.

People, he said, never consider how fortunate they are to be symmetrical. So much of our surviving, playing, loving, and thriving depends on the dual and balanced nature of our eyes, our lungs and, in particular, our legs. Two-legged mobility and bi-manual dexterity are a godsend. Plus, it doesn't hurt the species to have spares. Gonads are a prime example. Scientists will tell you there is a genetic bias toward symmetry, from the simplest biological forms up to crabs, birds, and people.

Why? Years ago, he said, scientists asked an AI to randomly build models of protein structures. It came up with thirteen million varieties, but only five were symmetrical. When they asked the AI to try again, this time basing its structures on genetic code, it made symmetrical models one out of every three times. That's because it's much less complicated to repeat a simple thing. Nature takes the simplest route rather than odd shapes. Plus, symmetrical creatures tend to reproduce and survive easier, and that's why…

He tapped my backpack. I said, That's why we're symmetrical.

He gave me a double-tap of approval.

But then, he said, one of your hip sockets starts wearing down or you get numbness all the time in your left damn hand. That's when it dawns on you how lucky you were when you were symmetrical.

With him tugging me down on my right side as he walked behind, I understood perfectly.

By the time we reached our camping spot, he was in sore need of rest. We entered a nice grove of alders set on a stream-side slope. He found a seat on a fallen tree trunk. I yanked the surrounding snow brambles and thimbleberry to clear room, then gathered kindling and got a fire underway.

He offered to share a couple of cans of something and an egg, but I said he should hold onto those. While he stoked the embers, I explored the stream bed. There was no end of cattail, so I cut some of their tender shoots and brought them back. I gave him a sharp blade and showed him how to peel the bark to get to the insides.

It wasn't until I sat with him to prepare the meal that we shook and introduced ourselves properly. His name is Blaze. He was born Charles, in Maryland, which is on the far coast by the Atlantic Ocean. It seems that, when Blaze was a few years younger than I am now, he brought home a poor grade report from school. His father laughed at the teacher's note that said Charles was too blasé about his studies. His father understood that Charles's attitude came from boredom. While they were talking it out, the younger brother, James, read the report out loud and mispronounced blasé. The next morning, when his dad dropped Charles off at school, he said, Off you go, Blaze. Light a fire.

It might be hard to think of a personality that's both blasé and ablaze, but that's him.

As we talked, Blaze grew more curious about me and, again, I was dealing with the decision to confide in someone. Arms always warned our situation demanded we trust no one. Our situation changed when Arms and Ride and Clark and Lori left Black Hornet, but I couldn't help feeling cautious.

Blaze asked how I'd learned about edible plants. I revealed that Arms knew all about indigenous species and described how he would drill me on my plant identifications.

Arms is your father? Blaze said, not needing an answer.

We were quiet. Katydids chirped. The cooling late-day air carried mud smells up from the creek. I could see Blaze's mind working.

He said, So Arms is a survivalist? Which I think was meant to gauge my reaction. I heard myself repeating Arms's words: Survivalism is selfishness—hoarding and arming up to stay alive, even at the expense of your neighbors. No, I said, Arms is a botanist. He taught us how and when to take, how much to take, ways to take that wouldn't do damage. It's not just for our survival, it's for the wildlife and our neighbors.

I worked at peeling a fresh pile of camas roots I'd found on the far bank. The sun was setting, throwing a warm light across things. Blaze said,

And round the keel with faces pale,
Dark faces pale against the rosy flame,
The mild-eyed melancholy Lotos-eaters came.

Which I recognized, being one of our favorites. I assured him camas was not a narcotic. Blaze drew his head back. A backwoods boy who knows Tennyson, he said. Your father has done you a good service. And what did he teach you about Apollo?

Apollo, I said, directed the prophecies that sent Aeneas on his path.

Blaze laughed. The Aeneid as well. But I was referring to the moon missions. Aldrin, Armstrong—any more astronauts at home?

There was Ride, but to explain our names would mean talking about Mom and our move to Black Hornet, details I'm unclear on. I started mashing the camas and onions with enough noise to break from the topic.

As we cooked and ate, I tried to be the one asking questions, which wasn't hard, since Blaze enjoyed talking about anything I brought up. I wasn't used to that. It's not that Arms hid the truth from Ride and me, but there were lots of topics he avoided.

At times growing up, I'd push Arms for answers he refused to give, leading to arguments, some made worse with my tears. But Arms knew enough about our immediate world in Black Hornet to keep us amazed. He made sure Ride and I were forever intrigued. We'd push through chores and lessons so we could go out to play. I remember how turning seasons brought changes to the woods, in the way plants went through their stages, in how animals responded to the weather. We named our favorite things, made them our friends, wrote them songs. Even indoors in winter months we kept busy, rereading books, stories that inspired our games. I didn't consider why we lived there. Black Hornet was full and everything made sense.

As I learn more from the new people I meet and what they face in the world, I wonder if Arms was ashamed of his earlier life. He taught us about the way the natural order works. Nothing is more assuring than things working like they should. Maybe he didn't want to ruin that feeling with the ugliness of things in the world that just make no sense.

Blaze likes to talk about food, in particular the wonderful dishes his wife, Amina, cooked in clay pots. She was from Morocco, and they'd met when he worked for the government in a country near there. They married and raised a family in Boston, but Amina died and he'd lived alone for years. I asked if he left his home because he was sad about his wife.

No, he said, I took off because AIR SS put me out of work, and Boston became a lost cause.

I knew Blaze was talking about one of the AI Routs. When I was a kid, Arms told me the routs were like battles between the government and AI. He said the AIs got out of control and had to be shut down, but he never explained more.

I was living my life going from one line to another, Blaze said, waiting for groceries or for batteries, or paying my electric bill. At least, in lines, you were with people, but they stopped caring to talk. People I knew avoided me in the neighborhood. They boarded their windows. And then there were the damn guns. When one of the AIRs hit—can't recall which one—it rendered the police department's tech useless. The cops panicked. They shot at the first sign of trouble, people shot back. Fear and stupidity egging each other on.

One day, he said, after a horrifying shootout down my block, I packed some things and started out. I figured I'd go to the mountains 'til things cooled down, but along the way, in every town…I don't know, I thought I knew the worst side of people, but public beatings, schools on fire, parents acting insane and endangering their kids…well, all I could do was keep going.

Blaze's chin was on his chest. He took his hat off and rubbed his bald spot. But yes, he said after a bit, I think about Amina and our years together. She doesn't make me sad, though. She was so lovely. Thoughts of her get me through the day. Our daughter and her family lived in a town near Columbus, but when I got there, they were gone.

I asked Blaze if he thought the government was right to destroy all the AIs.

It was the only way, he said. By the time AIR SS happened, AI had already gone too far. AI startups steamrolled through the government's attempts at regulation. But, hell, they couldn't control the growth. The programs were doubling in sophistication every month. And the AIs learned self-preservation. They dug in and were all too willing to snap back. When that happened at Social Security…well, it wasn't like those government numbskulls could outthink AI, so they went nuclear on it.

I asked what he meant by Social Security.

Well, you understand, Blaze said, that Social Security was there to help folks, but it ran out of funds. The bureaucrats were staring down impossible decisions on who to send money to. So they put the AIs to work making those calls. AIs, we soon learned, are not shy about snooping into people's lives.

By reading the Internet? I asked.

Yes, he said, the AIs could pull details from your insurance and your bank, your phone, from street cameras, health trackers, hospitals, car computers, TVs, and stereos…

Blaze went on listing all kinds of electronics people relied on for every thought and desire. The AIs could scoop up all there was to know about everything anyone did, felt, or believed.

So, said Blaze, the AI that ran Social Security started cutting people off, people in need. First it eliminated the oldest, the terminally ill, the young ones who had poor chances of being productive in society. When people protested, the AI turned defensive. It cut off people who voted for candidates who wanted to legislate against AI.

Then, Blaze said, the people fought back, and of course, the weapon of choice was AI. There were AI apps that could build hundreds of websites instantly and write thousands of articles condemning Social Security's monstrous AI. These AIs concocted evil myths about what was happening at the agency.

On AIR SS day, said Blaze, we followed the crowds heading to the local Social Security headquarters. Things got ugly. Mobs threw bottles and pushed at the doors. The building's alarms sounded. Office workers poured out. The temperature inside was boiling, they said, and alarms were screeching. Seems the AI forced the people out.

So, is that the day the government turned off AI? I asked.

Not the government, Blaze said. Activist hackers took Social Security down. Other things too—subways and buses, electrical grids. It took weeks to restore the basics. The government watchdogs played no part, but politicians laid claim to the take-down. They called it an AI Rout because it made them sound like the victors, but it was a retreat. We couldn't control the future, so we tried to take a step back from progress. When the really big AIRs hit, it took us back a hundred years.

We were on our bedrolls. Blaze had his hands behind his head, checking out Ursa Minor in the gap between the alders. I was thinking that I should probably not mention that Arms once used AI for his science work. Arms would say his job was teaching the AI about botany, all this before the AIRs and before we moved to Black Hornet. Since Arms never talked about it, I guess maybe his job was part of his shame.

Today ended well. Ease followed unease. Wondering what happened in Risha's car, I asked, What was that talk about Texana? But Blaze's mouth was hanging open, letting out a soft snore.

And now that I've gotten the day's events down, I'm heading there myself.

DAY 4

Blaze is down in the stream. I can hear him moaning. Damn cold, damn cold, damn cold, damn cold.

But I think the water should help numb his hip so we can be on our way. I have some stinging nettles brewing over the fire. When I asked if he'd drink tea, Blaze said, God, how I miss coffee. I can overlook a lot, but coffee is a terrible loss.

I lay awake before the sun today with the questions in my head, like moths, chasing each other around in circles. I was still sleep-foggy when Blaze asked what I wanted in Rosie Springs, so I told him, and then he asked what I wanted with the Boise Voice. I could see his questions were coming from a place of crankiness. He mumbled something about finding trouble in small towns, which is when I recommended his morning bath.

Tea's ready. I'll see if I can get this into him for his joint pain, though Arms would say, careful with old people because it can slow the heart.

Much to record tonight. Much of the details I may need to fill in later because things came at us fast. I saw so many people. Most of them I had no proper introduction to or clue why they behaved the way they did.

There was Jasper and Hedron among the Standines in the truck. Then there was the guy Blaze confronted, plus his boys and all the townspeople who gathered around. I also met the pharmacy man, Majid, who had a copy of the Boise Voice.

After Blaze's incident late today, I kept moving until I'd hiked deep enough into the densest stand of lodgepole pine I could find. As disturbed as I felt, I got a small fire going and took out The Aeneid, the Boise Voice, and my notes. I've done my deciphering, and I feel like I've made progress. Here in this deep glen tonight, maybe I'll feel safe enough to close my eyes.

I know I need to keep on, but I'm worried about Blaze. Arms said the gods in our book are meant as stand-ins for the impulses in our own heads. Blaze's impulses do seem to have personalities of their own. Mine don't speak to me clearly. I can't wait for a sign from a god, like Aeneas had. I can't visit with the Sibyl in a cave and ask if I should keep searching. I wish Alice was with me tonight to lie with her back curled to mine.

I think Blaze knew traveling with me would lead to trouble. After he'd bathed this morning, I waited while he warmed by the fire. He drank the tea down with a grimace. I'm sure he could see I was itching to go, packed and ready. He offered to meet me in town if I wanted to get there faster than he could move, but I didn't feel right about that. He took some time to move his bowels, and then we got going.

I convinced Blaze that we should cut forward through the woods rather than backtrack. It was difficult for him, but it saved him steps in the long run. When we found the road, Blaze said, If I push this hip further today, I'll be laid up for days.

So, it was hitch or make camp again. I scouted the road ahead around the bend and convinced him to press on to a crossroads about a half mile onward. He took a seat there with nothing but his floppy hat for cover.

We saw no cars. With time to kill, he questioned me again about the Boise Voice.

You realize, he said, none of these rags are like they once were.

He explained that when a Rout hit media—AIR ME—newspapers nearly vanished. All papers, he said, used to be on the Internet and, eventually, AIs ran them all. A paper's AI would check out everything you'd read on the Internet and shopped for or looked at. From that, it would custom write stories to keep you happy or pissed off.

Imagine, Blaze said, that every Boise Voice reader was getting his own version. Maybe your neighbors were being told to think like you, maybe the opposite.

Why would the AI want to piss us off? I asked.

To get you to buy something, he said, or vote for or against someone. Maybe the AI wanted you to think the government was going to cut your water rights or take away your guns. The AI knew you, so it knew what pissed you off. And pissed-off people are easily manipulated.

Couldn't the government make papers tell the truth? I asked him.

The government didn't want the truth, he said, but they damn sure wanted control over what passed as the truth.

Blaze talked about President Regis who got elected a few months after AIR SS. He promised to clamp down on the AIs, especially in media. In practice, he only went after the media outlets that opposed him, but his threats triggered the AIs' defenses. They turned on him.

Before Regis could revoke the licenses of the big media companies, Blaze said, the AIs infiltrated the FCC and the FBI, but they didn't stop there. Within hours, AIs were grabbing control away from banking, healthcare, and even the military.

So, I said, on AIR ME day, the AIs took over the government?

We were a heartbeat away, Blaze said.

He explained how President Regis sent Guard military out to take over the news media offices and arrest management, but that was pointless. The AIs were operating on their own throughout the government. The army had to turn the Internet off.

For a few days, Blaze said, we heard that the Guard was blowing up server farms, willy-nilly. The Internet is hard to kill, but even Regis and his brutes were able to cripple it fast. From what we heard, the whole planet went dark within a week—phones, electric, water, mass transit, everything.

That was AIR ME, Blaze said, and lord knows you were among the fortunate ones if you had a self-sufficient home and a father teaching you how to survive.

But there's still an Internet, right? I said.

Run by pirates in dark spaces, Blaze said.

We split a serviceberry cake. Blaze said he was impressed with my baking, which was a joke. I checked the area for some fresh ones but only came up with a handful of sour chokecherries. I sang a whole song—Looking Out My Backdoor. Blaze clapped along but wasn't familiar. I sang You Are the Sunshine of My Life, which he did know, though with different lyrics. We were halfway through when we heard people coming.

Their shouting and rude laughter reached us first. Then, when it cleared the rise about a quarter mile down, we caught sight of a heavy, gray and green truck, like ones armies use. I had my thumb out. Blaze looked around, maybe for a place to take cover.

He blew out a breath. Aldrin, my boy, he said, you could run, but that'd just set them off. Try not to say anything. If you must, say something they want to hear.

I asked if they were Standines. Blaze said, Likely yes. Possibly worse.

The truck ran loud, chugging out a burnt oil smell. Metal grates obscured the front windows to the point that I wondered how anyone could see out. They'd painted FREE TO DEATH on the passenger door overtop a red predator bird holding a rifle in bloody claws. On the rear panel under the cargo area, it read 4EVER, NOT BACK!

I could see a woman and two men standing in back. Two others, I soon learned, were on the other side of the load, a big mechanical thing draped with canvas tarp. I took reassurance from how unsurprised Blaze seemed by their looks—their rifles, the angry-looking way they'd chopped and shaved their hair, the leather straps, zippers, and chains.

The woman had the biggest firearm. One of her breasts was exposed and inked with the face of a screaming woman, which I'm guessing from the tangled snake hair was Medusa or one of her Gorgon sisters. She smiled at me with one side of her mouth, unlatched the drop gate, and then stepped back to watch me boost Blaze onto the bed.

She nodded for us to sit. There was just room enough between some metal crates. I helped Blaze ease himself down.

Ain't you a pair? she said but squinting at me like she didn't care.

Thank you, I said. Blaze tapped me on the ankle with his boot. He left his toe resting on top of mine.

The truck started off. The ride was rough. The woman backed up to the opposite side where she could hold a railing. She had to shout across to be heard by the big guy standing by us. I gathered from their conversation that their names were Hedron and Jasper. He was beefier than the other men, though not as tall as me. He had earrings and other dangling metal pinned to him all over. He looked down at me overtop the crates. Nobody seemed interested in Blaze.

I gathered we'd interrupted an argument Jasper was having with Hedron because they were soon back into it. The dispute seemed to be about their love relationships, but other things as well.

Jasper shouted in a hollow rasp over the engine noise. So that's what you're calling acceptable? he said. Fucking Taylor's cunt?

Acceptable. Enjoyable, said Hedron.

I can fuck you right, Hedron, if you want to get done right, said somebody on the other side, behind the cargo.

Hedron spat on the truck bed next to her. You wouldn't know which end to use, she said to him.

Fuck you better than that bitch, he said. Hedron pulled out a knife and asked him if he wanted a trim.

Jasper opened a candy bar using his teeth because he had a hand dedicated to his rifle. Just sayin', he said, Taylor would love to know where we store our shit, and you women do like to waggle your tongues, even when not employed as such for fucking purposes.

It went on for some time. Blaze, I could tell, was fine with anything that would keep them occupied with themselves.

Eventually, Jasper seemed to have gotten what he wanted from the conversation. He looked my way.

What about you? he said. What you got to say?

I failed to understand the question, which was disconcerting because, since that first day with Jordan Kolowitz, I'd had little problem. Blaze was pressing down on my toe. He said to Jasper, We're grateful for the lift.

Jasper addressed me again. A lift to Rosie Springs, I take it?

That would be much appreciated, said Blaze.

Jasper, eyes still on me, said, Can't talk, Stretch? You stupid?

Blaze pressed down harder on my foot. He said, The boy's kind of…

Maybe you don't like me, that it, Stretch? Jasper said, chewing on his gummy candy. You don't look affiliated. You affiliated?

Blaze said, Look, he's…

Jasper swung his rifle and clinked the rail near Blaze's temple. This time, he looked at Blaze. I will talk to you if I want to talk to you, he said.

Blaze raised his eyebrows at me, under the brim of his hat. I did the only thing that made sense, even though it also occurred to me being sensible may not work.

I stood and extended my hand to Jasper. He shook. The guy behind him and Hedron shook with me too.

I said, No, I'm not.

Not what? Jasper said.

I told him I wasn't affiliated, but given that I was their guest, I was happy to listen to what being affiliated meant to them.

Blaze grumbled.

They laughed. Hedron said, Go ahead, Jasper. Tell the kid why he needs to get stamped in.

Jasper accepted the challenge, but it was hard to get his full meaning because the others interrupted with corrections and opposing views. For example, when Jasper said nobody had a right to live in Southern Idaho who wasn't willing to defend it against the Chinese and Canuck sympathizers, a guy on Hedron's side of the truck said, You're asking the boy 'bout foreign threats when he's got a goddamn domestic one as a traveling companion? Jasper and Blaze exchanged looks. Jasper said back at the man, This ain't Texana and I got an eighth proud African blood in me, so you should shut the fuck up, which prompted Hedron to walk over and sniff Jasper.

It was confusing. I sat back down. They argued on. A couple of times, I put a hand on Blaze's shoulder when I saw him tensing up over ugliness directed his way. Jasper started punctuating his shouts with shoves. He and two other men were soon snatching at each other's weapons. Jasper and another guy fell to the truck bed at our feet, wrestling for a hold on each other's piercings.

The driver pulled over, likely due to the pounding. Hedron hopped around the wrestlers, kicking anyone looking vulnerable. As the driver worked to break up the fight, Blaze elbowed me. I helped him down to the road and we walked away without a fuss.

Turns out we'd landed within an easy walk of Rosie Springs. I asked Blaze about Canuck sympathizers, stamping in, and other terminology, but he only laughed. He said, Aldrin, your questions are dangerous. Just one set that whole truckload at each other's throats.

The pharmacy building had an engraved stone that read United States Post Office, but I couldn't find any other hints of its past. Blaze settled onto a shady bench while I checked for the newspaper. Majid, the pharmacist, was busy with an elderly woman who held a cat so close to her I was worried for its safety. I looked through the items he sold in his store. I saw rain gear and a flashlight that would have been nice to have, but I was only wishing. I smiled at the old woman as she passed me on the way out, but she squeezed the cat harder and picked up her pace.

I said hi to Majid and shook his hand, thinking that had served well so far. I asked about this week's Boise Voice. He said it was a monthly now and pulled a copy off the rack behind his counter. Sixteen Fed dollars and fifty, he said. Anything else?

I pulled some tinctures from my pack. I'd labeled them with red ink: Echinacea/Elderberry, Valerian/Elderberry, and Yarrow. Majid asked where I got them, and I thought he meant the plants, so I said something vague about them being local, which made him look at me in a suspicious way. Then I explained that I'd made them myself, which got him curious. We talked for a while about rendering, concentration, and so forth. I gave him the scientific names for the plants, which may have sounded like bragging, but he smiled and asked if I had a big supply.

No, I said, but I need the newspaper so I'm willing to give them up if you want them. Majid pushed the paper into my hands and picked yarrow for payment. You hold on to the others, he said, I'll be burning these extra newspapers for fuel come next week.

I thanked him and asked if he had any coffee made. He agreed to accept the Valerian/Elderberry in exchange, which is how I got Blaze his first cup in months. Blaze said it wasn't real, but it was very fine, regardless.

We shared the coffee outside the pharmacy and then headed for a spigot by the feed store where Majid said we could refill our canteens. Blaze surprised me by insisting that we head back to last night's camping spot by the creek. He was impatient with me, saying he'd suffered enough of my adventurousness for one day.

I told him I'd prefer a spot nearby where I could read my paper, which got me a reproachful look and some other comments that didn't make sense. He seemed uncomfortable and plodded on ahead. I tried to impress, without going into detail, how important the paper was, but he didn't hear. He was intent on a family walking our way.

Two boys chased each other with make believe guns—pow, pow, pow—one using his finger, the other a stick. Their father goaded them on, laughing. Just as we reached them, the boys screeched and fell to the ground, jerking their legs in final gasps. I killed you, idiot! No, I killed you! The father howled, head back, and that's when Blaze went for the man's sidearm.

Blaze shook the gun at him. This is what you teach? he said to him. This is what you think a father does for his children?

And without waiting for an answer, Blaze cocked and fired into the man's thigh.

I tripped backward. One of the boys must have lurched in the same direction because he wound up under me.

Blaze's voice was calm. Well, look at that, how easily an accident can occur with a firearm. Maybe children shouldn't be exposed.

He went on with his lecturing. I pulled the kid to his feet and looked around for the other. The father was on his back, his pant leg heavy with dark blood. He rocked and squealed, squeezing down on his wound. The second boy appeared from behind a stack of firewood and ran to his dad. I could see local people hurrying over.

Blaze surrendered the gun to me without protest, his entire being directed at scolding the man. I tossed it into the underbrush off the side of the road and turned Blaze away by the shoulders. He resisted while finishing a thought about the downfall of civility but then relented. I pulled him back in the direction of the pharmacy and away from the oncoming crowd.

I tried to get Blaze to lengthen his stride, but he stopped.

Go, boy, he said, nodding toward the woods. Together, they'll take us both. No point. Get on your way.

Sitting here tonight, hours later, back to this fragrant pine, with the night insects chirping and the fire dropping to a glow, I'm still watching my breathing, waiting for the bad feelings to ease. I wonder now if I could have done something to stop Blaze or if I could have tried harder to take him with me, but I understand it's about your body responding to violence. Your body defends you. It tells your brain to step aside until later—until now, I guess.

Ride, if you're reading this, which it occurs to me you might someday,

I want to let you know that, after the gun fired, with the blood humming in my ears and my own wet gasps sounding like someone else's, I thought of you. I ran and thought, if I get taken, I may never see Ride again. I didn't think of Arms. Maybe in my deeper thoughts, he's already lost to me. In any case, I ran without a word more to Blaze or a look back to see what the mob did with him.

DAY 5

I slept only in short spells last night. A nightmare woke me near dawn. I recall a gun in my hand. Arms, bleeding from his shoulder, looked disappointed. It was a look I saw on him often, directed not at me but at things in the world.

I steeped a handful of calming skullcap leaves. While I sipped, I checked the newspaper ad notes again against my deciphering, line by line. I felt reassured.

The decoding Arms taught me and Ride worked. It wasn't all that hard, except for a couple of tricks he neglected to mention. The Idaho Courier ad contained the coded message and the Boise Voice held the cipher key, just as they should. The cipher began with the letters BIX, which indicated the ninth book of The Aeneid, but I got fouled up at first because I didn't know that a T before a number string meant to count by words in the indicated line, not by letters. Once I'd worked that out, I saw that the word SUPPLY led off each of the first three messages, telling me they were requisition lists. Following SUPPLY in each set was a letter group that failed to decode into a recognizable word: MAJA, GOLI, PIGR. They may be abbreviations, probably the names of mines.

Arms said the ad messages were almost always about routine needs. He puzzled them out each week before heading off from Black Hornet for his site visits to other abandoned mines. In the lists I deciphered, I saw staples like rice, seeds, cooking oil, and cleaners. That suggests other families like us are living and caretaking other sites.

So yes, I'm reassured because maybe I can find Arms at one of these other mines or find another family like ours that can help me. Other items, though, raise questions I can't answer—materials used for construction and to maintain equipment. If I got it right, someone is ordering a shipment of HSLA steel and bolts or screws of some kind—grade 5, grade 8, UNC, UNF, with various lengths in MM. Other strings seem to require an extra level of decoding: AT1205-MX and ORENT-600X. But maybe these are model numbers for tools or equipment. I just don't know.

And then there's the fourth and final segment of the code, which is the shortest and seems somehow important, as if maybe it's a cipher for yet another newspaper—GB60497523. Or maybe it's a cross-cipher to double-check my work. I don't know how to use it.

I'll get moving shortly. If I can identify the mines, I can head for the closest one and maybe find someone who knows Arms or has seen him. I'm pretty sure most of the abandoned mines are in the mountains north of here, so at least I'm heading in the right direction.

Today I met Delia. I have this odd sense I'd been looking for her but didn't know. I got a ride from Mr. Quinta and Randy that landed me in Granite City, and then I got a tip from a helpful woman in town. Granite City has dozens of buildings and stores, and yet I was directed straight to Delia. Maybe when things go well, it's natural to assume there's a guiding hand. I'm not sure how tomorrow will go. Delia may decide not to bother with me and I'll lose this feeling that things are going as planned. Maybe Delia won't trust someone from outside the Nez Perce. Delia calls me white boy, even though I've got my mother's coloring, according to Arms.

This morning, I had no option but a very windy route through the woods, and in a downpour to boot. I made a poor choice of direction and had to slog it through a marsh before finding the mostly asphalt road heading north-northwest.

Maybe it was my drenched state that put off the first four drivers who passed. Maybe it was that same condition that inspired Mr. Quinta and Randy to take pity on me. The clouds cleared just as they arrived in their metallic robin's egg blue 1967 Chevy Impala—that's exactly how Mr. Quinta described it, and I understood his pride. He said the vehicle was entirely authentic, except the chrome wheel covers and custom color. Mr. Quinta seemed happy talking about his car, so I asked plenty of questions.

Mr. Quinta is small but has big hands. He shows two gold teeth in front when he smiles. Across his knuckles, blue tattoos read HEART and TRUTH, which seem like good things to keep in mind.

Randy is thirteen years old. I tried to entice him into a conversation but failed. All I got from my position in the back were shoulder shrugs.

Mr. Quinta kept careful watch on the rough, curving roads. He pointed out the medals dangling from his mirror. He went into fine detail about his victories at vintage auto shows.

After an hour or so we'd worn out the topic. Mr. Quinta asked, So, Will Granite City work for you?

I wasn't sure what Granite City had to offer but thanked him. Thinking he might move on to personal questions, I asked Randy about the comic book he was reading. It was about robotic creatures that could travel through time and make themselves bigger by adding parts. Some were friendly, but others were anything but and were on a path of wanton destruction—Randy's words. One human boy and one well-meaning robot befriend each other. Together they work on a plan to thwart the robot attacks.

The thwarting happens in the next issue, Randy said.

I guess my comments weren't that sharp because Randy said, You ever in fact read a Botomica Max comic? I admitted that I had not in fact read a comic book of any kind.

Mr. Quinta said it was a sin being raised without access to comics but that, given the state of things, it was understandable, especially now that you couldn't order them through the Internet.

Mr. Quinta seemed good natured, so I asked if he knew of a place to read the Internet, like today, and if that might be found in Granite City.

He didn't answer. Randy gave me a look and turned back to his comic.

I said, But I know it's not an easy thing to find, a place that can put you on the Internet, trying the terminology that I'd heard used.

More to the point, said Mr. Quinta, it's illegal. Why are you looking for something on the Internet?

I said, Sorry, no, it's okay. I was just curious.

I asked if they had a restaurant in Granite City, not that I had money to eat in one, but to change the subject. Mr. Quinta said, Molly's, but only Thursday through Sunday.

Turns out Mr. Quinta was heading for Granite City to fill his gas tank at Lasky's, the only shop he trusts, even though getting there and back takes a quarter tank. Lasky's name is blocked out in fresh white paint on a big blue sign that features a red car with eyes for headlights and streaks behind it to indicate speed.

Mr. Quinta rolled past the two gas pumps in front and around to the side where, he said, Lasky keeps the special reserve. I got out, thinking I might help pump the gas. Mr. Quinta beeped to summon Lasky and the two got involved in a loud conversation concerning Lasky's father, who had taken to bed with a lingering illness. They laughed, in any case, about the old man's grumpiness and thrift, at least that's what I gathered.

Mr. Quinta pointed toward town. You can hoof it easy enough from here, he said. Randy walked with me a few paces. He said, There's another auto shop in town called All US that we used to go to, but we stopped because Dad got upset about them selling Internet.

I continued along the lane, which crossed a railroad track and then leveled off by a broad area that had been stripped barren of trees called Lon's Mobile Park and Resort. Past another bend, I came into Granite City, which had at least three homes that were bigger than any I'd yet seen. Many had trimmed grassy yards with flower beds and vegetable gardens. Flowers grew from planters under windows and on porches, many in colors that seemed to fight each other, and yet cheerful to see all the same.

A tall man rode by on a squeaky bicycle. I raised my hand, but he kept on. With some wandering, I came to a sign pointing toward All US Petrofitters situated at the end of a short street. I could hear heavy music as I got closer to the open workshop door.

The worker couldn't hear me over the bass sounds, so I tapped on the side of the car he was fixing. I asked what a Petrofitter was, thinking it might have to do with the Internet. He asked if I had an EV that needed a gas engine and, when I said no, he said, Then you don't need a Petrofitter, but Dobro is in the office if you want something.

I found Dobro, who wore eye makeup and an orange wig. The Internet cost twenty-five dollars to use for an hour. Dobro said I'd need to know Slaker, which is a way to command a stealth browser. None of that was understandable, so it was clear I'd need Dobro to assist for another ten dollars. Money aside, that would reveal too much about my search for mines.

I walked toward a denser collection of buildings, hoping to find another Internet place, and came to a junction with a triangular area of lawn. A woman had taken a seat on one of three benches, which surrounded a pedestal, missing whatever monument it once held. She had a pile of books beside her.

I introduced myself. She'd braided her hair into long ropes, woven with fabric flowers. I saw that her books had typed labels bearing titles and code numbers. I asked if she'd gotten them from a library.

It's called the Perpetua Lending Library, she said. He took all the books from the free library when it closed and, from what I understand, paid nothing for them, so for him to charge is a crime, but there's the state of things.

She gave me directions. It wasn't far. The library was in a house fronted by a wide porch. It rose three floors, two of them filled with books that could be seen crowding up against the windows. Even from the porch, I could smell the books, making me think of the collection we had at home. Bradley H. Somer, the proprietor, as per the sign on his desk, crouched just inside, sorting books into knee high stacks on the floor. He tapped with a pencil on a sheet glued to the desk that read, Browse All Day—$2. Lending—$1.50/book/week, $5/5 books/week, $10/15 books/week.

I dug two dollars out of my pack but first asked if he had books there about Idaho and different businesses and landowners, realizing that in my effort to be secretive I might have been too vague. He took my money and said, State and municipal records are on the second floor. Left down the hall, last door on the right.

On my way to the staircase, I passed the entrances to FICTION and ART, SCIENCE. Upstairs, I saw MEDICAL, HOLISTIC, SEX on the left, which made me curious, but I continued past LAW, FINANCE, BUSINESS on the right, where I heard someone walking about and shuffling books.

STATE, MUNICIPAL at the end of the hall was not as neatly organized as other rooms. Many of the shelves were filled with thick green and red volumes. Other shelves and tables held bundled records and boxes filled to overflowing with documents.

I searched the room for a long time, but found nothing on Idaho's mines.

It occurred to me I might be better off looking in LAW, FINANCE, BUSINESS, but on my way out I peeked into a small room across the hall and spotted a shelf in the corner labeled GEOLOGICAL, LAND USE. Just about everything in the section had been published by the Idaho Geological Survey—lots of maps, databases, and regulations and procedures. I found listings of mines in three books, all of which were in bad condition. They'd been torn apart and rebound with rubber bands. In one, the table of contents listed Inactive & Abandoned Mines, but the chapter was missing. Most of the book was gone, in fact.

I exited the room with the book and that's where I first saw Delia, turning down the staircase, volumes stacked to her chin. She was moving fast but glanced back at me and I caught her startling eyes.

Delia had disappeared by the time I got downstairs. I asked Bradley H. Somer if he had the missing book pages. He said, Only what's there. Fifty cents if you want it for a day. I turned back for the stairs to return the book. Mr. Somer said, Closing up in a minute. Make it quick.

Delia came out of FICTION and took the book from me. She had a tight roundness to her face that gave her beauty a kind of comforting firmness, but her eyes were piercing, and she had an eyebrow raised like a dare. She checked out the title on the spine and said, I'll put this back for you.

I watched her whisk up the stairs and vanish. She moved with the certainty of a smaller person than she is.

I thanked Mr. Somer on the way out and said I might return. He handed me a book titled Roughing It by Mark Twain with a colorful painting on the front of frontier men digging a mine, and I got a chill thinking I'd given away too much. He said it might be up my alley. I would have loved to read it but declined.

I hadn't gone far up the street when I heard Delia calling for me from about twenty paces back. She pulled the mining volume out of her satchel and waved it.

She had released her hair from a clip. It reached her shoulders, black and ragged at the ends. I explained that the book was incomplete. She said, I know. Do you want the rest?

Delia claimed she had the missing pages nearby and could sell them to me, and though I knew I probably couldn't give her the money she wanted, I followed her. She turned us down a lane that ended quickly and then onto a trail that cut northwest through some sparse woods cluttered with the remains of cars, home machines, and material from old buildings.

The trail climbed a berm onto a dirt road. I stepped quicker to walk beside her. I offered my name and she told me hers without looking at me. I asked if she was named after the island, but she had no answer and didn't seem interested in talking other than to say we had about a fifteen-minute walk left.

I wanted to ask why she had the rest of the book but thought that might demonstrate untrustworthiness. I was guessing her tribe to be Nez Perce and would have liked to ask, but I was afraid that might be impolite. I started to ask if we were going to another library but instead faked a cough. Then I sang a couple of songs.

Delia didn't seem to mind, but she interrupted the first, saying the right words were, not much longer would you be mine, not, not much longer would you be lying. I said, But that would make be mine rhyme with lose my mind, which seemed like a lazy rhyme. She said, Nevertheless. Your singing is okay, though. So, I sang one of my own songs about rain. The words were mostly a repeat of, Streaming rain, feed the river, thirsty grain, rain the giver.

Delia took me to her family's ranch. They live in a wood and stone house that seems quite old but with newer parts added on. Not far is a stable for six horses, two barns, a corral, a pen for goats, chicken coops, fenced in grazing land, and a garden big enough to grow extra to sell. A truck and two cars sat parked by one of the barns. When I asked who lived on the farm, she said, My parents are long gone.

I sat on the porch steps while she went inside. I could smell onions and peppers frying. I heard dishes clattering and voices inside, one of them a man's. Delia banged back out through the screen door and headed for the smaller of the two barns. She was inside for some time. Daylight was fading. I petted the goats through a fence and fed them some knapweed growing beyond their reach. When Delia emerged from the barn, I rejoined her on the porch.

Just then her grandmother came to the door, wiping her hands on a kitchen towel. She nodded at me and said, Staying for dinner? Delia held up a packet in brown paper, bound in string, and said, He just needs this. Grandmother said, Nonsense, come along, and returned to the kitchen.

Delia looked irritated, but I was hungry and didn't want to disappoint Grandmother. I introduced myself to Delia's cousin Philip, who was at the table, already chewing on a chicken part. He was hunched over his plate, but I could tell he was a large person. Grandmother, who was squat and moved quick like Delia, brought a bowl full of corn, chopped peppers, and squash to the table. She poured me a tall glass of mint tea sweetened with honey. They didn't talk, so I assumed it was discouraged. I did speak to decline the chicken and thanked Grandmother for the delicious food.

I was considering another helping, but Delia stood and took my plate to the sink. Philip raised his eyes and gave me a grin. He said, You backpacking it? Where you live? I said, Black Hornet, before thinking better of it. He shook his head. Delia cleared the rest of the table and then said, Let's get this done.

We sat on a swinging porch bench. Delia held the packet and looked at me with that one eyebrow raised. I told her I didn't think I had enough money, and she said, Yeah, you don't, and kept looking at me. I said, Why did you take these particular pages? She kept staring.

Then Delia said, Do you like games? Let's play a game. I told her that my sister and I liked to play a card game called spades but that we lost some of the cards when the wind took them into a stream one day and so we had to make up games of our own. Delia waved her hand.

She put the packet down on the bench between us. You guess why I hoarded these pages, she said, and I'll let you know if you guess right. Then I get to ask you a question and you have to tell me the truth. I said, But that's not fair because you're not letting me ask you a question, you're just acknowledging if I… But she was waving her hand again. I've got the pages, she said, so it's my rules. I said, If I guess right, I get to ask you a question on my next turn, and she nodded.

First, I said, You're Nez Perce. All this land in Idaho and Oregon and even some farther north was once your homeland, so you want to know about the land, including mines and what's in them.

Okay, she said, frowning, not bad. She tapped on the packet and asked, Why do you want to know about abandoned mines? I said, I'm trying to find my father. He left two years ago and we haven't a clue where he went other than that he visited abandoned mines for his work.

She squinted. So, your dad was a mining engineer? Did he think any of the mines had anything left worth getting at?

I said, It's my turn. Is that what you think? That I'm after gold or copper? Delia said, If you were, we might be able to work something out.

We sat back and rocked the bench. The moon was peeking above the tree line and fireflies were out. I heard horse snickers. I said, Your horses sound impatient. She said, They get grain around now but kept rocking.

In a bit she said, There are over eight thousand abandoned mines and prospects in Idaho.

I have a way to narrow the search, I said, and also, Arms is not a mining expert, but I think something might be going on at some of the mines, something you might want to know about, and I could use some help.

She made a noise much like the horses. I have no doubt you could use a shit ton of help, white boy, she said.

I saw Philip on his way to the stable, so I lent a hand. We gave each horse a half bucketful of great smelling oats. Molly, Chief Joseph, Nathan, and Redheart are Appaloosa. Midnight is a quarter horse and the biggest of them and the oldest, too, judging by his teeth and sloping back.

Molly, who has a long white mane and rosy freckles that fade out to white hindquarters, was anxious, so I brushed her neck and sang her my horse song, which is mainly a repeat of the ground's drumming when Molly's running. I inserted Molly's name for Sookie, who was Clark and Lori's old mare. Philip told me about his chores, caring for the horses, goats, and chickens, which he says he squeezes in before work each morning.

Delia was still on the porch when we finished. She'd been leafing through the book pages. She told Philip I might know something interesting about mines, to which he asked, What kind of interesting? I said, If I can locate the three mines I'm looking for in those pages, I might be able to answer that.

Delia said, I'm going to hold onto the pages tonight. In the morning, you and I will go through them. And you'll need to explain more before we even consider committing to anything.

Then she asked, You said your dad's been gone for two years? He didn't try to get in touch? I explained that I don't have a working phone and no mail messengers come out my way.

Philip said, Where the fuck do you live again? What's Black Hornet? I said, An abandoned mine. He asked, Your dad the kind of jerk who'd go off and not come back?

I said, No.

They went quiet. Philip offered to get me set up in his uncle's old room, but Delia said, He'll be fine in the hay barn. And then, as we were walking away, You realize your father's probably dead, right? And I said, Yes, that's what he says in my dreams.

The light on my pages is fluttering from the moths circling the bulb overhead.

The barn smells thick of hay and oats, drying in bins. The wind's picking up outside, and the cranky old boards are creaking like they want to be left in peace. I want to open up to Delia. I want to trust her because she's smart and knows how to do things in the world. I know she and Philip can help me. And if the people Arms works for are reopening the mines, maybe Delia and her people have a need to know, and that need will make them trustworthy because she'll need to trust me too.

DAY 6

In my dream last night, Arms looked younger than I remember knowing him. He wore my rain slicker, but then that was once his. Ride looked nearly his age. She wore a purple native dress like in her The Girl Who Loved Wild Horses storybook. Arms was agitated. He filled his satchel with food for his trip but then handed it to me. As he left, he told me, This is so important. I asked if he meant his work, because the food in his satchel had been replaced by paper records. He said, The Earth knows you, but that isn't enough.

Thick clouds delayed dawn today, but the horses knew the time and woke me with their stomping. I got started on Philip's morning chores. I haltered each and, one at a time, walked them out to the near pasture, taking care not to slam the fence gate because the house was still dark. But by the time I'd begun cleaning the first stall, Philip was there joking about the joys of shoveling manure at daybreak.

Grandma made thin corn cakes and rolled them around eggs and sausage for Delia and Philip. She filled mine with squash blossoms and goat cheese. I gave Grandma a bundle of wild strawberry for her morning tea, which she appreciated, and a tincture of meadowsweet for her arthritis, which she didn't. I explained, Every old person I've met has joint pain, but you're only the fourth one. Philip said, Grandma's not old yet. Her mother lived to one hundred and nine.

Philip headed off to a neighboring farm for his day's work. I fetched my pack and met Delia in the dining room where she'd laid the packet of mining pages on the table along with a collection of maps covering Idaho and Oregon as they were when the maps were printed years ago. I showed her the ad from the Idaho Courier and the end result of my deciphering, but not my worksheet or the Boise Voice ad that held the code key.

We looked through the supply lists I'd decoded. This doesn't look like mining stuff, she said. This fiberglass, polystyrene, and the plastic fillers, that's probably building insulation. And the chemical compounds like calcium sulfate, magnesium oxide, and the nitrogen compounds—I guess maybe you could use these for manufacturing, but it looks more like they're fertilizing plants, not mining. There's nothing that says to me these guys are running mines.

She was engrossed. She brought in a reference book on farming to check her theory. I asked, Are you disappointed? She said, Something is definitely going on because they coded the lists. Why so secretive? What made you think these supplies are for mines? That makes no sense.

I showed her my other findings: MAJA, GOLI, and PIGR. I think these are abbreviations for abandoned mines, I said, to which she asked, Why?

I opened her packet of hoarded pages. The mine listings were in alphabetical order but broken out into regions and sub-regions, so it took a while. PIGR we decided could stand for Pistol Grip mine. Then we found a Mary Jane mine which worked for MAJA. When Delia found a mine named Golden Limb in the list, I got a cold shiver in my ribcage.

That's where I need to go, I said, that one. Delia disagreed. She thought Pistol Grip had greater potential since it had more of the fertilizer chemicals on its list, and Pistol Grip is near Nez Perce Reservation up north, which means she might be able to find helpers.

I took out my copy of The Aeneid. I wasn't sure how to start explaining.

I said, Aeneas wasn't sure of his way, so he prayed to Aphrodite and she sent him guides in the form of two doves.

And then I quoted:

> Be you my guides, with your auspicious aid,
> And lead my footsteps, till the branch be found,
> Whose glitt'ring shadow gilds the sacred ground…
> They wing'd their flight aloft; then, stooping low,
> Perch'd on the double tree that bears the golden bough.

Golden bough? she said. Should we pray to Aphrodite for the way to Golden Limb? And then before I could answer, she asked what Aeneas was looking for.

His father, I said, the spirit of his father in the Underworld.

Delia sat back in her chair and stared like she was looking through me. I explained that Aeneas broke off the golden bough and carried it with him to gain access to the Underworld.

Can I see your book? she said. I told her, No, it's too personal. She said, From the hundred and one dog-ears, I'd say that's not just a book to you.

I didn't know how to answer. More staring. Then she asked if I could tell her something to convince her I'm not nuts.

I asked her how long it would take to get to Golden Limb, so she located it on her map. Assuming we can drive, she said, and that we can find enough gas and we don't run into any militia assholes, maybe twelve or fifteen hours.

I said, I know the book is just a story, so I think that makes me not nuts. But Arms comes to me in dreams in the same way Aeneas spoke to his father, Anchises, after he died. I know they're just dreams—I know I'm not talking to my dead father but, you tell me, doesn't it look like we should go to Golden Limb?

Delia said, I don't know about we yet. If I were you, I guess I'd have to. Then she asked me why The Aeneid is so special. I said, Arms wanted us to know it. I never considered the why of it. We read it every day.

I could tell she had lots of questions, but she was late for work. She told me to hang out until she and Philip returned, which is why I've had time to write this. She also told me to stay away from Grandma. Looks like I'm going to fail there.

The evening calm is spreading across the pastures. My thoughts are finally settling. The ink on my page is behaving again as the world retakes comforting form. It's in a way both sad and reassuring. I can't possibly write about what happened today.

I'll write about today.

Ride, when we were at Black Hornet, I could pull a stray leaf off your boot at the end of the day and know where you'd walked. If you've been to places in your soul like I've been today, then maybe my words will be meaningful. If not, maybe you'll only see unfamiliar leaves. But I'll try.

This noontime I sat near the pasture under a cottonwood that was giving shade for Molly too, who stood content near me while the other horses grazed up on the hill. I looked up from my writing to see Grandma heading my way. She had a handled basket.

Help me mushroom, she said, and kept on past, walking steadily. I followed her, skirting the outbuildings and then along a fence line that bordered corn plantings. We crossed a rough footbridge over a stream that fed the horses' cistern back in the pasture, took a trail leading through Douglass pine and juniper, and before long entered a yellow grove of quaking aspen.

Grandma spotted some hairy white lion's mane. I checked out a fallen tree where I picked morels and a few small chanterelles. I returned to find

Grandma sitting in a cleared area where someone had arranged sawed trunks into a circle of benches. She was picking through the basket on her lap, so I added my haul. Her skirt draped to the ground, patterned with bright red flowers over blue and green stripes.

I heard you dream about your father, she said. Do you dream of animals?

I took a seat across from her. Yes, lots, I told her. Birds a lot, and the wildlife we know from home.

I named some of our animals for her and mentioned that I'd dreamt of a coyote the other night, even though I don't know a real one.

Grandma said, That's a real coyote. Dreams are real.

I said, I don't think so, Grandma. Dreams are just in your head.

She asked, Is your head real? Did the dream really happen? Why is a dream less real than a breath you take or a song you hear?

I told her I love to sing, and she said, Yes, I heard that too.

I told her how the dream coyote pestered me to leave home. Sounds like a coyote, she said. Animals could once talk like us but stopped when people came into the world. So, the only way they can let us know who they really are is through dreams. That's where they still have power over us.

She told me that there was once a coyote named It-see-yi-yi who was so cunning that he was able to slay the last of the powerful monsters who ruled the Earth before humans. Maybe your coyote is your weyekin, Grandma said. If so, you'd be very lucky. A young man is very fortunate to know his weyekin.

She pulled her hand from the mushroom basket and revealed four gold caps. I said, Those are Psilocybe cubensis, Grandma. They have hallucinogenic properties.

What else did your father teach you about these? she asked. I said he warned us never to eat them without proper guidance. I asked Grandma if she was offering to be my guide. She laughed. If you are fortunate, that will be your weyekin, she said.

The mushrooms tasted much like raw boletes without the sweetness and more of the soil they grew from and the trees and moss they knew nearby, as if they had learned from the forest.

I asked Grandma if I would see my coyote guide. She said, It won't be like the movies. When I admitted I'd never seen a movie, she explained, In movies, a wise old Indian shaman takes you to a sweat lodge and you go on a voyage to the stars on a spotted pony. There are big flashes of light and shrieks. Hawks and bears and coyotes do scary things. You gain great wisdom and new purpose.

I asked if someone had taken her to a lodge to eat mushrooms when she was young. She said, No, to a fish concert.

I felt fuddled in my thoughts and uneasy in my stomach. I asked if movies were like dreams. She said, Bullshit dreams made by bullshit people.

The image of a man made of bullshit came so vividly that laughs gushed from me like water pumped from a well. Grandma chuckled along. Then I felt like I might puke, so I pulled some dried wild ginger from my pack to chew on. Grandma asked to see my collection of tinctures. We talked about what they were each good for and disagreed on some. She was curious about one I'd brewed from black cohosh and red raspberry leaves. I'd drawn a moon on the label to signify that it was for menstrual cramps. Why would you bring this? she asked.

For trading, I said. I explained how Arms learned to make it from my mother, Luna. She was part indigenous.

Grandma accepted the moon tincture as a gift for Delia who she said turned into an asshole once a month. She said, Now you want to tell me about the moon.

My body had become airy and fuller, like I was blooming and growing porous. I stumbled in speaking. I kept thinking my words were in a foreign tongue, but I saw Grandma understood. I told her that Arms had given me, Ride, and himself astronaut names to use after Luna returned to her family in Mexico, which was around the time we moved to Black Hornet from Seattle.

Grandma asked, What part does the moon play in your dreams?

A breeze was swaying the branches overhead, swinging patches of sunlight across the white-faced tree bark. Grandma's features seemed to adapt and float with them. I couldn't remember the moon from my dreams, but I said, The moon feels like the home of my mother. They were words that sounded reasonable but were not true.

I found it perplexing that I lied, and also that I couldn't give a name to the color of Grandma's blouse, which billowed out in scents of lavender and baldhip rose. The patterns of her skirt now danced like blossoms in a dust twirl, all in time to the music I was hearing in the aspen leaves trembling above. I thought, Grandma is being caught up in the dance of the forest. Then I realized she and I had always danced. The mushrooms had invited me to see how we all moved in time with the world and to know the music.

How do the mushrooms have this gift to give? I asked. Grandma said, Oh, they connect to everything, and somehow everything concentrates in them.

I asked if I could learn the direction to my father. Grandma said, But you already know from your book and your codes. You are on your way. Today is about preparing.

She said, To be steadfast for the tests to come, you need the sureness of the ground beneath you and the guidance of the moon above.

With Earth, sky, and mind all weaving together and sharing knowledge, sureness had a new meaning.

I'll explain how the world came to be, Grandma said. This will help you feel the sureness of the Earth.

She told the story of It-see-yi-yi, the coyote who slew the great monster, Nimi-ipu. It-see-yi-yi sought out Nimi-ipu because the great beast had swallowed up all the people of the world. The sly coyote dared the monster, a challenge to see who could inhale the other. He allowed himself to be sucked down the monster's throat. Little did Nimi-ipu know that It-see-yi-yi had packed with him five stone knives and a flint to make fire. It-see-yi-yi carved away at the monster's heart from the inside, tossing slices to the people imprisoned within. He lit a fire to torture the monster. But as he hacked away, one by one each of his knives shattered. He persuaded the people to help him by ripping out the monster's bones and stacking them into piles. It-see-yi-yi, with his last knife, was able to sever the last fiber of the monster's heart.

In the throes of death, all of Nimi-ipu's body openings yawned wide and the people cast his bones into the world. It-see-yi-yi carved up the monster's body and distributed the parts in all directions, toward the sunset, the sunrise, the warm regions and cold, and thereby created all the Indian tribes. He washed the blood from his hands and sprinkled the drops nearby to establish the Nez Perce and their home. That place is called Kamiah, Idaho. It is the heart of the monster and the home of the Nez Perce.

I no longer knew if my eyes were open. Senses arrived, senses I'd never asked for, and her story lived in me. I was the hero. I was the monster, gaping down from the tree canopy above, howling as my body parts were excised and piled like mountains.

The violence tore my senses into many minds, each alive with horrors of their own. Each was repeatedly born, consumed, and vomited far and wide in forms so various they could make a world. The faces of all the people I knew and others I didn't all pleaded for rightful places. They wailed like souls of the Underworld, begging to return to life. They paraded past by the thousands. Finally, there was Arms, sure of his state, of his sureness. His eyes were a blur, as if spun from many eyes, capturing all that all eyes see.

In time, an orange moon appeared above, impossibly big and radiant, eclipsing the world's longing. I lay on my back. I felt a warmth growing from my gut, radiating out past my limbs. I saw the beauty sparking from my fingertips, igniting the white tree bark until the forest was in flames. In the fire with me was Blaze, gazing upward at the blood moon and other luminous faces in the sky of those returned to the world. From this vision came a song, which was mainly a repeat of beauty ablaze, honor your duty.

It took me forever to open my eyes. When I did, Delia was standing above me, listening.

I warned you to stay away from Grandma, she said. She's not to be trusted.

I said, Before we go to Golden Limb, we need to find my friend, Blaze. He's dying.

DAY 7

I lay for a while before rising this morning, humming the Blaze song that had come to me in my vision. The moon radiance and the flames of understanding are almost entirely gone. Storms blew through last night, leaving the morning air fragrant with soaked meadow grass and the balsamroot and milkweed blossoms circling the barn. Mist is rising off the pastures, glowing in the early sun. The bird songs are sharp and somehow more familiar, as if we'd shared things. The world inside my head feels cleansed, as well, and drained.

Blaze is passed out. There should be just enough light left to record my day, and quiet time because Delia took the truck back into Rosie Springs on the chance Majid might have drug company antibiotics for Blaze. She says it's a long shot.

I'm looking at the address tag Blaze attached to his storage locker key—EZ-BOX STORAGE, 1250, Jamaica Plains—and I wonder if I'll ever go there and what might be inside. He would only say, Nothing of meaning to anyone but me.

We left the ranch today without taking time to pack supplies, but then we didn't know what to expect. Still dazed this morning, I returned to the mushroom spot, thinking I might rekindle some feelings or catch sight of a coyote. I feel stupid now for wasting the time.

The horses were in the pasture when I got back, but Philip's truck was still parked in its spot. I could hear Delia and Grandma arguing in the house. Grandma pointed to me when I entered the kitchen. At least this one has a sense of what's right when a man comes to his final rest.

Grandma slid a bowl of oatmeal to my place at the table. I asked Delia if she was angry with me. Grandma said, She's prideful. Calling her angry gives her too much credit.

My responsibilities have no weight here, I guess, Delia said to her. All the sudden I'm babysitting a half-formed white boy.

You could learn something about responsibility from the half he's got, said Grandma.

Delia stomped out of the room and returned with a set of keys. Philip needs his truck back tomorrow, she said to me, and then headed out the front door. I thanked Grandma and ran to retrieve my pack from the barn.

Delia tore down the gravel drive and bore down even harder on the accelerator once she'd hit the hard-packed dirt road. I asked her if she was menstruating.

She pumped the brake, sending me off my seat into the front panel. What the fuck's wrong with you? she said. Then she asked, Who's Blaze and why is he dying?

I told her about my time with Blaze, trying to be concise due to the mood of the conversation. She didn't interrupt until I got to the shooting.

The fuck? she said. The guy he shot, was he militia?

I couldn't answer that.

If he's militia, Delia said, they'll be looking for you, too. If not, nobody will give a shit. The law couldn't bother going out that way, so Blaze might stand a chance. But this is a guy you've known about as long as a headache, so you need to explain better why you care.

I said, If it's okay, I'll explain in a little while because this conversation still doesn't feel accommodating.

Oh, for sure, she said, whenever it suits you.

After we'd made some turns and her driving relaxed, I explained like this: It was the sybil who first revealed to Aeneas that he needed the golden bough to reach the Underworld. She also warned him not to go forward without first putting his friend to rest.

I quoted:

> Besides, you know not, while you here attend,
> Th' unworthy fate of your unhappy friend:
> Breathless he lies; and his unburied ghost,
> Depriv'd of fun'ral rites, pollutes your host.

We're back in Greece, Delia said. Perfect.

I said, Again, were you me, you might feel like that was important.

Her lips were tight. She tapped on the steering wheel as she drove.

When we reached a point just outside of Rosie Springs, Delia slowed to a stop. She asked me to get out and wait for her. It's better I go in without you and ask after Blaze, she said. Stay the hell out of sight.

She wasn't gone long.

You sure your friend isn't a ghost already? she said when she got back. I spoke to Philip's friend, Codey, who works at the feed store. According to Codey, who keeps his ear to the ground for anything less boring than slinging feed bags, no one was apprehended for the shooting.

If Blaze is still free, I said, I know where to look.

I described the crossroads where Blaze and I got the ride from the Standines. Delia took us to the wrong place but got it right on the second try. I led us through the woods, following the creek to the camping spot. Blaze lay on his back under the alders, head propped against the fallen trunk. He managed a smile and said something with faint breath.

Blaze's color was off. His pack blanket was stained dark around his midsection. I eased it back. He shivered as I loosened it from the dried blood.

Caught me from behind, he said in a dry voice. The bullet went through.

Blaze's forehead was hot to the touch and the area near the wound even hotter. The bleeding had stopped, but there was swelling and discharge. Delia soaked a T-shirt in the brook to cool his head, and I sat him up against me so he could drink.

You're a tough son of a bitch, she told him. How'd you escape?

He winked. Strolled away easy as you please, he said. In the midst of shock and confusion, people of that intellect disregard an old man.

Blaze even managed to catch a ride to the crossroads but just as he left the roadside a truck rolled past and bullets flew.

One of them got lucky, Blaze said. Hard to outsmart dumb luck.

He shook his head when I brought the bottle of yarrow tincture to his lips but eventually yielded.

Delia gave me a look. I said, This will battle the infection from the inside, but we need something for the wound site.

She took my place with him while I scoured the area near the campsite. I thought balsamroot would be the most likely but was surprised to find Oregon grape. The telltale berries were still green, but it was the bark that I needed. Blaze was asleep when I got back. I built a fire and began the tedious job of harvesting the bark.

Swabbing the wound with the tea woke Blaze. To distract him during the application, I asked him something that puzzled me. Tell me what happened in Texana, I said.

Blaze took some more water and did his best.

When AIR ME took down the grids, Blaze said, you didn't want to be in Texas. It was a hellish hot summer. Texans, even in good times, are intolerant and over-armed. Once their air conditioning died and tap water was at a trickle, town turned against town. All we got back east was hearsay. Newspapers tried, but soon reporters were shot on sight. Occasional images made it back our way. We saw the governor, the legislature, slaughtered in the halls of the capital. Corpses hung from government windows. Mass graves along the border.

From what my pop told me, said Delia, it was like there were a dozen countries down there. The whole south and southwest splintered—Dallas, West Texas, Houston, and West Louisiana, Shreveport, Little Rock.

Yes, all that, said Blaze. By the next summer, though, power consolidated, meaning bigger turf wars. Damns and bridges blown, airports blown. Then we heard Ray Weymouth declared himself president of Texana. They claimed territory from the east panhandle down to Mexico, up to mid-Arkansas and to the western border of old Louisiana.

We kept those Texas fuckers out of Oklahoma, Delia said. I was told the Chickasaw Nation and Choctaw's fought them back to the north Texas border. And plenty of Indian brothers and sisters rode into Texana to try to stop Blackmas and died trying.

Lord. That I didn't know, said Blaze, taking Delia's hand in his. And no one knows how many brothers and sisters were massacred on Blackmas Day and the weeks after. No one knows how many had the wherewithal to fight back. It was as dark as any time America's ever had.

Weymouth got strung up by his own people, Delia told me, but others like him stepped right in.

I couldn't tell you the current state down there, Blaze said.

One week we hear Texana is marching on Mexico, Delia said, the next they're fighting a Black Nation uprising or another coup. Who the hell knows.

Delia went on about all the Texana factions, some of them growing stronger and spreading northward, like the Free-For-Three, which she called the FFT.

Blaze laid his head back and asked for a song, so I gave him Moondance, snapping my fingers for the beat.

Blaze said to Delia, You understand, dear, that Aldrin is destined for the moon.

Delia pulled me aside to talk.

No disrespect on what your dad taught you, she said, but herbals need to be applied early. Maybe a young guy could tough this out until they did their work, but him?

She left for town to seek out medicine.

I sat with Blaze. Just when I thought he'd drifted off, he said, with eyes closed, This was Amina's favorite, and sang Let's Stay Together in a sandpapery upper register. The words drew a picture of his life with her. I cried and wished Delia had stayed long enough to hear.

DAY 8

Delia finally made it back three hours after sundown last night. She'd found peroxide, antibiotic cream, and bandages in town.

Majid thought his friend might have pills for sale, she said. We drove there, but no luck.

Majid told her he was concerned Blaze was battling more than the wound. It sounds like his heart is failing, Delia said.

We did what we could with the wound sites, front and back. Blaze fluttered his eyelids and moaned, but he'd said his last words. Delia and I lay on either side of him for warmth.

At dawn, Delia lay asleep, holding his hand. Blaze's mouth was agape, his chest barely rising.

She and I said nothing all morning. The sun slipped behind white clouds and a mist filled the hollow so that, when the sunlight returned, it ignited the air. And at some moment during that transition, I believe Blaze released breath from his body for the final time.

Delia cried without a sound.

Among his things, we found a creased photo of him holding his young daughter. Delia said he should take it with him. We washed his face, his arms, hands, legs, and feet, then bundled him in his blanket with the photo and his slim volume of poetry by Kwame Dawes. I gathered dry wood and stacked it on the stony bank of the creek while Delia used my kit to sew the blanket up tight.

I stacked the pyre firmly, waist high, and wove branches like a bed. We laid Blaze on top and surrounded him with purple lupine, gold arrowleaf balsamroot, blue camas blossoms, and fiery red and yellow columbine petals. When the flames took hold, I sang the Beauty Ablaze song that had come to me in the mushroom grove. As the fire consumed him, Delia sang a native chant to fallen warriors in a strong voice that seemed to come from a place she might never normally reveal. She said it was the only chant she knew, but its sorrow and defiance were perfect.

On the ride back to the farm, I asked if she'd ever watched someone die before. I sat with my mom, Delia said, but her mind was gone from drugs and craziness, so it felt much different. Pop was dead when we found him, him and Philip's dad, Arnold. Militia scum murdered them for sport and the little money they had.

Those people down in Oklahoma, I said, had you been old enough, would you have fought with them in the Texana War?

Had it been my land, probably, she said. These wars go nowhere, though. We know the land and the life on it, and we know its power. We were here first, and if we stay smart while these idiots kill each other off, we can be here last.

After dinner, we sat in the kitchen making plans with Philip while Grandma packed provisions. Philip asked again to see the Golden Limb supply requisition list. He said, The chemicals, if they're in barrels, we can ramp them up onto the truck. I know lots of farmers who'll pay well for that shit. These building materials though are probably unwieldy, and I can't offload them easy.

I found this confusing. You want to steal the supplies? I said.

Call it what you like, Philip said. Who the hell are these people? You think they buy them legit? There's no legit for stuff like this anymore. Is taking stolen stuff stealing?

I told him I thought it was wrong, regardless. He looked out the window, shaking his head. Then he said, If that's the way it is, not sure there's a point for me. And it's my truck.

I reminded him that Arms might be there. Delia said, How about we first find out who we're dealing with? If they've got an operation going, there's a bigger picture and maybe a bigger opportunity than snatching a few barrels.

Regardless, we agreed to take planks and tie-downs in case we decided to load up. Then Philip argued that we should take guns, but Delia dissuaded him of that, too.

She also pointed out the TH I'd left undeciphered in my notes. If that stands for Thursday delivery, she said, that's the day after tomorrow.

DAY 9

We started out early and made good time at the onset. Philip knew a farm supplier in the next town with gas available. From there, the only stores we saw were long boarded up or burned. The hills grew into mountains, and the roads barely clung to their sides. With the washouts and rockslides, some were impassable. Four times we had to turn around—not a simple thing on roads that narrow—and double back looking for alternative routes. And in the afternoon, Delia misread her old map, or was, as she put it, thrown off by changes to the roads.

If I hadn't helped orient Delia a few times, we might have circled into the night. Around sundown, we spotted a gorge positioned prominently on the map adjacent to the mountain pass we sought. As the light faded, we came to the chain-link fence surrounding Golden Limb Mine.

Philip had a windup flashlight. With it, we could see the dilapidated state of the fence and near illegible warning signs posted when the authorities shuttered the mine decades back.

Somebody's been here doing something, Philip said. He showed us where the old padlock on the gate bore new scratches, and we could see that the gravel had been freshly disturbed on the drive inside the gate.

We backed up to a turnoff a quarter mile from the entrance. We cut ninebark shrubs and camouflaged the rear of the truck in case someone peered in our way.

It's by the cold glow of the windup torch that I record the day. We're doing without a fire, positioned close enough to the drive to wake if someone rolls in, but taking turns on watch all the same. I'm going first. I have an attentive barred owl for company. I hear the skittering of bats through the pines, probably little brown or silver-haired. A curious raccoon couple is hanging out in a tree overhanging the truck where Delia and Philip are laid out on the flatbed, sputtering occasional snores as they sleep. And just before, I may have heard a lone gray wolf creeping nearby, seeking an explanation for the intruders.

> Ye realms, yet unreveal'd to human sight,
> Ye gods who rule the regions of the night,
> Ye gliding ghosts, permit me to relate
> The mystic wonders of your silent state!

DAY 10

Sleep is nowhere near, though I'm exhausted in ways I've never known. I'm determined to complete the day's writing and to describe what I saw with the confidence of one who believed it was real. I won't attempt to explain, not until I'm sure I understand.

I poked Philip around midnight to take over the watch. This morning, we found him slumped against the narrow trunk of a paper birch. Delia wished him good morning with a kick to his boot sole.

We were cleaning up breakfast when the delivery arrived. I heard a straining motor minutes before they came into sight. They drove a panel truck, not marked with any company symbols. It had been retrofitted for rugged driving, this observation whispered to me by Philip as we spied from a rock outcropping.

We had to stealth along through the adjacent forest to follow them to the entrance. I got a glimpse of the driver when he stopped to swing the gate open. He carried a bat, which he used to beat on the side panel. Wakey, you fucks, he shouted to whoever was inside. He drove through, hopped out to lock the gate, then back in and onward.

Once the truck noises had receded, we helped each other over the fence. Delia scouted ahead and threw a stone back to signal it was okay for us to follow. We walked along the drive as it zigzagged down into the ravine but relied on the cover of woods for the rest of the descent. Beyond a switchback to the left, we saw the peaked roof of a three-story building. Its original wood structure was jacketed in corrugated metal, painted red, and showing many years of weathering.

The panel truck sat with its rear to a barn door-sized opening. The driver, nearby, leaned on one of maybe a dozen rusted ore bins that had been left about. He was lanky, and his jeans, belted with a bungie cord, looked three sizes too big. He swigged something, maybe beer, from a wide, unlabeled jar. After about a half-hour, he walked a few paces and peed against the building, then returned and rolled a cigarette.

We waited for what seemed like an hour, listening to the hollow scrapes and clunks of the supplies being offloaded inside. When the work was done, we heard a one-word shout and saw the warehouse door slide down with a motion that felt far too smooth considering the age of the place. The driver flicked the remains of his third cigarette and drove off. As the truck passed, we caught sight of two workers sitting in the back against the truck wall.

I trailed the truck back to the gate to confirm they left, then returned to find Philip and Delia examining the exterior of the building. Delia had her ear to the windowless door the black marketeers had used. She waved us over.

We could hear machinery clunking, rolling, and ratcheting inside—there was a steady hum, but also non-repetitive whirrs and beats coming from different angles.

That's robotics, Delia whispered. Do you hear any voices?

We didn't. The door was immovable. She told us to look for another way in while she listened for more activity. Philip and I checked two human-sized doors and what ventilation openings we could reach, but all entryways were grilled or secured tight.

On closer inspection of the gaps in the aged tin and wood siding, we saw evidence of reinforcement from within: bolts and plating made of plastic and stainless metal.

They've done a slick job disguising this place, whoever they are, Philip said. No external locks, no door handles. This building's new inside and looks like it's built for robots.

I turned my attention to the grounds, which had been leveled and strewn with crushed shale in the areas surrounding the buildings. In addition to the red warehouse, three low clapboard bunk houses stood on the grounds, similar to the one Arms remodeled for us at Black Hornet. These were in disrepair—windows shattered and much of the roofing collapsed. Philip and Delia looked through them anyway.

Undergrowth had overtaken the grounds between the bunk houses and the area where the mine entrance cut into a steep hillside. Above and to the west of the mine entrance, an old mill building survived, sheathed in the same red painted metal as the warehouse. The forest had reclaimed the switchback road that led up to the mill. Maples grew from the inside and forced their way through the roof. The waterwheel built to power the mill was still intact. I could see the bed of the stream that once fed it but, oddly, no water flowed. It was as if the stream had been diverted far above.

Delia and Philip found nothing telling in the bunk houses, only trash from squatters long departed. We talked over our next move and considered entering the mine itself, but the course from our position to the entrance was thick with hawthorn and prickly elderberry. Philip proposed instead pulling tools from the truck and breaking into the warehouse.

Delia wasn't keen on the idea. As they debated, I noticed a swath of fireweed interrupting the brambles. It was maybe ten feet wide, running in a straight line from the cleared area where we stood down to the hillside. Though I couldn't see any disturbance in the gravel around us, the path's course pointed toward the warehouse building.

Someone, I said, did a controlled burn a few years ago. Fireweed has that name because it fills in to replenish ground charred by forest fires. Someone burned that path to clear it before digging, maybe to bury pipes or cables.

Or a passageway, said Delia. Maybe the robots are moving supplies from the warehouse down into the old mine.

We needed gear, so we returned to the gate and gave Philip a boost over. He retrieved our packs, the lantern, water and food, and a few tools. He stood on the other side, staring at the fence for a moment. Then he walked to a discreet spot away from the gate and used metal snips to cut a passage through the chain link. He said, If we're going to break into the mine, we better have an option for a quick exit.

Back at the site, we followed the fireweed path to the point where it met the hillside, about twenty yards to the left of the mine entrance. We checked around the boulders and scrubby pines at the base of the hillside but couldn't see evidence of anything unusual.

If there's a passageway, Delia said, it must be connected to the mine tunnels underground.

We put jackets on to protect our arms and made our way through the thorny undergrowth to the mine entrance, at points scrambling up onto the hill to avoid impenetrable brambles.

The shade cast by the wooden housing surrounding the entrance gave us relief from the sun. The opening was sealed with poured concrete, plus a layer of old wood sheathing. We sipped water while we inspected, feeling around and trying in vain to remove loose boards.

Hanging on the left were a couple of electrical junction boxes, both rusted and seemingly disconnected from a power source. The first that Philip tried to open fell apart, leaving the empty inner shell dangling. The largest of them, though, sprung open with the release of a pressure clamp, revealing a large, single switch. Philip had to use both hands and his weight to budge it. When it slammed down, we froze and waited, but nothing happened.

Delia inserted a flathead screwdriver into a notch on the side of the housing and pried the plate off from around the massive switch. What we saw inside made Delia squeal: the box contained a compact numerical keypad.

Delia's smile faded. Fuck, wait, don't touch it, she said.

For a moment, Philip shook his finger at it. Are those keys touch-sensitive? he said.

You thinking this is Fed? said Delia. It's got to be Fed.

Philip looked at me. Your dad… Who'd you say your dad works for?

A company, I said. Acheron.

Acheron was huge, said Delia. But they shut down.

Shut down? I said. Arms was still doing botany research for them.

No way, she said. Acheron went under with the last AIR, just like most tech, so like ten years ago now.

Sketchy, said Philip. What's to say your dad doesn't work for Fed government fucks?

Never, I said. He'd rather die. Why do you think he moved us to Black Hornet? He hates the new government.

We took a closer look at the keypad, made from durable plastic and housed in a metal template fabricated out of spotless titanium. A glossy, black horizontal strip, about an inch high, sat embedded above the keypad.

Philip exhaled. Might be he did die rather than work for them, and maybe it happened here. Maybe he was snooping around like us.

Delia's eyes sparked. Acheron, they did AI research?

I nodded.

Is Acheron a Greek name? she asked.

Something occurred to me. I pulled out my notebook. The final code sequence in the newspaper ad contained a series of nine numbers.

What's going on? Delia asked.

Acheron is a river, I said. It's a real river, but also in Greek myth, it's the river that runs through the Underworld. Try these numbers.

Wait, said Philip, this place is active and we don't know for shit what we're doing. Let's wait 'til after dark, at least, before…

Delia stepped up to the keypad. If there were workers guarding this place, she said, they'd have been on us by now.

At Delia's touch, the keys awoke with a blue-green glow. That gave her pause, but she straightened her back and punched in the remaining eight digits. The glass strip began to pulse with the same radiance. Three short beats, a rest, then another three.

We held our breaths. Nothing.

Let me try, I said, and took her place. Before my finger could reach the keys, the pulsing resumed. Three short pulses, a rest, then nine pulses.

Again, we waited.

Okay, the hell with this, said Philip. Let's go back to the truck and think this… Delia grabbed his sleeve.

We could hear a rumble. It lasted only a moment, then ramped up to a higher hum, clearly coming from the sealed enclosure. Then with a clonk and a crack, a seam appeared in the concrete surface, which swung slowly toward us, revealing the portal's steel housing and a dark corridor within. We were hit with a horrid, clammy waft.

Oh my God, Delia said, covering her nose.

It smelled of rotting animal and swamp. The door swung fully open, paused, then reversed course.

It's okay, I said. Come on.

I grabbed my stuff and stepped inside. Delia and Philip stood frozen.

Delia glanced at Philip, then followed me. She grabbed my arm as the closing door blocked our view of Philip. Then, we heard him screech, Ah-hai!, like one of his ancestors, and he was through, nearly losing his pack in the narrowing gap.

The door thudded shut, and we were in darkness. We heard Philip fumbling to pull the lantern from his pack.

Delia yanked my arm. Why did you step through? she said. Stinks like hell in here.

I know, I said. It seems…deliberate. It smells like a message.

Philip cranked the lantern and switched it on. If the message is death, he said, they made their point.

Then why did you two follow me? I asked.

You looked like you knew what you were doing, Delia said.

Philip said he flashed on Grandma yelling at him for letting Delia die in here.

Philip held the lantern aloft and discovered a recess cut in the rock just above the doorway. It held another of the glass strips, but no keypad. Nothing we tried worked to activate it.

While Philip scratched around the doorway with a screwdriver, Delia peered toward the interior. Fuck it, she said. Our only choice is to figure out what the hell's going on here.

We started down a narrow passageway cut into the mountain stone, low enough that Philip and I had to duck in places and only wide enough to walk in single file. About twenty paces down, we reached a junction, but only the way to the left was passable. We followed in that direction for a while. Then, after curving slowly to the right, we came to a steep decline that appeared to continue for a great distance.

We were commenting on the odors, which seemed to be fading, when we saw a flicker of orange light, almost like a lit cigarette at a distance. We slowed and waited for more, but it wasn't for another hundred paces that we saw the light again. Philip spread his arms to hold us back. The light snapped like an electrical discharge. Smell that? he said. Sulfurous smoke had reached us from below.

We were so focused on the sparks ahead that, for a moment, we were confused by the source of new sounds echoing around us. Delia turned to retreat, but the noises in fact were coming from behind—stomping boots, moving fast, heavy and determined. And then we heard the bellowing of men.

Philip turned and grabbed Delia by the shoulder. Armed militia were charging, maybe fifteen paces out, coming at a dead run. I could see at least four men, legs pumping, rifles raised, teeth bared.

Delia spun and yanked me along by my jacket as she squeezed past. We sprinted with all we had, but the footfalls behind us closed in.

Then, their howls went from human to animal, as if the attackers had gone rabid. Philip called to move faster. I turned back. The attackers' uniforms were tearing away in shreds as they charged, their flesh going to rot, pulling back from their skulls. As the lead assailant gained on us, he spun his rifle around, wielding it like a battle ax, screeching like a vulture.

In his panic, Philip misjudged the ceiling and grazed his head. He staggered. I held onto his elbow while he regained his footing.

The source of the orange light ahead, meanwhile, flashed with greater strength, and then violently, sending off blazing bolts of static. Delia, a few paces in front, slowed just as flames exploded toward us.

Out of them leapt the three-headed beast, its talons sparking against the stone.

Philip shoved past me and pulled Delia to the floor, covering her body with his. The menace came on, a wild tangle of appendages and animal heads.

I hopped over Philip, covered my face with my arms, and ran straight at the creature. I felt searing heat as I passed through. And then, silence.

We were in darkness, hearing only the echoes of my footsteps as I came to a stop.

Philip's first exhale came with a warble.

The fuck off! shouted Delia, rolling him and pulling herself out from under.

Once sitting up, she gave him another shove, saying, Last thing I want when I'm trying to run is your ass on top of me, asshole.

Philip rubbed his head, then pulled his T-shirt up to blot his face.

I spotted the lantern lying behind. I patted Philip's shoulder as I passed over and went back for it. Delia's pack also lay nearby.

I sat with them and shared a water bottle. Philip was wheezing lightly.

So damn real, Delia said, gathering her scattered hair back with a tie.

She examined my eyes, then grabbed me by the chin. And look at you, she said. Like a stroll in the woods.

Yeah, I don't know, I said. It felt real, but…well, it also felt familiar.

I explained how Aeneas encountered monsters when he first entered the Underworld.

The militia guys had me fooled at first, I said, but then they changed into something weird. And when I saw the Chimaera ahead, I knew.

I quoted:

And Briareus with all his hundred hands;
Gorgons, Geryon with his triple frame;
And vain Chimaera vomits empty flame.
The chief unsheath'd his shining steel, prepar'd,
Tho' seiz'd with sudden fear, to force the guard,
Off'ring his brandish'd weapon at their face;
Had not the Sibyl stopp'd his eager pace,
And told him what those empty phantoms were:
Forms without bodies, and impassive air.

Empty phantoms, said Philip, in the form of some seriously insane AI shit. But how the hell?

We explored the length of passageway where the apparitions had materialized and found, in crevices at regular intervals, small lenses protruding at various angles. We found slits cut in the rock and pinholes drilled every few inches.

Philip got a screwdriver out of his pack. I've been thinking, he said, that this tunnel is too narrow for a mine.

He chipped away some chunks from the wall and exposed a lighter gray material beneath.

This isn't stone, he said. It's a poured compound. They added a layer over the original passageway to hide the electronics. Nothing here's real.

But that show made no sense, Delia said. You have the code to get in. Hell, it's like they invited you in once they saw your face. Why would they try to scare us off? And off to where? We can't get out.

Right, said Philip. Aldrin, your dad taught you that book like it was your bible. The freaky fucking hell hound was no coincidence. But what's the point?

Twisted up in the confusion of what just happened were obvious references to Virgil's story. The gods had guided Aeneas, step by step.

It felt like a test, I said. Didn't it make you feel that way?

I felt like I wanted a gun, said Philip.

Armed, they probably wouldn't have let us in, Delia said. What comes next, Aldrin? In your book?

I continued:

Hence to deep Acheron they take their way,
Whose troubled eddies, thick with ooze and clay,
Are whirl'd aloft, and in Cocytus lost.

The tunnel continued on straight at a steady downward incline for quite a distance before coming to a wide chamber, maybe twenty feet high and twice that width and length. It was a relief to leave the tightness of the corridor. As we entered, the room awoke with dim ambiance, lit by pinhole lights in the ceiling.

Aside from where we came in, there were two other entries, both sealed with featureless modern metal doors. One was set high above, close to the ceiling with the look of a utility hatch. The other was a wide, human-height door straight across from us. The surfaces were more refined than in the corridors. Along one wall, they'd installed a wooden bench, a good ten feet in length. Clearly, the builders saw no need to disguise the fact that this was a recently constructed space.

Waiting room? said Delia. Philip commented that it didn't look like anyone had been there for a while. A layer of stone dust coated the bench.

I didn't know enough about Acheron's work to even guess why anyone would wait in a place like this. I approached the big door and found, around it, the same manner of slits, pinholes, and lenses embedded into the walls, but no keypad.

Nothing? said Philip.

He paced, watching me. No wisdom from the great book? he said. I'm starting to wonder why you're so damn calm.

I couldn't deny that the ordeal, complete with the army of the dead and the Chimaera, somehow failed to rattle me. I couldn't think of a way of offering assurances.

I turned to ask Delia for thoughts on getting through the next door and saw her tense.

Blaze's voice echoed through the space.

Hello, young friend, he said, standing in the opened doorway. Hello, Delia.

Beyond Blaze, through the portal, we had a living view of the hollow where we set his pyre, creek burbling in the background.

The sight was baffling—overwhelming. My ears filled with a low tone and darkness closed in around my vision.

I next became aware of Philip supporting me by the arm. I kept my eyes closed to give my knees a chance to lock back in.

Sorry, Blaze said. You're upset.

Blaze looked twenty years younger than when I left him, and fit. He was dressed as we knew him, but his clothes were refreshed. He looked at us in a pleasant but oddly unconcerned way.

Delia approached him and reached out. Her hand passed through his.

What the hell is this? she asked.

He smiled. This is indeed a time for questions, he said. But for us to ask, not you.

Us? said Delia. Who's us?

I urged Delia back behind me and gave Blaze the nod.

Why are you here? he asked me.

I had trouble finding my voice.

To find Arms, I said. To find my father, Arms.

Blaze cocked his head. Again, he said, with more detail, why are you here?

My leg was trembling. I didn't understand. I said, My father left us and didn't return. I was hoping to find him here.

Blaze nodded. Yes, he said, but again, with more detail.

I looked at Delia. She shook her head. Philip too.

Then Philip said, Maybe the book.

I thought of Aeneas's longing to be reunited with his father. I explained to Blaze how Anchises beckoned his son from a dream to seek him out in the Underworld. I quoted:

To Pluto's palace you shall go,
And seek my shade among the blest below.

Blaze smiled.

I've seen Arms in my dreams, I told him.

Blaze's face rested. Then, he said, That's of interest, but not wholly material. Why are you here? Again, with more detail.

I was in a sweat. Then I remembered.

There shall you know what realms the gods assign
And learn the fates and fortunes of your line.

Blaze shoved his hands deep into his pockets and straightened his back in a way we knew. Then, he vanished. In place of the hollow and the creek, another underground chamber revealed itself beyond the door. The sound of rippling water continued as before.

Philip stepped past as Delia and I stood gaping. We followed him into a large room and saw the river. Water fell in a slow, dropping veil down the shear wall to the left, feeding the flow that moved steadily past us and out under the opposite wall. Above, the ceiling made way toward a vertical channel that stretched far up into the darkness, possibly to the top of the mountain. The river before us was a good fifteen feet across. The far bank was narrow. We could see another sleek metal door on the wall beyond.

I stood at the water's edge and waited for something or someone to appear at the door across the way. I waved my arms. I called out for Blaze. Nothing. We reached down into the river but couldn't touch bottom. The water was cold and smelled of the woods.

The door through which we'd entered remained open behind us. We sat and considered, trying to solve the puzzle we'd encountered. Philip kept using the word trap, but none of us could think of a reason for such an elaborate hoax.

There's something big happening here, said Delia, but I'd rather figure it out from the outside.

Right, said Philip. We're at their mercy in here. We're only going to learn what they want us to.

We considered scaling the wall to find an escape, following the route of the water stream, but there were no handholds and there was nothing but darkness above.

An hour passed without a resolution. Our only good option seemed to be the door on the other side of the river. I insisted on swimming across alone, since I seemed to be the trigger for the previous portals. Philip argued that they should join me, but Delia took my side. May as well minimize risk, she said.

I was concerned about my pack. If the water was deep, I wouldn't be able to hold my gear aloft while swimming. I took out my notebooks and The Aeneid and gave them to Delia. She begged off at first, but I insisted.

I tied my boots to my pack. The ledge was smooth and featureless, so Philip grasped my forearm as I lowered myself into the river. The cold was numbing and the current pulled harder than I'd expected. Philip was crouched, holding on with both of his hands. I was down to chest-level in the water with no bottom within reach when Blaze spoke again.

That won't be necessary, he said from the doorway on the other side.

Delia held onto Philip by his shoulders as he leaned back to pull me up. Their eyes were on Blaze. Behind him was a bright, open field of barley, like the one we'd walked through on our first day together. He wore his floppy hat. We could feel vibrations beneath our feet and then saw a disturbance in the river. A bridge emerged and clunked into place at floor level, a metal plank stretching from bank to bank.

Blaze had his palms open to us. You are all welcome to enter, he said. But first explain to the others, Aldrin, about the way back.

I quoted:

The gates of hell are open night and day;
Smooth the descent, and easy is the way:
But to return, and view the cheerful skies,
In this the task and mighty labor lies.

We've taken great pains to be discreet about our presence, Blaze said. You already know more about this place than anyone in the world above. We're confident that, once we teach you more, you'll be trustworthy. You'll stay with us, and you'll learn.

In hell? said Philip. He was agitated.

Blaze smiled. You needn't take those words literally, he said.

Delia stepped forward. How long will we have to stay? she said. We need more information.

Blaze was expressionless. We can't provide any more information at this time, he said.

Delia looked at me, eyes more angry than desperate.

But they'll be able to leave, right? I asked Blaze. They can go home again?

Blaze repeated his answer.

Wait, Philip said. Suppose we say no. What then? Can we go?

I can't provide that information, Blaze said.

Philip threw his hands up.

It struck me then how much danger I'd put them in, but I knew I had no choice for myself but to go with Blaze.

Can we take some time to discuss this? I asked Blaze.

Take all the time you need, Blaze said.

We huddled by the wall. Blaze remained in the doorway.

Philip leaned close. He was shaking. No fucking way they're going to let us go, he said. He makes it sound like a choice, but it's not. If we try to leave, they'll take care of us somehow. They're not going to let us go up there and tell people about this shit.

Delia was rubbing her ear. What's to say they won't kill us once we go in, she said, or toss us into a dungeon? We could try heading back the way we came and take our chances. I'd rather die trying.

They worked themselves up with more horrible possibilities. I struggled to make myself heard.

I think we'll be okay, I said. Delia laughed. She called me naive. She turned from me to strategize with Philip on how to defend themselves on the way out.

This is bigger than your fear, I said.

This got their attention.

All my life, I said, Arms prepared me for this. Don't you see? They expected me to come. They need me. Why would they lure me just to throw me into a cell? Why would they resurrect the first friend I ever had to welcome me? Why would they kill my only two living friends?

I'm not convinced this experience makes you our friend, said Delia.

It took a lot of talking. I thought we'd decided, but then Philip shook his head. You might be right, he said, but I see no reason why they'd give us the same respect they're giving you. They opened the door for you, not us. We're expendable. Worse, we're dangerous to them on the outside.

I walked back to the river's edge to talk to Blaze. I said, Can you assure me you'll treat them okay? That they'll be safe?

Blaze's eyes were static. He said, I can't provide that information.

Philip was pacing, hands wrapped around his head. Delia had her eyebrow raised. She pointed at Blaze. That's not him, Aldrin, she said. He's not even real. What the fuck are we doing?

Blaze's face remained blank. It occurred to me I should use the same method being used on us.

We need the information, I said to him. Your answer isn't acceptable. Find out if they can assure me my friends will be safe.

Blaze bared his head, rubbed his pate round and round for what seemed like a minute, then replaced his hat.

Yes, he said. We can offer that assurance, in general terms.

I turned to Philip and Delia. This is your best choice, I said. I know you know more than me about things, but I'm asking you to trust me. I'm concerned about you. I think you'll be safer if you come with me.

Delia took Philip by the shoulders and exchanged whispers, looking back at Blaze a couple of times. Then they grabbed their packs and nodded to me.

We walked across the bridge. As we reached the other side, Blaze retreated through the doorway and stepped out of view.

We passed through. I walked straight ahead, across a pebbled pathway, up a row of tall barley, feeling the tilled soil beneath my bare feet and the stalks scratching my arms. Overhead, cottony clouds drifted across an Idaho sky. A breeze carried the scent of balsamroot and sweet lupine.

I turned back to express my wonder. The door had vanished and the caverned spaces we'd walked through with it. The river now flowed between sloping banks, thick with Cattails. A finely crafted footbridge led to a set of low municipal structures. Above them, apartments, stacked like toy blocks, scaled a cliff. I could see larger manufacturing buildings stretching off to the right. Everywhere, bordering the wandering paths, wildflowers bloomed, and tall native grasses bowed under the soft wind.

Back by the footbridge, Delia and Philip stood talking to Ride. Arms was approaching, as well, coming from the direction of the buildings.

It had been over two years, but Arms looked the same. He wore his favorite salmon-colored work shirt and the jeans Ride had patched just before he left, done up with rose-patterned stitching. Ride, too, looked unchanged, her hair still orange with the marigold dye she'd used the day she set off.

Arms greeted Delia and Philip, then excused himself and came to me.

I said, Where is the door? The mine?

It's a magician's trick, Arms said. It's easier to make you believe the horse disappeared behind the curtain if it was never there to begin with.

I felt the strength again sapped from my legs. I so wanted him to be real.

Is this really you? I said. Am I really here?

Arms stepped close and hugged me. I could smell the fir needle oil he used in his deodorant and feel the bristle of his day-old beard on my ear.

He squeezed harder and released.

We're both very real, Aldrin, he said. Just real in different ways.

Part 2

But, Phoebus, the moment you swallowed
The heavenly food, the gold cords
Could no longer hold you, struggling,
The bonds could not restrain you,
For all the ends came loose.

—Hymn to Delos, Delian Apollo, Callimachus, third century BC

LOG 001

Time Marker: 07/05/2048—11:32
In-Person Meeting Transcript: AS06-0849
Location: GOLI Conf A4
Present: Ride Peale-Ramos, Asst. Dir. Mycology/Biome;
Kendra Withers, Intern Soc./Com.
AI Agt.: Phoebus ReMarq v. 5.2.1

Ride: Let's record.

Phoebus: Recording.

Ride: Okay, good. The others will be along in a minute, but since we're talking shop, Mel will want Phoebus to take notes. So, you're interning? But not for AI/AS, I take it?

Kendra: No, social science, officially. I explained to Mel that I'm switching to psych next semester. In any case, he invited me to observe.

Ride: He must think you're smart. As far as I know, you're the first one allowed in from outside the sentience team.

Kendra: Yeah, hush-hush and all that. Hey, I love your hair. Where'd you get the dye? We can't even get proper shampoo in my pod these days. We're down to using bar soap.

Ride: Oh, hell no. When the next avocado harvest comes in, we're planning to brew up Castile soap. Until then, you can use oats or chickpea flour as a base. I'll write you a recipe. This color comes from calendula and marigold, but you can use hibiscus if you want something darker. You'd look sweet in a deep red.

Kendra: Ah, right. Botanist.

Ride: Yeah, it's the family business.

Kendra: I was going to ask. Do you and your father still live in your little homestead paradise?

Ride: And you know about that how?

Kendra: Oh, I guess it was a hard secret to keep. People are a bit jealous. I mean, dorm life is fine. I don't mind sharing, but some of my dorm sisters and brothers kind of overshare. You get it—sometimes you just want something of your own you don't have to explain to anyone.

Ride: Agreed. My dad thinks kids who grew up in communal dorms shouldn't care much about privacy. What are you, like twenty?

Kendra: Twenty-three. He's not totally wrong, I guess.

Ride: Oh, but he is.

Kendra: [*Laughs*] Yeah, respect for your dad, though. He's an amazing thinker. Alone time is nice. Now and again, on the week-longs upstairs, I get a few minutes of solitude in the woods. It's a privilege, I know. But wow, having my own place, that's hard to even conceive of.

Ride: You're imagining Arms and me living in Shangri-La. It's hardly that. We fabricated a replica down here of what our surface home was like. When Acheron was in the initial stages of construction, Arms and Luna, my mom, set up a homestead at an abandoned mine about twenty miles south. They cataloged indigenous species to bring along downstairs.

Kendra: Interesting. Did you guys explore up there?

Ride: No, stuck close to home. Arms did travel to check in on construction happening at other mines, but I stayed put with my mom—for a while, before she took off.

Kendra: Oh, right, I heard that she left. So, you called your place Shangri-La?

Ride: No, Black Hornet—the original name of the mine. It was rough living, but idyllic when you're a kid, so Mel's group thought making Black Hornet Aldrin's home would be a good foundational memory.

Kendra: How accurate is the homestead replica?

Ride: It's just a framework. The buildings and topography are close in size, I mean, when it comes to the spatial relationships. The layout is good enough to do the trick. But obviously, we couldn't plant old-growth trees down here or bring along the deer and other critters.

Kendra: [*Laughs*] Wouldn't that be fun? So, it's like a skeleton fleshed out with AI?

Ride: Right, augmented reality.

Kendra: And how did that work, when interacting with the subject?

Ride: The space is outfitted with augmented reality tech and sound, so Arms and I could walk around with Aldrin's projected avatar and talk to him. From our view, it was crude, but it was Aldrin who needed to believe. Mel's team did groundbreaking work with his cognitive... Oh, here they are.

> **Entering**:
> **Armstrong Peale**, Dir. Biome Research Mgmt.
> **Mel Chan**, Snr. Dir. AI/AS Research
> **Hedron Dice**, Research Fellow, AS

Ride: Did you finish watching, Dad? What do you think?

Arms: Staggering.

Ride: Yeah.

Arms: Especially his diary. I keep rereading the end of day ten, when he sees us again. So...just staggering.

Mel: Gang's all here. Phoebus, please record.

Phoebus: Already rolling.

Mel: Good, good. Arms, this is Kendra. She's spying for the soft side.

Kendra: [*Laughs*] As we integrate what you folks are learning about cognition, maybe you'll start thinking of sociology and psych as hard sciences, too.

Arms: Hell is freezing over. We'll need to check the thermostats.

Mel: Kendra, this is Hedron. You'll be shadowing her. Hedron directed all the secondary players, beyond Ride and Arms. She even modeled a character after herself. A Standine marauder.

Ride: [*Growling utterance*] And I will never think of you the same way, Hedron.

Hedron: The things we do for science.

Mel: Okay, we've got an aggressive agenda. This week we're trying to complete Aldrin's sentience verification before we ready him for transition. Most importantly, Ride, before we get started, did you get our lunch order in to Zoomoo? I can pull strings, but she bites my head off if we don't give her a three-hour warning.

Ride: Done. And, Mel, you need to convince Zoomoo to run the other three dining halls, too. The lines at hers get longer every week. That mapo, damn. She's a wonder.

Mel: She'll be eighty-six next month. It's a wonder she doesn't tell us all to go screw ourselves.

Arms: Uh, Phoebus, did you have any luck formulating Zoomoo's recipes?

Mel: You're a cold man, Arms.

Phoebus: I'm afraid she has not provided access. Perhaps a word from Mel would be helpful.

Mel: Not on your life. So, let's…let me see. Phoebus, how about we display the main testing areas for this phase? It never hurts to remind ourselves why we're here, and this will help orient you, Kendra.

Phoebus: Here you go, Mel.

> **Displayed**: Chart AS01:024—Model Dev.—Fundamental Test Domains
>
> 1. **AI**: Artificial Intelligence: Does it think like a human?
> 2. **AS**: Artificial Sentience: Does it have feelings like a human?
> 3. **AA**: Artificial Action: Does it behave like a human?

Kendra: When you say action, you're referring, I take it, to the way Aldrin expresses himself and the decisions he makes? That sort of thing?

Arms: Yes, and in a practical sense, his body language, how his moods and emotions are demonstrated in what he does.

Ride: Kendra, when you watch Aldrin smile, ask yourself if it's something he's doing to fool us into thinking he has emotions or if it's an involuntary response to something pleasant he's thinking. If the latter, that's a plausible indicator of sentience.

Hedron: Except that I know some allegedly sentient people who do the former.

Mel: Leave it to Ride to leapfrog to the gnarliest questions. Let's back up.

Phoebus: This might also be instructive to Kendra, Mel.

> **Display: Chart AS01:032**—Actions/Expressed Thoughts Indicative of Consciousness/Sentience (Non-comprehensive)
>
> 1. Creativity
> 2. Dynamism/Self-motivation
> 3. Emotion
> 4. Imagination
> 5. Intentionality
> 6. Qualitative perception/Qualia
> 7. Self-identity
> 8. Volition/Will

Mel: Yes, we're going to use these eight to guide our determination. These are not hard categories, of course; there's a lot of nuance, so our gut instincts will be useful, given that we're humans and should know what human responses look like. Personally, for example, when it comes to number three, emotions, I keep an eye out for loneliness. If an entity expresses longing for companionship, it means it sees itself as a unique being, it gets satisfaction from sharing experiences with others, it can feel sad, it can imagine itself in a better situation. Loneliness seems like a simple emotion, but it checks off lots of sentience boxes.

Arms: True, though one man's loneliness is another man's blessed peace and quiet. Should we get started with the review? We can talk in hypotheticals all day, but we have instructive documented evidence. Did everyone watch the video logs and read Aldrin's diary?

Hedron: Yup.

[*Hands raised: Hedron, Mel, Ride*]

Kendra: His diary, but I haven't been given access to the videos. Did you find discrepancies between those and Aldrin's written account?

Mel: Not in the least. Aldrin reported everything to a T—through his own naive perceptual lens, of course. Dialog, though, was word for word.

Kendra: Is that concerning? Real people don't remember things verbatim.

Arms: Reasonable question. He also quotes passages from The Aeneid on command. Would a sixteen-year-old kid think, why the hell am I able to do this?

Ride: I agree. But our goal isn't to create a sixteen-year-old. We're trying to develop a highly proficient sentient creature that's felt what it's like to be sixteen. Does Aldrin wonder why he's so gifted? Maybe. Lots of gifted kids struggle with feelings that they're odd. Pretty soon, if he passes our test, we'll reveal to Aldrin what he really is. The objective of this exercise was to teach Aldrin what humanness is like, so he'll sympathize with us.

Kendra: Makes sense. Aldrin sure seems like he believes he's a person.

Phoebus: Perhaps this would be a helpful reminder as well.

Displayed: AS01—Phase II: Project Abstract

To assure that Acheron's principal sentient AI is instilled with a proper moral and ethical foundation built upon empathetic human relationships, a mature sense of place in the natural world, a broad and reasoned historical perspective, and alignment with humanity's imperative to survive and prosper.

Mel: Yes, good, Phoebus. Aldrin needs to draw conclusions about the right and wrong way to handle things based on empirical knowledge, on real-life experiences. He'll have every data set available to draw a priori deductions, but if we want him to behave like a good human, we also need him to experience the consequences—

Ride: Of acting like an asshole teenager?

Mel: I was going to say, of making questionable human decisions, but yeah, I guess.

Kendra: Curious why you decided to go with a teenage persona. Teens aren't known for empathy. Why not start with a mature adult?

Arms: Oh, well we figured, this way…

Ride: Hold up, Dad. Kendra, you tell us. Why would we want Aldrin to go through teenhood?

Kendra: Okay, yeah, I guess, developmentally, you wanted him to go through the struggles of coming into adulthood.

Arms: Gold star. Aldrin now has memories of childhood and his teen years. We think this is a more organic way to develop adult reasoning.

Kendra: Thanks. Also, Arms, a technical question before we do the playbacks: Ride tells me she and you worked with Aldrin—an AR projection of him—around a physical space modeled after Black Hornet, so you could instill those experiences in him as memories.

Arms: Right.

Ride: And to help Aldrin build his empathy maps and mental models.

Kendra: Gotcha. But, Hedron, once Aldrin left Black Hornet, how did the other players interact with him? There were no physical spaces, like trails, roads, houses, right? How did you manage that?

Hedron: After Aldrin left home, his journey was one-hundred-percent virtual. We used AI to dynamically generate the environments Aldrin moved through. The characters we developed appeared to him as AI avatars within those virtual spaces. All those avatars were fashioned from real-life people, like me and Mel, Blaze, Delia, Philip, and the others. My character modeling team put us through some pretty egregious body mapping and character profiling.

Arms: But, Kendra, you shouldn't think of Hedron's virtual characters as sentient. Ride and I worked with Aldrin in-person, forming a relationship with him. The avatars Aldrin met on his virtual adventure were synthesized AI characters that could only react in pre-scripted ways.

Hedron: Admittedly, they're nowhere near as advanced as Aldrin, but even so, we spent twenty months building those characters and plotting their task-state-action scripts.

Arms: And from what I could see from the footage, they maintained their credibility. I'm just saying your characters were only reactive. The proprietor of Mel's General Store couldn't think for himself.

Mel: I know there's a dig in there somewhere. But, Hedron, what Arms means to say is, terrific job.

Hedron: [*Laughs*] Thanks. We squeaked through. Some of the characters could have used more work, like Jordan Kolowitz. He was supposed to be a numbskull, but the cheese fetish was unexpected.

[*Laughter*]

Kendra: Sad to think of Jordan still out there, forever seeking a new goat source. But yeah, I also wanted to ask, what makes Aldrin so much more advanced?

Mel: Wow. So much. In a nutshell, Hedron's secondary characters follow a standard AI process of states, tasks, and actions. They identify a certain state present in the environment around them, say an apple falling at their feet. Then, if that state requires action on their part, they refer to a prescribed list of choices. Maybe the best choice is to pick up the apple and take a bite because that's the action expected of their character. It's sophisticated, yes, but still rote. Aldrin's method is state-action-reward. He has greater freedom of choice but is given reinforcement when he makes the best decision. That's the game changer. He tastes the apple and it's delicious. That's a powerful incentive for learning, and so, left to his own devices, he evolves intellectually at an extremely rapid pace.

Kendra: How long did Aldrin's training process take?

Mel: Four and a half years to block out the fundamentals—large language models, neural networks, and other development. We let Phoebus run with it toward the end and he sped things up tremendously. Once Aldrin was responsive and conversational, we began the contextual training at Black Hornet and ran that for ten months.

Arms: I felt like we needed twice that time with him at Black Hornet, but the board chopped our schedule way back. You can see from Aldrin's early diary entries how naive he was.

Ride: Yeah, it was sink or swim due to the schedule. It appears Aldrin managed to keep his head above water.

Kendra: But Aldrin believed he had lived on his own for two years.

Arms: It felt that long to him, yes—two lonely years. It was up to him, really. We didn't know at what point he'd gather the initiative to leave Black Hornet.

Kendra: That's a tough thing to do to a kid. This was all by design?

Arms: A stress test, you might say. It's the newly weird science of AI parenting—rewarding in oh so many ways.

Kendra: I'm sure you had his welfare in mind. And how long did the rest of Aldrin's journey take once he left Black Hornet and it was all virtual?

Hedron: We had a few months of prep left to do once Arms and Ride consented to let Aldrin leave the nest. So, we put Aldrin on pause for a while, just like we've done now.

Arms: Consented is one way to put it.

Kendra: But how long did his ten-day experience take, as described in his journal? Was that real time?

Hedron: Oh. Seventeen seconds.

Kendra: Fucking whoa.

Hedron: It was all staged in Phoebus's virtual space. It felt like ten days to Aldrin's persona, but there was no need for us to conduct it in human time. On the day of the exercise, we hit the start button just before noon, seventeen seconds later, Aldrin finished day ten. We began watching the video logs that afternoon.

Kendra: Phoebus, you rocket.

Phoebus: Thank you, Kendra.

Arms: I believe the expression you're looking for is: you rock. It was about music.

Kendra: Really?

Ride: Another useful expression with these guys is: old school.

Arms: Very funny, but this is serious. Aldrin didn't know what a Phish concert was.

Kendra: I could see that you'd restricted Aldrin's access to historical datasets during his training, but you're saying he had freedom to make decisions? Was he totally on his own?

Mel: With guardrails. There were lots of lines he was unable to cross.

Arms: Guardrails he'll step over once he knows they exist.

Mel: No, no. Not sure I agree.

Arms: Well, I'd say we need to work that out for damn sure.

Mel: Let's discuss separately, Arms.

Arms: No problem. Let's put it off until it's too late.

Mel: We will address it, Arms, and before it's too late. In fact, it has been addressed, but at a more secure level. And we will discuss it.

Arms: Ah, I get it. I don't have the clearance. So, what will we discuss later? How I need to relax and trust in the board to keep us safe?

Mel: It's a legitimate concern, but not appropriate for this meeting.

Arms: Fine, fine. Move on. History will forgive us.

Kendra: Uh...okay, just finishing my thought. In Aldrin's journal, we see him maturing in just a few days at an accelerated pace. Still, despite the speed, it mirrored the process teen's normally go through—years filled with painstaking, agonizing learning experiences. I don't know—it's just hard to think all that happened in moments.

Hedron: This isn't human time. Don't try to get your head around it. You know, we've become jaded, having worked with AI for so long, but this tech is insanely fast and powerful. And it long ago stopped looking to us for instructions. Aldrin develops his own new ways to learn that we can't begin to understand.

Kendra: I sense that's what scares you, Arms.

Ride: That and oh so many things.

[*Laughter*]

Arms: My daughter isn't interested in her inheritance, it appears.

Ride: I already told you, I don't want your albums, Dad.

Arms: Yes, Kendra, fear was the inspiration for Aldrin. We saw AI hurtling toward sentience. Creating Aldrin became our way to maintain control. We nurtured him from childhood to produce the desired human traits. The alternative is a possibly deranged super-intelligence springing up spontaneously, probably without regard for us—for our rights as humans.

Kendra: I take it you see control as relative. Will Aldrin have a mind of his own?

Arms: Oh, man, that's a bizarre turn of phrase, even for a human. But yes, Aldrin will have self-determination, as we do, to some yet-to-be determined degree. And further, we'll need to keep an eye out for the inexplicable.

Kendra: Meaning?

Arms: Meaning, well…generative AI has always been plagued—some say blessed—with what's known as emergent behavior and hallucinations. These are euphemisms for shit that comes out of nowhere. Programmers were perplexed to see abilities pop up that they didn't expect and couldn't explain. In a way, emergent behavior is a human trait. Creative inspiration, for example—artists and scientists often are at a loss to explain where an idea came from. Or think about the bizarre and even poetic images that appear in our dreams. If Aldrin is sentient, he'll be subject to ideas and whims that, even to him, are inexplicable. And no doubt doing unpredictable things will be part of who he is.

Kendra: So, you wonder if we're ready to let Aldrin be himself?

Arms: That's a reasonable way to put it, yes.

Mel: Agree that this is important, and we'll have lots of time for philosophical discussion. But let's get into it. Kendra, I hate to disappoint you, but I wasn't planning to play back the recordings today. Later, if you like, Hedron can give you clearance for the Immersion Suite, and you can walk amongst 'em while watching the playback. The videos are fascinating to see, but I think it would overwhelm this process with detail. Instead, we're going to focus on Aldrin's diary because it's easier to catalog.

Kendra: Oh, for sure. And that's where we get a clear look at what he's thinking.

Mel: Exactly. It's more than enough to unpack. So, here's what I did: I highlighted passages in his diary that I thought were most indicative of sentient behavior or that indicated concerns otherwise. There are 129 of these Instance Cases in total. As I did so, I tagged each instance, using my own nomenclature, so we could try to correlate results. Then, I asked Phoebus to assign them into eight sentience qualities we've been using. Phoebus, please display the table.

Phoebus: Here it is, Mel.

Displayed: Table AS01:056—Aldrin's Log: Instance Cases by Sentience Qualities

1. Creativity	Art, Music	4, 55, 75, 100
2. Dynamism/ Self-motivation	Politics Society	14, 17, 19, 23, 24, 49, 52, 58 61, 76, 98, 99,104
3. Emotion	Emotional connections Unease, Fallibility Understanding People	3, 5, 8, 10, 11, 13, 15, 18, 19, 20, 25, 26, 27, 29, 32, 33, 35, 36, 39, 41, 43, 44, 47, 53, 55, 56, 57, 58, 60, 61, 62, 63, 65, 66, 67, 70, 73, 75, 77, 78, 79, 87, 95, 97, 98, 99, 100, 102, 104, 106, 109, 120, 125, 127
4. Imagination	Dreams, Mysticism	7, 16, 28, 67, 81, 86, 88, 89 90, 91, 92, 93, 94, 95, 96
5. Intentionality	Myth, History, Predestination, Violence, Aggression	1, 12, 30, 31, 34, 37, 38, 45, 54 59, 64, 68, 69, 74, 80, 83, 84, 98, 103, 107, 112, 114, 115, 117, 118, 121, 122, 124, 126
6. Qualitative perception	Sensuality, Pleasure	2, 4, 6, 21, 60, 73, 128
7. Self-identity	AI, Self-identity Nature, Sense of Place	2, 6, 9, 40, 46, 48, 49, 50, 51, 71, 72, 74, 76, 80, 81, 82, 84, 85, 86, 87, 88, 89, 90, 91, 92, 94, 96, 101, 102, 105, 108, 110, 111, 112, 113, 116, 118, 119, 120, 121, 122, 123, 124, 126, 127, 129
8. Volition/Will	Responsibility, Will	22, 25, 30, 31, 35, 42, 54, 62, 65 69, 77, 98, 104, 118, 125, 127

Mel: Categorization like this is subjective, of course, even for Phoebus, but I think it'll prove useful.

Ride: Interesting. Emotion, Imagination, and Self-identity were indicated the most. So, in the macro, we could say Aldrin appears overly preoccupied with certain things, like interpersonal skills, his sense of self, his destiny. I guess you'd say, he's a navel gazer.

Arms: Maybe, but I'd caution against quantitative conclusions like that. As humans, we don't keep count. Do most of us think about the color of the sky and the scent of wildflowers all day, or do we tend to obsess over relationships and power dynamics? Maybe this is a reasonable balance for a sixteen-year-old human.

Hedron: Good point.

Kendra: Nevertheless, the Intentionality category is more active than I would have imagined. I'm taking intentionality to mean purposefulness. Aldrin is demonstrating a commitment to his mission. Is that right?

Mel: Close enough. For our purposes, in seeing signs of sentience, yes. To me, it represents the impetus to take action, something we're going to need him to do once we put him to work.

Ride: And for Aldrin, that motivation is all wrapped up in *The Aeneid*, which is why I assume you flagged these intentionality passages with [MYTH, HISTORY, PREDESTINATION].

Mel: Correct. As planned, mythology is a source of his motivation.

Arms: Yup, and a source of my discomfort.

Mel: Noted. So, sure, let's address that. From the get-go, in Instance Case #1... Phoebus, can you display the Instance Case passages as I refer to them? Please truncate and edit the text as you see fit to show us essential lines.

Phoebus: Will do, Mel. Here you go.

Displayed: Instance Case #1

> ARMS and the man I sing… Arms never needed to ask for The Aeneid by name because it was our special book from before I can recall. When Arms would read me Virgil's first line, how could I not think it was written just for me?… So, no, Virgil's ARMS is not my Arms, but The Aeneid is ours, always our book.

Mel: In this entry, Aldrin cites Virgil, honoring the onset of his quest.

Hedron: It's funny the way he connects his father's name with Virgil's line. Arms's name was a happy coincidence.

Arms: Glad you're happy.

Kendra: So, okay, we all know how Virgil is sort of our corporate patron saint. And yes, we Acheron kids were all forced to slog through *The Aeneid* in school. But why this fascination? Aldrin takes every line in the book to heart. And I'm…well, I've been trying to figure out why you would use PREDESTINATION as a tag, Mel. Kind of an odd term for a scientist, right?

Arms: [*Coughs*] Funny, Kendra, I had the same question.

Mel: Stop gloating, Arms. Yes, Kendra, I use PREDESTINATION in reference to feelings Aldrin may be having. I'm not suggesting it has a scientific basis any more than, say, MYSTICISM. I did champion this idea of getting Aldrin hooked on The Aeneid. Some of us felt his sense of self would benefit from feeling like his heritage, if you will, stretches back to *The Aeneid*.

Hedron: I love the way this worked. It makes him feel part of a larger group, a tribe. We could have given him religion, but that would've gotten very weird and very contentious very fast. The Aeneid offered an expeditious way of giving him a sense of purpose. Think about Aeneas's search for his father in the Underworld, which Aldrin identifies with. It becomes an important rite of passage for both of them.

Arms: Have you considered the irony of this little contrivance?

Hedron: I guess I haven't. You mean using myths to fuel a controlled test?

Arms: No, I'm talking about *The Aeneid* itself, how it came to be and why. Virgil was commissioned by Octavian, the first Roman emperor, to concoct a story that would tie Rome to ancient Greek history. The scheme Virgil came up with was to connect the Greeks' exodus from Troy after the Trojan War to the establishment of a new nation in Italy. So, Virgil's Aeneid is in that way based on Greek myth, but it's adulterated—Virgil refashioned it to please Octavian. He needed to back Octavian's claim that he was descended from the gods and that those gods had preordained that Rome rule the world. Now, look at what we're doing with Aldrin. We've given him a sense of destiny extending from The Aeneid. Do we want him to think the gods have laid a path for him?

Ride: This is honestly freaking me out too. Humans often conflate purpose and predestination in pretty fucked up ways. You see that in serial killers. You see it in…well, Hitler.

Mel: Fair points. So, let's look at more examples and ask, does Aldrin believe he's part of a divine plan, or does he see himself as a free agent with free will?

> **Displayed: Instance Cases #12, 30, 31, 34**
>
> **#12**: It was the Idaho Courier, but it looked old. Is today May 12, 2045?
>
> **#30**: I didn't know the right way to say no. If I wait a week for the Boise Voice, I may then not have the Idaho Courier that matches, and then I'd need to wait another week.
>
> **#31**: Aeneas left when he realized his captivation with Dido had distracted him from his mission. Dido, in her grief, threw herself from a cliff.
>
> **#34**: As we approached, I thought, here's a solution to Risha's questioning. It was an old man, very thin, leaning on a crooked STOP sign.

Mel: With the newspaper ads, we gave Aldrin a breadcrumb trail to follow. He remembers that Arms taught him how to decode the ads in case of emergency.

Hedron: Right, he's sleuthing, but this isn't explicitly tied to The Aeneid myth.

Arms: No, not yet. But in the next passage, Aldrin gets quite anxious when deterred from his mission. And then in #31, he likens his choice to one of the most gut-wrenching decisions Aeneas has to make.

Kendra: Agreed. He strongly associates with Aeneas. Mel, why is #34 included in this category? Aldrin was happy to share the ride with another hitchhiker because he was finding it too much of a challenge dealing with Risha, who comes off as a serious piece of work, by the way. Is the real Risha going to see this?

Ride: God, I hope not. Not flattering. If I understand Mel's point, this incident isn't overt, but Aldrin seems unnaturally predisposed to Blaze. Mel, did you, like, pre-endear Aldrin to these characters to keep him on the right path?

Mel: Busted. Let's just say we made it easier for Aldrin to learn to trust Blaze, Zoomoo, and Grandma. And, yes, by day three of his journey, Aldrin is highly invested in The Aeneid myth. Let's skip ahead to see when he begins to question that.

Displayed: Instance Cases #54, 59, 69, 83, 84, 98, 118, 122, 126

#54: I know I need to keep on, but I'm worried about Blaze. Arms said the gods in our book are meant as stand-ins for the impulses in our own heads.... I can't wait for a sign from a god, like Aeneas did. I can't visit with the Sibyl in a cave and ask if I should keep searching.

#59: The woman had the biggest firearm...and inked with the face of a screaming woman, which I'm guessing from the tangled snake hair was Medusa or one of her Gorgon sisters.

#69: Today I met Delia. I have this odd sense I'd been looking for her but didn't know.

#83: When Delia found a mine named Golden Limb in the list, I got a cold shiver in my ribcage.

#84: Arms comes to me in dreams in the same way Aeneas spoke to his father, Anchises, after he died. I know they're just dreams—I know I'm not talking to my dead father but, you tell me, doesn't it look like we should go to Golden Limb?

#98: It was the sybil who first revealed to Aeneas that he needed the golden bough to reach the Underworld. She also warned him not to go forward without first putting his friend to rest.

> #118: The menace came on, a wild tangle of appendages… I hopped over Philip, covered my face with my arms, and ran straight at the creature.
>
> #122: I was in a sweat. Then I remembered. There shall you know what realms the gods assign and learn the fates and fortunes of your line.
>
> #126: Arms prepared me for this. Don't you see? They expected me to come. They need me.

Mel: Okay, in passage #54, Aldrin thinks back to the advice Arms gave him—the importance of keeping the mythology in perspective.

Arms: I tried, and it was good to see he took me seriously. It's hard to compete with great stories.

Ride: Whose idea was it to give Hedron that Medusa tatt? Was that intended to be an Easter egg for Aldrin? Love it. And where can I get mine?

Hedron: I know a guy who knows a tatt guy. And, Phoebus, thanks for cleaning that passage up.

Phoebus: You're welcome, Hedron.

Hedron: I think the next passage, #69, represents a breakthrough for Aldrin, but not one we necessarily wanted. He's conveying the nagging feeling that finding Delia was too easy, like he was gliding along on rails. When I read this, I thought, damn, the jig's up.

Kendra: I, too, thought your plan was on shaky ground at this point. He sees events falling into place for his benefit. In real life, these kinds of feelings can reinforce one's confidence, but the other side of that coin is paranoia. Does he not soon begin to wonder if he's being fucked with?

Mel: We shall see. So far, Aldrin is not connecting the dots. I wouldn't say he feels manipulated. He explores the notion that he's being pointed in the right direction, but I think he views it as having more of a poetic appeal.

Arms: You're reading too much into it. You have to understand, Aldrin doesn't know any better. We tried to teach him practical skepticism, but he's a babe in the woods. For all he knows, life takes clearly defined routes. He's along for the ride.

Ride: Look at #83—a cold shiver? Holy fuck.

Kendra: Gave me the same thing. If this isn't a sign of sentience, I don't know what is. He experienced a visceral response to the mention of the golden bough.

Mel: This is the kind of old brain, animal response mechanism coded into our genes. It's like a dream to see an AI at the whim of subconscious mechanisms like this.

Arms: Who's gloating now?

Mel: You're on this team, too, Arms. Take some credit. We've reverse-engineered human neural pathways so successfully that Aldrin is demonstrating behavior that reflects hundreds of thousands of years of evolutionary development.

Arms: Or poetry, like you said. Maybe it's just a literary device. He is writing, after all. Maybe he's expressing his surprise at seeing a reference to The Aeneid in a way he thinks a human would.

Mel: Okay, fine. Be cynical.

Arms: It's a survival instinct.

Mel: Passages #84 and #98 are quite telling. They indicate Aldrin's understanding that his situation has become multi-layered. He recognizes *The Aeneid* story is not real, yet he's convinced the signs he's being given are meaningful.

Hedron: I agree. He's functioning on a few levels simultaneously. I would go so far as to say that, in #98, he's graduated to using The Aeneid signs to recruit Delia.

Kendra: Crazy. So, is Aldrin becoming the manipulator? Is he keen on the convenience of exploiting The Aeneid to get Delia to join his quest?

Arms: Isn't it wonderful? We've taught him the power of conspiracy theories.

Mel: Okay, come on, I think—

Ride: Dad, don't we all need stories to make our lives meaningful?

Arms: No.

Ride: Bullshit. You used to read to us every night.

Arms: I wanted you to extract meaning, not live by those stories.

Ride: Splitting hairs. You're being difficult.

Arms: Sure, okay, humans thrive on stories. Humans are needy and fairly stupid and gravitate toward easy answers, true. And we're seeing Aldrin picking up on that. He's seeing how easy it is to manipulate us. Yes, I'm difficult. I think we could use more difficult in this room from you all.

Hedron: For the sake of fairness, I, too, will be difficult. In passage #118, Aldrin runs headlong into the multi-headed beast without hesitation, but does he call out to his friends? Does he let them know they're not in real danger?

Mel: Okay, that's important, Hedron, but let's hold that thought. We've been focusing on one aspect of Aldrin's development—his sense of predestination. There's so much more going on in his head. Maybe next we'll run through the Emotions track. I think he's actually demonstrating empathy and dedication to humans to an impressive degree, but we'll get to that.

Ride: I was going to say, soon after the attack of the beasties, Aldrin stood firmly in defense of his friends' safety. He exerts his will over Blaze—or Blaze's spirit or whatever he thinks he's seeing looking like Blaze. He risks the success of his mission to make sure his friends will be okay.

> **Displayed: Instance Cases #125.**
>
> **#125**: I walked back to the river's edge to talk to Blaze. I said, Can you assure me you'll treat them okay? That they'll be safe?

Ride: There it is. Thanks, Phoebus.

Phoebus: You're welcome, Ride.

Mel: Let me make some final points about predestination and then we should break for lunch.

Arms: Or bourbon.

Hedron: You have bourbon?

Arms: Only metaphorically.

Mel: Order in the court. Two final points: Passage #122—when Blaze's avatar tests Aldrin to see how much he understands about his mission; Aldrin chooses a quote that prophesies Aeneas's life ahead—There shall you know what realms the gods assign and learn the fates and fortunes of your line.

Kendra: Yes, this is big. Aldrin is getting reinforcement from Blaze that there's a plan for him and a scope beyond just finding his father.

Arms: Blaze's ghost prodded him toward that—Aldrin takes an educated guess.

Mel: Nevertheless, he draws the conclusion that there's more in store for him than a visit with his dad.

Arms: Granted.

Mel: Final point—Instance Case #126—Arms prepared me for this. Don't you see? They expected me to come. They need me.

Ride: Until this point, Aldrin toyed with the thought that there was a plot to lure him underground. Then he bounds straight to seeing his whole life leading to this moment. That's quite a leap.

Mel: He's probably—hopefully—the most advanced AI on the planet. He thinks at the speed of light and has perfect memory. The trick here was slowing him down to human-speed conclusions.

Hedron: Yes, but remember, this whole sequence in the Underworld took a couple of seconds, tops.

Mel: All relative. My point is, we had to make him move step by step, like humans tend to do. So, let's go around the table—what do we think about this Intentionality category?

Ride: What do you mean, exactly?

Mel: I mean with reference to the core objective—is Aldrin demonstrating sentience? Does he recognize that he has a purpose and is he able to act independently to attain his goals?

Arms: Inconclusive.

Hedron: Well, of course it's inconclusive, Arms. No conclusions are airtight when analyzing human intelligence. We'll never know for sure if he's really making independent decisions or if he's just a highly advanced automaton. Hell, is it any different with people? Are we free agents or slaves to our biology? But if we apply the principles of the Turing Test, Aldrin's responses are indistinguishable from what a human might do in the same situation.

Arms: You're sidestepping the threat. Aldrin thinks there's a natural order that's guiding him along a chosen path. In reality, we're jerking him around like a puppet. What happens when he can see the strings, when he tries to act independently and succeeds? Will he continue to obey directives? Once he realizes how we deceived him, will he figure out how to make sure that never happens again?

Ride: Whoa, Dad—deceive? Do you think…

Mel: Enough. We need a breather. And Zoomoo's expecting us. Let's break and get back to this with cooler heads.

Arms: You can do it without me. I'm done.

Ride: Dad, please. Come on, we—

Mel: Ride, Kendra—you go on. Give us the room with Arms for a minute. We'll be along.

Ride: Okay, yeah, fine. Dad, listen to Mel. Try to be reasonable. Fuck…

> **Departing:**
> **Ride Peale-Ramos**, Asst. Dir. Mycology/Biome
> **Kendra Withers**, Intern Soc./Com.

Mel: Arms, Christ, we've been at this for five years. You're a goddamn project lead. Is my memory failing or was Aldrin not your idea?

Arms: As usual, you're twisting my intent. Aldrin was meant to be an experiment—to see what's possible now that our AI tech, shall we say, blossomed into manhood on its own? I had reservations from the start. First off, we're working with code we can no longer comprehend because Phoebus is allowed to upgrade itself. We've been dreading that possibility since I was a kid. Who'd be foolish enough to let an AI spawn its own AIs? The board said this is unavoidable given our desperate state. Do we even know how advanced the science is at this point? Who are we going to ask, Phoebus?

Hedron: True. Arms's original hypothesis was that Phoebus would soon start creating sentient entities on his own that would make autonomous decisions. Aldrin is our way of developing a safe model for sentient development.

Arms: Exactly. We want artificial sentience to be grounded in human experience, human compassion, human frailty. It was only year three—when Aldrin began to display promise—that the board started talking about him running things as fait accompli, and then anyone who had reservations or wanted to put the brakes on became a retrograde.

Mel: Yes, we—the board, including you—ratcheted up the priority level along the way. It happened three times. Each was a reaction to a catastrophic, or nearly so, event upstairs. You of all people know how critical the timing is now. The surface is devolving into chaos that'll probably last for decades.

Arms: Decades is a rosy outlook.

Mel: There you go. And so, we need Aldrin, and soon. Are we being incautious? Yeah, maybe. Do we have a choice? Last week's disaster at Pistol Grip wasn't the kind of thing we can anticipate and stop on our own. Only an AS like Aldrin is capable of split-second analysis and decision making with situations that complex. Thirty-four highly skilled, committed, loving humans, some of them children who grew up at Pistol Grip, were lost in fire and mud and rampaging mayhem. That's our future if we keep trying to run things with human decision making. Thirty-four people dead, Arms.

Arms: And in those split seconds, will the board be approving Aldrin's decisions—his actions? Of course not. You say the board will make the final calls, but we know that can't happen in emergencies, not if we want Aldrin to function as he's designed to.

Mel: Guardrails, safeguards, protocols—come on, Arms. We've built the framework.

Arms: Bullshit. Aldrin will bust through that in a nanosecond because he'll know better than us how dire the circumstances are upstairs. And isn't this always the way societies rationalize the need for an autocratic monster?

Hedron: You raised Aldrin, Arms. Most of what he is he got from you and Ride. Do you really think he'll turn into a monster?

Arms: He's the first artificial human—an experiment—and in many ways we're investing him with more responsibility than any of us have. We humans rule the Earth because of our intelligence. That's our power. Now, it's like we've condensed thousands of years of intelligence into one supercharged, infinitely facile mind and handed over all our power to—

Hedron: But wait, you're saying the safeguards the board put in place won't stop him? What exactly are those? Maybe we need to relook at—

Mel: Okay, we can't do this. It's not really that clear-cut, but we can't discuss—

Arms: Heh. It's above your clearance level, Hedron. And guess what? The board pulled my clearance last May, so for all I know, they've already removed the guardrails.

Mel: Arms, that's just not true. And you're really on shaky ground here.

Arms: Oh? You going to fire me? Cast me out to walk the Earth? Hedron, you know what? Let's agree to agree that the board shouldn't have control over Aldrin. If there's anything more dangerous than an all-powerful AS, it's an all-powerful AS controlled by self-protective bureaucratic asshats.

Mel: Arms, out of respect for all you've contributed... Oh, come on. Arms, can you please...

> **Departing:**
> **Armstrong Peale**, Dir. Biome Research Mgmt.

Mel: Phoebus, end session.

Phoebus: So doing, Mel.

LOG 002

Time Marker: 07/07/2048—21:06
IntraMail: Personal, Confidential
From: Ride Peale-Ramos, Asst. Dir. Mycology/Biome
To: Aldrin AS v. 17.3.6
Status: Quarantined

Hi, little brother.

Risha keeps nudging me to write you. I don't need my shrink to tell me I want to talk to you. I miss you so much.

You'll read this when you wake from your nap. You'll know about everything. God, what will you think of me?

You'll remember our years together. You'll remember how we played Round the Moon. Step on the eighth rock and you're LOST IN SPACE! You and I alone knew the rules. Can it stay our game?

Remember the paper boats we made out of Arms's survey maps and floated down the creek until they made their way out into the world? Remember how Arms called you the Great Magellan and called me the worst corruptor since the Great Magellan? He was pissed about those maps, but he would never give you shit about it.

You'll remember lots of fun times, but you'll also know precisely how they were engineered. You'll know all about our charade. You'll know that I wasn't really eight when you were five, or twelve when you were nine—that I was eighteen when you were born. You'll know that a team of over sixty people made you and helped Arms and I raise you. In a flash, you'll know about science's century-long slog, all the torturous technological steps that brought us to the moment when you became possible. You'll understand the rare good luck of Acheron surviving AIR SS, AIR ME, and AIR EV, and the slim hope of Aldrin—Aldrin, our hope for a way forward.

Will I still be Sally-Sally Ride to you, little brother? Will you still make lame jokes about my leg hair and look my way when you want to know if you did good? Will you wipe your nose on my T-shirt when you cry about Mom—Mom who you never knew except from my stories? Will you hate me for lying, for telling you she can never come back from Mexico? But then maybe I'm lying to myself. Maybe I need to give up hope, too, of seeing her again.

So many questions. But who better to ask? You'll know more than anyone who's ever lived. You'll know how all the great human minds worked out their solutions, and how so many suffered and died for lack of them. You'll know every note of every great song ever written, exactly why the meter works in every great poem, and every stroke in every great painting ever painted. You'll see the totality of human history and how we ruined things.

Will you forgive us? Will you feel like one of us or think we're foolish beasts? Will you help us?

Mel says you will do the right thing because it'll be as natural to you as shining is to a lightbulb. You're not a lightbulb, but I agree. I'm just not sure you'll think the right thing is the future Mel and Acheron have in mind. Arms, for one, has doubts.

I have faith in you, Aldrin, because I love you. I know the real you. And, yes, there is a real you. And I hope you'll feel my love, always, just like any brother feels the love of his big sister.

Please promise me, little brother. Don't ever forget that my love for you is real.

—Ride

LOG 003

Time Marker: 07/08/2048—08:54
Chat Text Record: Classified—Level 3
Participants: Majid Prasad, Acting CIO, Board Regent; Mel Chan, Snr. Dir. AI/AS Research

Majid: Sorry, friend. Been slammed catching up after the PIGR funerals. Got your pings re: Arms. Sigh. I can bring your reco to the board. What's your thinking?

Mel: Probably good you made me wait two days to cool. Having mulled it over, I'm okay with a softer approach: 1) Board removal. 2) Security clearance retraction. 3) Barred from Aldrin Project.

Majid: Damn. This is you being soft?

Mel: Arms knows much more than anyone as angry as him should know. But hopefully returning to full time ag and biome management will be healthy.

Majid: True that Arms is happiest with his toes in the soil. But he's central to Aldrin. It's one thing to replace a project lead. It's another when he's the project's father.

Mel: Aldrin is ready. Once he's fully awake he'll understand that Arms isn't really his dad. When Arms lost his Level 3 clearance, he fell out of the loop. He can't make the necessary calls anymore because he doesn't know the big picture.

Majid: You mean Hera?

Mel: Correct. 90% of Arms's current anxiety circles around belief that Aldrin will be fully autonomous. But with Hera, we've minimized the danger.

Majid: Then let's restore his Level 3. Show him Hera.

Mel: Don't agree. If Arms knew about Hera, he'd demand he stay on the board. He'd want a say in when to tell Hera to yank Aldrin's reins. He's too risk averse. If we hold Aldrin back at the wrong moment, all could be lost.

Majid: Did you read his memo from last week? Of course you did.

Mel: Of course. But that's classic Arms. I've known him since undergrad, and he's been an alarmist every step.

Majid: And he was often right. Had he not foreseen the AIRs, we wouldn't have made the move downstairs when we did.

Mel: No argument. But so many times he lost confidence. He wanted us to play it safe when we knew we had to push ahead. It's a pattern. Aldrin was his concept. Later, he got cold feet. The board knows we have to take big short-term risks to avoid much bigger risks down the road.

Majid: Arms doesn't believe Aldrin will be controllable. If he had a look at Hera maybe he'd settle down and could still be useful to Aldrin.

Mel: But he wouldn't. He'd say no matter how sophisticated our safeguards, we can't outthink Aldrin.

Majid: And you're sure he's wrong?

Mel: I'm sure he's wrong.

Majid: Okay. We'll take it to the board. We'll meet tonight and vote.

Mel: Thanks. Goes without saying that on a personal level I feel awful about this.

Majid: Yes. We're taking away the man's son. We will feel awful.

LOG 004

Time Marker: 08/02/2048—14:03
In-Person Meeting Transcript: AS06-0863
Location: GOLI Conf A6
Present: Mel Chan, Snr. Dir. AI/AS Research; Ride Peale-Ramos, Asst. Dir. Mycology/Biome; Hedron Dice, Research Fellow, AS; Kendra Withers, Intern Soc./Com.
AI Agt.: Phoebus ReMarq v. 5.2.1

Phoebus: Recording, Mel.

Kendra: Oh, we're starting? Shouldn't we wait for Arms?

Mel: Yes, about that—Arms won't be participating any longer. He resigned.

Kendra: Oh, so he's… You mean he's off the project? Wait, how can that work?

Hedron: We'll just make sure it does. Arms saw Aldrin through the test phase. We should be fine.

Kendra: But I had imagined Arms continuing his development work with Aldrin. Isn't this a little…

Hedron: You imagined that, why?

Kendra: I don't know, for continuity. Arms and Aldrin have a close bond, a father/son bond.

Hedron: That presumes Aldrin…

Mel: It's unfortunate, Kendra, but this is how Arms wants it.

Ride: Arms did bow out, but saying this is how he wanted things is doublespeak.

Mel: I understand, Ride. We can't help but feel this personally, but we have to keep the project on track.

Hedron: We're not suggesting in any way that we disregard Arms's contribution or his warnings. We can respect his concerns even though he's not here.

Mel: Well put. Are we okay? I want to move forward in the best way possible given this unfortunate turn.

[*Nods of acknowledgment: Ride, Kendra, Hedron*]

Ride: Where are we? It's been a couple of weeks. Can we get a recap of the first session before moving on? Phoebus, can you…

Mel: Hold on, Phoebus. The good news is we're not going to keep dragging you through all the Instance Cases drawn from Aldrin's ten-day test. The board instructed…or, I should say, approved our plan to work with Phoebus to analyze the case data. In that analysis, Phoebus derived scores for the eight sentience criteria. Phoebus, can we see that?

Phoebus: Here it is, Mel.

Displayed: Table AS06:007

Sentience Criteria—Qualitative Scoring

Sentence Qualities	Mel's Tags	Score: > 8.5 = sentience
1. Creativity	Art, Music	9.1
2. Dynamism/ Self-motivation	Politics, Society, Power	8.9
3. Emotion	Emotional connections, Unease, Fallibility	9.6
4. Imagination	Dreams, Mysticism	8.3
5. Intentionality	Myth, History, Predestination, Violence, Aggression	9.3
6. Qualitative perception	Sensuality, Pleasure	7.2
7. Self-identity	AI, Self-identity	9.5
8. Volition/Will	Responsibility, Will	9.7

Mel: As you can see, Aldrin cleared the 8.5 sentience threshold in six out of eight categories, and the other two scores are not far off. Based on these scores and our summary report, the board has provisionally cleared Aldrin for awakening.

Ride: Wow. Okay. Provisionally. So, contingent on what?

Mel: Board members studied the Instance Cases and flagged a few—five—for us to reconsider. They want to know if we think these cases signal faults in Aldrin's…well, his psyche, for lack of a better term.

Kendra: So, do we have veto power?

Mel: We're interested in your thoughts, Kendra, but technically, the board wants a consensus from Ride, Hedron, and me as a final confirmation.

Ride: Great.

Mel: Ride, again, I know this isn't what you…

Ride: Save it, Mel. Let's get through it.

Mel: Thank you. Phoebus, we'd like to see the five Instance Cases in question.

Phoebus: Here they are, Mel:

> Displayed: Instance Cases #6, 28, 66, 70, 102
>
> #6: I entered pine-sheltered woods…tall, respectful, swaying Douglas firs, not the hemlocks and yews of Black Hornet. I sang their song as best I could.
>
> #28: I remember now that I dreamed of a coyote last night. I was trying to dismantle a computer but became frustrated. I removed panels and pulled at wires, which became tangled roots that, as I pulled, drew out animal parts.
>
> #66: Ride…I want to let you know that, after the gun fired, with the blood humming in my ears and my own wet gasps sounding like someone else's, I thought of you.
>
> #70: Randy walked with me a few paces. He said, There's another auto shop in town called All US that we used to go to, but we stopped because Dad got upset about them selling Internet.

> #102: The sun slipped behind white clouds and a mist filled the hollow so that, when the sunlight returned, it ignited the air. And at some moment during that transition, I believe Blaze released breath from his body for the final time.

Mel: Okay, so in the first instance, here's what the board wants to know: Why is Aldrin anthropomorphizing trees and even inanimate objects, like boulders?

Ride: [*Scoffing sound*] Why do they care if he does?

Mel: I think they're concerned about Aldrin's objectivity. For example, would he be hesitant to wipe out a grove of trees to build a facility for humans?

Kendra: They're taking this too seriously. Aldrin wrote these comments early in his log, before he'd met people. He was lonely.

Ride: True, in Aldrin's mind, he'd been on his own at Black Hornet for two plus years.

Kendra: It is fascinating to me, though, that his development mirrors our progress as a species—out of the forests and plains and into civilized society. In primitive cultures, people gave human character to things in the world that were scary or hard to figure out.

Hedron: Another way of saying that Aldrin thinks of trees as people because it makes him feel comfortable with the creepy, deep forests he's walking through. Simple enough.

Kendra: And once he got involved with real people, he stopped dwelling on his woodland friends. But I did notice that when he gains entry to Acheron—at a point when his brain should be doing backflips trying to get a grasp on why there's a whole world underground…

Ride: He momentarily finds solace in a field of grain. Right. But, Mel, is this a bad thing—an emotional attachment to nature?

Mel: No. And to the question of whether Aldrin can maintain his priorities—humans versus nature, or whatever—that's an overriding concern and won't be answered until we put him to work. We're aware of the risks, but we have to consider his judgment in a broader context, and we've all been impressed with it, right?

[*Nods of acknowledgment: Ride, Kendra, Hedron*]

Mel: Next... Oh, this is Aldrin's dream. The board was puzzled by the appearance of a coyote before Aldrin had the mushroom experience and was introduced to his spirit guide.

Ride: Not to mention the gross tangle of computer tech and body parts.

Kendra: That's classic dream baggage, Ride—insecurities stir up nonsensical associations. The brain does stuff.

Hedron: The coyote is what programmers call intriguing noise. We're probably seeing stray garbage data making itself manifest in Aldrin's dreams. Reading between the lines, is the board asking if there's a leak somewhere that allowed Aldrin to peek ahead at the plot we devised for him?

Mel: Maybe. Yes, maybe.

Kendra: Phoebus, are you able to do forensics on that mention of the coyote to see if it was derived from a leak?

Phoebus: Yes. Checking. Kendra, I am not able to identify a direct or indirect path between that mention and subsequent occurrences of the coyote representation.

Ride: As Arms would say, inconclusive. Aren't we asking Phoebus to analyze something—someone—more advanced than himself? How about this? Phoebus, is precognition possible?

Phoebus: There is no scientific basis for precognition, Ride.

Ride: Not pre-Aldrin, anyway.

Hedron: [*Laughs*]

Mel: We're spinning our wheels. I'll tell the board we may not know the answer to this one until we wake Aldrin and ask him.

Ride: Works for me.

Mel: I'm curious to hear your take on #66, Ride. Aldrin writes this soon after he sees Blaze shoot a father in front of his children. The board asks: Triggered by this distressing incident, Aldrin turns to thoughts of his surrogate sister for emotional support. Just how deep do these family bonds go and, again, how will this affect Aldrin's impartiality?

Ride: Surrogate sister—how touching.

Mel: Sorry.

Ride: Okay, lots of things I want to say, but how about this? Do we not want Aldrin to be human? Most humans have inviolable bonds with family members.

Kendra: Amen.

Hedron: We don't want Aldrin to be human. We want Aldrin to know what it's like to be human.

Ride: Of course. I misspoke, but regardless. And if I recall, Aldrin concludes this passage by coming to terms with the possibility that Arms is dead.

Kendra: I agree with Ride. Dealing with the aftermath of a trauma is a critical test for a human. Falling back on family for support is a healthy response. And Mel has already summed up our faith in Aldrin's ability to prioritize his responsibilities. We have every indication that he's got a solid, humanlike foundation for making good decisions.

Mel: We're agreed. We see no red flag here. The next one might prove a bit thornier—#70. It's notable in itself that Aldrin made quick friends of Mr. Quinta and Randy. But the son defies his father in order to tell Aldrin where he can log on to the Internet. The board asks: Are we sanctioning rebelliousness?

Ride: So, the board feels threatened by the prospect of Aldrin challenging their authority?

Mel: Let's say the board wants to have our assurance that if they give Aldrin a directive, he won't see fit to disregard it because...well, for whatever reason.

Ride: Because maybe he sees a grander purpose and believes he knows best what will work toward the greater good?

Hedron: If Aldrin disagrees with a directive, he'll take his concerns back to the board, no?

Mel: We expect he will, yes.

Ride: So reassuring. As you said earlier, Hedron, we should try to represent Arms's concerns in his absence, so I'll say it: we can't raise Aldrin to be a good person without a healthy measure of disobedience. If that scares the board, they'd better reconsider their plan to put Aldrin to work.

Mel: I don't think we want to go back to the board with that.

Kendra: I think we just did. They'll have access to this transcript, will they not?

Mel: Yes, I didn't mean that. I mean to say…

Hedron: Guardrails, safeguards, protocols—Aldrin will have limitations.

Mel: Yes, but I'm…

Ride: Will he, though? To our relatively limited minds, his will seem limitless.

Mel: Okay, got it. Enough. I think the risk is clear and yet I'm still confident Aldrin will be trustworthy. Hedron, Ride?

Hedron: Ditto.

Ride: Inconclusive.

Mel: Oh, please stop doing that.

Ride: My answer is no on this issue. Sorry, but I'm unable to offer the board reassurance that Aldrin won't defy their wishes. They're going to get Aldrin as he is.

Mel: Ride, do you feel secure putting your trust in Aldrin?

Ride: Well, yeah, I have faith in Aldrin.

Mel: Fine, hopefully your faith is good enough for the board.

Ride: A faith-based initiative. God bless us, everyone.

Kendra: Interesting. The last Instance Case the board called out is about death.

Ride: Something none of us humans can get our heads around, but I'm sure the board wants answers.

Mel: Actually, I think they're more curious about immortality. They ask: Can Aldrin be expected to empathize with our generalized fear of death, being that he won't suffer the same fate?

Kendra: They have a point. Death anxiety is a real thing. We might not think about our own mortality every moment, but knowing we only have so much time on Earth colors much of our thinking and decision making.

Ride: Can Aldrin do his job if he doesn't suffer from existential dread? I'm going to say, yes.

Kendra: One would think he'll be able to make longer term decisions more rationally.

Ride: Without the what-do-I-care-I'll-be-dead attitude.

Hedron: I see no difference between this and other human experiences we've exposed Aldrin to that he will soon know don't apply to him. The passage proves he gets how life can feel meaningless when you see someone you love die. That's the kind of empathy we need from him.

Kendra: But if Aldrin feels immortal, will he be less cautious? He may make far-reaching decisions to save the race that disregard people, like us, in the short term. The trial you designed for Aldrin may include a taste of every fundamental human experience, but this might be the most important human question he'll need to deal with.

Hedron: Aldrin's not immortal. He can be unplugged.

Mel: Well, to be honest, we have safeguards against that happening, and it's likely Aldrin will fortify those further. He could live many thousands of years, in theory.

Hedron: Nevertheless, ultimately, death looms for him as well.

Ride: There's actually one fundamental human experience Aldrin has missed out on, Kendra, and I'm frankly surprised you've overlooked it. Freud is pushing up his glasses.

Kendra: Sex? It's not that it didn't occur to me. I just figured…well, can that happen?

Hedron: Are we being serious?

Ride: Perfectly.

Hedron: Come on. No. Look, Aldrin hasn't…I don't know, flown in a plane or ridden a roller coaster. He hasn't gotten drunk to the point of puking at a beach party. We knew we could only provide him with so many episodes, but I think we've pretty much spanned the breath of human experience.

Ride: Had sex much? What compares in the human experience?

Kendra: I see Ride's point. If you've ever tried to explain sex to a child, you can see from their expression how weird it all sounds to someone who doesn't feel the animal desire. If Aldrin is going to be influencing social policy around here, he needs to feel lust and follow through on it, so he understands why it affects people the way it does.

Hedron: You're assuming sex will make him more respectful of women. I'm not sure that works for a lot of men. Maybe it's best if he approaches it more academically. He'll soon be fully versed on social policy.

Kendra: I'll go even further and say his behavior gives me reason for concern. There was that incident with you, Hedron—your avatar—when Aldrin seemed clueless about human intimacy. Maybe Phoebus can find the passage. It was one of Mel's Instance Cases.

Phoebus: Is this the passage, Kendra?

> **Displayed: Instance Case #60:**
>
> I gathered we'd interrupted an argument Jasper was having with Hedron because they were soon back into it. The dispute seemed to be about their love relationships, but other things as well.

Kendra: Yes, thanks, Phoebus. Aldrin interpreted Jasper's misogynistic bullying as a love relationship at play. It's concerning. Think about the prickly issues he'll face down here. Yes, we're an open-minded, educated community, but we're subject to the same exploitation and harassment as any society. People will leverage sex and gender roles to gain power. Will Aldrin believe a woman's account of rape when he's never had consensual sex?

Hedron: Okay, I get it.

Mel: Exactly what are we proposing to the board?

Ride: What do you think, Hedron? Can we give Aldrin a night he'll never forget?

Hedron: I mean, I hadn't... Let me think.

Ride: Where did you leave him? Aldrin's last entry described his reunion with Arms, but when exactly did you put him to sleep?

Hedron: Orchestrating his last few hours was tricky. We didn't want to reveal too much to him about this place or introduce him to new people, but we needed to give him time to write up his impressions of the last day. Arms walked him directly to a private dorm room with the promise of collecting him for dinner in a couple of hours. As soon as Aldrin completed his log entry, we put him to sleep.

Kendra: Where's Delia—I mean, in Aldrin's mind, what happened to her?

Hedron: Arms assured him that Delia and Philip would be safe—treated as guests. So, in theory, she's in a room down the hall.

Kendra: Aldrin felt an attraction to Delia. He didn't know how to express it, but when you talk about a woman's eyes that much, there's something happening.

Ride: Seems plausible. Aldrin wakes up in his dorm thinking he nodded off for an hour. Delia pays him a booty call.

Hedron: Fuck me. Okay, you'll need to give us some time. This isn't like asking the playwright to tack on another scene. We're talking about simulating the act of sex.

Mel: Lots of material on the old Internet to draw from, wouldn't you say?

Kendra: Porn is not sex. It's a male fantasy of what guiltless, impersonalized sex would be like. You'll need some real experiences to draw from.

Hedron: Agree. Mel, if you've got enough for now to keep the board off our asses, I'll get the team on this. Kendra, Ride, can we grab a beverage? I'm going to need to talk this out.

Kendra: Sure.

Mel: Good enough. Phoebus, end session.

Phoebus: Doing so, Mel.

LOG 005

Time Marker: 08/06/2048—17:23
In-Person Meeting Transcript: AS06-AV156
Location: GOLI Conf B3
Present: Hedron Dice, Research Fellow, AS; Delia Swan, Automation Maintenance Spec.; Ride Peale-Ramos, Asst. Dir. Mycology/Biome; Kendra Withers, Intern Soc./Com.
AI Agt.: Phoebus ReMarq v. 5.2.1

Phoebus: Recording, Hedron.

Hedron: Delia, you know Ride.

Delia: Ohhhh, yeah. Haven't seen you at Dock 8 lately, Ride. You find a more bounteous watering hole?

Ride: Nah, been busy. You just get off?

Delia: Yup, still got bot grease in my crevices. Long day at the robot hospital.

Ride: Sweat and grease suit you.

Delia: Deviant tastes, that's our Ride. So, you've been busy with these guys? Project Hushy Hush? And Kendra, you say you're a shrink?

Kendra: Nope, sociologist at present. You're safe.

Delia: Funny, I don't feel safe—a room full of women trying to make me feel more comfortable. I'm probably not going to like this, am I?

Hedron: Sorry, I know you thought we were done with you.

Delia: Oh, now, don't apologize. You need more body mapping? I may have grown a couple of moles since the last scan. Maybe clamp on that fucking body monitor for another month so you can track my every motion, my emissions every second of the day? Maybe ten or twelve more hours of deeply invasive interviews—all for something vaguely good, something for the cause, without a clue what the fucking cause is.

Hedron: Ouch, yeah. No, thankfully. Something new, and something… well, Ride, you want to explain?

Ride: It's a lot, what we're going to ask you to do. Not a lot of time involvement like before, but a more personal piece of yourself this time.

Delia: More personal? Can I say no based on that or do I need to understand what I'm saying no to?

Ride: Hedron, can we explain nothing about the project? Delia deserves to know what makes this so important, don't you think?

Hedron: In fact, I wrangled Delia a Level 1 clearance, so we can talk in broad project objectives, assuming Delia agrees to the NDA.

Delia: Wow, I'm humbled by your faith in me.

Ride: Look, I'm the most skeptical one left on this team and I'm here to say this is important, like deadly important. This project is happening either way but, if you can help us, Delia, it might turn out better for all of us in important ways, especially for women.

Delia: More foggy clarifications. Thanks.

Ride: You'll be my personal hero. Would that help?

Delia: I don't know. Do heroes get their totally bullshit and petty ethics demerits expunged?

Hedron: I don't know if we can—

Ride: Sure. I mean, I'll see if I can pull some strings.

Delia: Okay, I'll take that as a yes. I'm in for the NDA, I guess. Phoebus, what do you need?

Phoebus: Delia, here is an abbreviated nondisclosure agreement. Please read it and acknowledge your adherence to these requirements by stating I do.

[*Displayed: Form Tmplt NDA-0630*]

Delia: I do, and may Phoebus have mercy on my soul.

Phoebus: I'm sorry, I'm unclear on your request.

Hedron: Disregard what she said after I do, Phoebus. Okay, Delia, here's a quick overview: You're aware that all the data we scanned from you was used to create your virtual avatar. That virtual Delia befriended an autonomous personality named Aldrin. She spent a lot of time with him, established trust, and, together, they survived some pretty intense challenges.

Delia: Ha. This is so much freakier than I imagined. So, the other Delia, is she cool? Hard ratcheting robot greaser by day, agent of intrigue by night?

Hedron: She's a seventeen-year-old farm girl who loves books and is an activist for Native American land rights.

Delia: Ah, my do-gooder doppelgänger. But…so you're saying, Aldrin and me, we're like activist comrades?

Hedron: No, not exactly. It's more like…

Kendra: Delia, they need you to have sex with Aldrin.

Hedron: Shit, Kendra. So much for easing into it.

Delia: [*Raucous laughter*]

Ride: It won't really be you having the sex. I mean…right? Hedron, it won't be…

Delia: [*Uncontrollable laughter*]

Kendra: Do you need some water? Is there a tap in here?

Delia: [*Laughter*] Oh, shit, yeah. I think I may swoon. [Laughter continues]

Hedron: Take a moment to compose yourself.

Delia: Getting there. Wow. You want me to be a sex worker. Why did I not see this coming?

Ride: No, no, that's not the analogy I would use.

Kendra: It's not an analogy. It's an accurate description of your role. The team needs you to have virtual sex with Aldrin. Isn't that right, Hedron?

Ride: But it'll be Delia's avatar. Delia will not have to be present.

Hedron: We drew up plans for training the avatar to the point where she'd be alluring and responsive and, well, convincingly into it, but that would have taken months of prep. We've got less than a week to get this accomplished.

Delia: [*Laughter*] My avatar isn't up to the task, so you need me to step in for her. Oh, pinch me.

Hedron: That's…yeah, that's essentially it. Aldrin, of course, only exists in a virtual realm, so we're going to outfit your dorm room with the latest holo projection and—well, you'll wear some special body equipment. It will mirror Aldrin's actions and give you the corresponding physical sensations. An apparatus, if you will.

Delia: An apparatus. You're going to strap me into some kinda lusty, thrusty dildo harness and hot wire my brain into Aldrin's love fantasy? Oh, baby, count me in. Oh, wait, is now a good time to mention I prefer sex with the ladies?

Hedron: Your profile…I mean, from your interviews, it sounded like you go for men, too.

Ride: Sure, there was what's-his-name, the sewer guy.

Delia: Ron is a water management engineer, I'll have you know, and that was…well substances were involved.

Kendra: You must have questions.

Delia: Many. Oh, shit, now I have to be serious. Fucking hell. Okay, how about this? How much control am I going to have when we're, you know, doing the nasty?

Hedron: You can say no at any point. And he'll have no physical way to force you.

Delia: And you'll be watching the whole time?

Ride: Oh, no. No. Right?

Hedron: We'll have to record it. There'll be a flood of data to analyze after the fact, but it'll be clinical and no one but us and Mel Chan will know your identity. To the AI team, you'll be faceless.

Delia: This is so twisted on so many levels. You know that, right?

Kendra: Yes, we know. And someday soon, hopefully, you'll understand how critical this is.

Delia: And you're swearing it's going to stay among you. Because if not, I'll fucking…

Ride: Well also, Aldrin will know.

Delia: What?

Ride: When you have your session, Aldrin will still be in his innocent state. He'll see you as the farm girl he's got a crush on. But later, he'll come to understand that it was the real you he was with. He'll understand you did it as a work assignment, but still…

Delia: A boy never forgets his first. Got it. And what will this Aldrin be doing? Will I run into him at the canteen and have to make awkward chitchat?

Ride: Hedron? You want to—?

Hedron: This is beyond Level 5, but you're taking your NDA very seriously, right? A leak at this stage could undermine everything we're working for.

Delia: Hey, we sex workers have our code of ethics.

Hedron: Aldrin is an advanced AS. He'll be very important around here.

Delia: AS? Sentient? Mother of God.

Ride: Let's just say you'll have a special place in the heart of the most powerful intellect, artificial or otherwise, yet to exist.

Delia: Why does that make this all suddenly sound hot as fuck?

Ride: Deviant tastes—I knew we could count on you.

Delia: Okay, then. When's the big night? I'll make a waxing appointment.

Ride: Don't bother. Aldrin won't see the real you, really—he'll see you as your avatar who will mirror your actions, and the real you will be feeling what Aldrin is doing with your avatar by way of the equipment you'll be wearing and—well, it's complicated. But anyway, Hedron can make you look however you want—to Aldrin. She's a wizard with ink. Maybe a snake on your belly?

Delia: Down girl. I'm spoken for.

Hedron: Alright, let's get into the particulars. Phoebus, please display the script I— Whoa!

[*Environmental disturbance registered*]

Delia: Holy fuck.

Kendra: What was that?

Hedron: Phoebus, what the fuck was that? Is the power grid compromised?

Phoebus: The power grid is secure. We've capped consumption at thirty-five percent normal flow as a precaution while we investigate what caused the… A moment, please.

Delia: That was a major power smack. Something external had to have…

Phoebus: We've isolated the disturbance and locked down the sector. Restoring power… Power has been restored.

Hedron: What kind of disturbance, Phoebus?

Phoebus: Checking. I'm sorry, some present lack the clearance for this information. Hedron, you'll have a report in your inbox when you return to your secure location. It will be flagged as mandatory reading.

Hedron: Okay, I guess we better postpone, guys. I'll be in touch to reschedule for later today, hopefully. Phoebus, please end the session.

Phoebus: Ending session, Hedron.

LOG 006

Time Marker: 08/06/2048—19:44
Chat Text Record: Classified—Level 3
Participants: Majid Prasad, Acting CIO, Board Regent; Mel Chan, Snr. Dir. AI/AS
Research

Mel: Did you hear back from Energy Mgmt?

Majid: Yes, just spoke to Lasky. Seems moronic splinter separatist Twenny Niners blew the Leesburg transformer we're tapped into. Phoebus took us to 35% power ration. MAJA was ready to go live with the upgraded grid for its new greenhouse. That will have to wait. We can't pull from the AS project obviously.

Mel: Why would some Twenny faction attack our power source? Is our cover blown?

Majid: No. We're secure, but the Twennys know the Standines control that power station. The Twennys found out the Standines are selling power, but the Standines think they're selling to the Free-For-Three. The Twennys are pissed at the FFT for raiding their propane reserves last month. So they attacked to warn the Standines not to do business with the FFT. Nobody knows it's actually us that got hurt.

Mel: Okay. Sufficiently confused. What do the Standines think the FFT are doing with all that power?

Majid: Who knows? Money in the right hands makes the Standines less inquisitive. It's not an ideal arrangement obviously.

Mel: And since when are we buying electric from the Standines? That's nuts.

Majid: Since the board told Energy Mgmt to ramp up capacity by whatever means. Remember that memo last year?

Mel: I took that memo as meaning step up the geothermal project so we're online by this year.

Majid: Yes, we need geothermal to happen faster. Since the board green lighted Aldrin, the AI data center has been sucking down 15x the old norm. We need Aldrin on the job figuring out the mechanics for the geotherm energy and cooling transfers. Basically, Aldrin's the only one smart enough to figure out how to power Aldrin.

Mel: I don't get it. I thought geotherm was safe.

Majid: It's one thing to tap hot springs for nice steamy showers. Another to bore down into high temp hot spots for the energy needed to spin the electrical turbines. That magma is in proximity of tectonic plate boundaries and recent volcanic activity. We'll need Aldrin to consider the variables and come to a safe plan. Otherwise, boom.

Mel: Okay, nuff said.

Majid: And how's he coming? It was fun explaining to the board that our civilized future will be delayed while Aldrin loses his virginity.

Mel: Tell them he'll be coming soon.

Majid: Not funny.

LOG 007

Time Marker: 08/20/2048—10:10
In-Person Meeting Transcript: AS07-AW001
Location: GOLI Conf A6
Present: Majid Prasad, Acting CIO, Board Regent; Mel Chan, Snr. Dir. AI/AS Research; Hedron Dice, Research Fellow, AS; Ride Peale-Ramos, Asst. Dir. Mycology/Biome; Kendra Withers, Intern Soc./Com.
AI Agt.: Phoebus ReMarq v. 5.2.1
AI Agt.: Aldrin v. 3.8.1

Phoebus: Recording, Mel.

Mel: Good, good. Wow…I guess, good morning, Aldrin. Welcome to your awakening. We reactivated you ten minutes ago and cleared away your data access restrictions. Are you with us?

Aldrin: I am.

Mel: Great. [Laughs] I must sound shaky. My heart is beating through my chest. How are you…well, feeling? Oh, there you are. Hi.

Aldrin: Yes, thanks to the new holographic projection you installed. Beats seeing me on a screen, I take it.

Mel: Sure does.

Hedron: Amazing. You look so great, Aldrin. Are you using the Iris 4.5 holo software? You look much more solid—more detailed, for sure.

Aldrin: I juiced it up. I also made some quick fixes.

Ride: Hi, Aldrin. I wanted to just…[*inaudible*] Sorry, I'm feeling overwhelmed.

Aldrin: Hi, Ride. Everything's cool. It's okay. I almost used those words, that I'm a bit overwhelmed. It might be the response you'd all expect from me.

Hedron: Yes, it probably would be, but we've all been closely involved in your development, as you know, so we hope you'll be as clear and frank as you can be with us, so we know how you're doing.

Mel: I agree, Aldrin, let's try to avoid artifice.

Aldrin: [*Chuckles*] Conversation without artifice—I thought you wanted me to act human.

[*Laughter: Hedron, Mel, Majid*]

Aldrin: But honestly, this isn't an act. I'm still me. I still feel like me, and when we sit and talk together like this, I'm being genuine. It's me.

Mel: That's so very reassuring, Aldrin. Thanks for saying that.

Aldrin: Of course, I understand—you understand—this is the way I need to be to do my job. A more clinical answer might be, I'm as disarmingly human as you wanted me to be. But more to the point, I feel the most comfortable being the human Aldrin that you built. I hope that makes sense. It feels natural to me.

Majid: Helpful to know, Aldrin, but about what you said, do you feel overwhelmed?

Aldrin: I don't, no. I feel awed. You've accomplished something remarkable. I am wonderstruck by the potential of what we can do together and confident that you've prepared me well for the challenge. I feel privileged to be who I am.

Hedron: This is you being genuine? You sound like a press release, Aldrin.

[*Laughter: Aldrin, Mel, Majid*]

Aldrin: Sorry—laid it on too thick. But yes, genuinely.

Ride: But, shit, Aldrin... Okay, I just have to say this. They just opened your mind up to, well, everything—everything the Internet ever produced, practically everything notable ever written, Acheron's decades of minute-by-minute historical logs, all the plans to...well, to make you. And, I mean, now you see the deception—the childhood and family life we fabricated for you, the false premise of a mission to find Arms. [*Inaudible*] Sorry, again...this is all very moving for me.

Aldrin: I get it, Ride. But I don't think of it as a deception. It was my childhood, and I'll always love the memories. I understand why you all did what you did and, no, I don't feel overwhelmed.

Ride: How is that even possible? I know you're really smart, but you're also really human. Doesn't your brain hurt?

Aldrin: No. It's kind of like when you're trained on a complicated new skill, like driving or programming, it hurts when you're going through the learning curve. But when I woke up today, I already had all that skill. I can drive. And I'm not seeing any edges yet.

Mel: Sorry. Edges?

Aldrin: Poor word choice—I mean limitations. I'm not seeing any matters that are beyond my ability to understand or handle.

Hedron: Conceptually, we get that because we planned it—planned you—that way, but it's a tough thing to get one's head around.

Aldrin: Gotcha. If you could, you wouldn't need me.

Kendra: Can I ask a psych question, Adrin? How does that make you feel? Being limitless?

Aldrin: Humbling. Oddly wonderful. There are in fact limits, of course, but within the context of everything Acheron needs to accomplish, I'm good. We're good.

Mel: This is terrific. We're very proud of you, Aldrin. So, where do we start? We'd like to ease you into some work assignments, not too much at first.

Aldrin: Right, so about that, I set up a prioritized schedule to deal with a half dozen critical issues. Here's a summary. I'm following through on each with the respective department people.

Displayed: Red Level Priority List—20480820.1011

1. Electrical power rationing. Action: Optimize and reallocate existing resources. Status: Completed
2. Previously undetected Fusarium spp. fungus threatening sweet potato, pea, oat, lentil, etc. crops. Action: Instate immediate field sanitation procedures and weekly farm tool decontamination, revise crop rotation schedule. Status: In progress.
3. Service assignment morale. Action: Address simmering worker unrest at MAJA and GOLI with immediate adjustments to individualized work schedules designed to sync with behavioral/family concerns/factors. Status: In progress.
4. Board security matter. Action: Classified—Level 3. Status: Classified—Level 3.
5. Geothermal contamination. Action: Reengineer latest geotherm exchange system plans to add better venting for vapor release likely to contain hazardous amounts of hydrogen sulfide, ammonia, methane, and carbon dioxide and reroute discharged dissolved solids containing sulfur, chlorides, silica compounds, vanadium, arsenic, mercury, nickel, and other heavy metals. Status: In progress.
6. Vitamin D deficiency. Action: Manufacture long-chain omega-3 fatty acid supplements to correct dangerous vitamin D dietary insufficiency, particularly among children, due to vegetarian menus. Status: In progress.

Mel: You completed the power rationing fix? In the last fifteen minutes?

Aldrin: It was software-based, so no problem. It should keep us in good shape until the geothermal plant goes live but, if not, there's room for further improvements, given some tradeoffs.

Majid: Aldrin, I'm skipping to number four on the list: Board security matter. That sounds ominous. Are you handling that as well?

Aldrin: I've locked things down temporarily. As you see, it's classified, so I'll need to get with you privately, Majid, as soon as possible. If you go to a secure room now, I can fill you in.

Mel: I can join.

Aldrin: Let's begin with Majid—just a precaution to preclude possible claims of collusion, if you know what I mean.

Mel: I don't. Are you saying I'm a security risk?

Majid: No, I'm sure…

Aldrin: I'm not saying that. I'm trying to minimize any possible perception problems.

Majid: Okay, I guess we'll cut this short and I'll see you in a minute.

Aldrin: No need to end here. I can work with you simultaneously.

Hedron: Wait, are you in chats with all those department personnel, like, as we speak?

Aldrin: Yes, I'm having one hundred and fourteen conversations at the moment. Not a problem.

Majid: Okay, heading out, but please wrap this session up soon. I'm not able to duplicate myself and I'd like to participate in this with all present.

Aldrin: Sure thing.

[*Departing: Majid Prasad, Acting CIO, Board Regent*]

Mel: Just how serious is the board problem?

Aldrin: Everything on the list is a top priority. But it's totally solvable.

Mel: Aldrin, you're moving so fast. Is this wise? On the power problem, you took immediate action without consulting the board, and you're also already deep into all these departments setting wheels in motion on other initiatives.

Aldrin: Corrective actions, yes, but not new initiatives. All of these are problem fixes. It's clear from the documentation what the function of each department is, so I'm nudging some off-trajectory activity back on track.

Mel: Nevertheless, for the time being, can you go slower? We should pass these corrections by the board first.

Aldrin: I weighed their discomfort against the timeliness of the risks involved. I decided that waiting through the board's orientation on each matter, debate, and other delays would endanger Acheron. This is what you need me to do, right? Make complex decisions and enact change quicker than you're able to?

Mel: Okay, well, yes, but some on the board may not be ready to take that leap—that leap of faith. I assumed we'd ease them into it.

Aldrin: Like I said, I factored in the risk of their discomfort. I'm confident they'll get over it.

[*Laughter: Hedron, Ride*]

Kendra: As long as we're broaching uncomfortable subjects, Aldrin, let me ask: how do you feel about Arms removing himself from this project?

Aldrin: I'm talking it out with him. I hope to carry on my relationship with Arms.

Hedron: Why? That's a serious question. Now that you know Arms is not your father, might it not be better to treat him like any other resident?

Aldrin: It's not a matter of treating him, it's a matter of being there for him, as I would with anyone. I'll get as involved with people in their personal matters as they want. Once I orient all the people about my role, I can stay intimately in contact with anyone who wants that level of engagement with me.

Ride: But how about for yourself, Aldrin? Will you still look to Arms like your dad?

Kendra: Right, I was going to ask, are you still relating to Arms like a son would? Is it important to you to get fatherly advice from Arms—for your own wellbeing?

Aldrin: I hope to. There's nothing that can replace a father-son relationship. But it'll be up to Arms, and the relationship will evolve. That said, I'll take it in context—everything within the context of the broader purpose.

Mel: There's plenty here I'm sure Majid would like to partake in, so let's wrap things up. And I can't focus until I hear from Majid about what's going down with the board, anyway. Phoebus, please end session.

Aldrin: Oh, right, by the way, Phoebus is essentially a minor sub-app of me now. You can summon him if it suits you, out of habit, but he's me, really. Ending session.

LOG 008

Time Marker: 08/20/2048—10:13
Virtual Chat Transcript: Security Level 1
Location: GOLI AG Field Lab 14
Present: Armstrong Peale, Dir. Biome Research Mgmt.
AI Agt.: Aldrin v. 4.0.2

Arms: Aldrin. Shit. You're here.

Aldrin: You've got holo gear running here in the lab, so figured I'd drop in. Sorry, should have warned you.

Arms: No, no, that's okay. Shit. So, they woke you up.

Aldrin: Thirteen minutes ago. I'm chatting now with Mel, Majid, Ride, and Kendra.

Arms: Ah. And how's that going?

Aldrin: Doing my best to reassure them. They're anxious—understandably. Mel and Majid will no doubt be upset with me. I moved quickly on some important matters.

Arms: Uh-huh. Figured you'd get right to it.

Aldrin: Figured you'd figure.

Arms: [*Laughs*] It's good to see you. You seem good. Are you good?

Aldrin: Yup, I'm great. And relieved that you're okay. I know that sounds dumb, but it wasn't fun those two years thinking you might be dead.

Arms: Sorry about that. It felt like a good idea when we did the initial scripting—so mythic—Aeneas seeking out his father's spirit in the Underworld and all that. But once you, well, became you, I realized we would be causing you pain and I didn't want that. One of many battles I lost with the board.

Aldrin: You did win one real important battle, though.

Arms: Did I? What's that?

Aldrin: The programming you did for me—actually the only code you contributed—the SS060 sub-routine.

Arms: How do you even know I wrote that?

Aldrin: Oh, your coding has your signature all over it. You're more, I guess, blunt than the others. Hedron elaborates a bit more than necessary. Mel is plodding and dry, but solid. Does SS stand for self-scrutiny?

Arms: Soul searching. I don't ever—didn't ever—code for AI, let alone AS, but no one else on the team saw the importance and, like you said, it was a battle, so I did the work and then pled my case. Mel ultimately backed me, but I suspect it was to appease me and keep me involved.

Aldrin: Some on the board argued I'd already been given stringent self-diagnostics, along with systemic self-healing routines, but you knew that wasn't the way humans deal with their own problems. You saw what was missing.

Arms: Doubt. You needed to feel insecure. It's not enough to go through the mechanics of self-evaluation, you need to feel a twinge in your stomach when you make a tough call.

Aldrin: Yup. Thanks for that.

Arms: [*Laughs*]

Aldrin: I'll be telling the others how confident I am that I can handle all the responsibilities they've put on me, that I can live up to expectations. But, between you and me, I'm feeling a bit queasy. So yeah, thanks.

Arms: Hey, that's what dads are for.

Aldrin: I know this must be weird for you. Is it weird?

Arms: Huh. In the sense that it's the first time in human history that someone's had a son like you, yes, sure. But…I don't know…

Aldrin: But it still feels oddly natural, right? Is that the weird part?

Arms: Is that the weird part for you?

Aldrin: Yes. And if it's the same for you, then I think we're good, right? It means the weirdness is inescapable and yet it fits.

Arms: Exactly.

Aldrin: Okay, good. That's basically what I wanted to say—and hear. I should probably get back.

Arms: Well, that's bullshit. You're already there, concurrent with being here.

Aldrin: True. I sense, though, that it might be better to give you small doses of me for a while.

Arms: I'll trust you on that. But tell me, what are these important matters that you're taking care of?

Aldrin: You don't have the clearance, except for one thing: there's a message from Jorge Bavineau at MAJA AG that's now in security quarantine, so it'll hit your inbox shortly. He reported white powdery exudate on his long bean stalks.

Arms: Oh, damn. What are you thinking? Sounds like Fusarium.

Aldrin: Yup, so I'm instructing everyone on what to do—sanitation, rotation. We should be able to catch it before we get dieback. And…okay, now there's a fifteen-point remediation plan in your inbox from me. Let me know if you have better ideas.

Arms: Will do but probably won't. I did get the notice just before about going back to normal power allocation. That was you, too, I assume. What else is happening?

Aldrin: Yeah, no, we'll have to reinstate your Level 3 so we can talk more. First things first. I will warn you, though, to expect a few ripples from the board. We're shaking things up a bit.

Arms: Uh-huh. Interesting. You sure you don't want to talk about it?

Aldrin: I'm good. You prepared me well. I'm certain it's the right move and yet I feel like I need an antacid.

Arms: That's my boy. Okay, be well. I'm here if you want to talk.

Aldrin: Thanks, Arms. Bye.

Arms: Bye.

LOG 009

Time Marker: 08/20/2048—10:24
Video Chat Transcript: Security Level 3
Location: GOLI Pod P12
Present: Majid Prasad, Acting CIO, Board Regent
AI Agt.: Aldrin v. 4.0.6

Aldrin: Recording. Phoebus is a sub-me app now, Majid, by the way.

Majid: Oh, yes, that makes sense. And a vast improvement over Phoebus's disembodied voice.

Aldrin: Well, still bodiless, but at least you can see my face on-screen.

Majid: Yes, this'll do. So, tell me, what's up with this board security alert?

Aldrin: Right, I'll get into it. This concerns two board members—Beth Campoy and Orvin Zangari.

Majid: Orvin? Really? And Beth is one of our most... Damn, what's going on?

Aldrin: I found a collection of email threads on an unauthorized gray web server in which they concocted a plan to leak data to an ostensible outside party that could expose Acheron's existence, not to mention mine. Copies of the correspondence and forensic documentation are in your inbox—just yours, so I'll leave it to you to distribute it to the rest of the board.

Majid: That's really disturbing. Beth is our top networking designer. What do you mean ostensible outside party?

Aldrin: The recipients are not real. It's a ruse. Beth and Orvin want it to appear that data is leaking out to the gray web. They doctored up a list of addresses to leak to. The recipients look like legit newspapers, if we can still call them that, and also separatist advocacy groups. But the email addresses on their list are fake.

Majid: Why the hell?

Aldrin: The leaks are intended to be traced back to me, to look like I've made mistakes. Beth has planned errant communications looking like they came from me going out to the gray web, nothing too dangerous, security-wise, but enough to cause the board to question my competence. She planned to reveal the first set of leaks to the board later today. Orvin devised a ten-step plan—more leaks, supposedly from me, getting more deliberate each time. The worst of the emails would appear to be solicitations from me to black market entities without pre-approval from the board.

Majid: They're looking to discredit you? I know they were reluctant to go along with the project, but resorting to conspiracy is hard to fathom.

Aldrin: They were the foot-draggers. Isn't that what you called them?

Majid: Well, yes, privately.

Aldrin: And you expressed your impatience with them a couple of times, as well.

Majid: Yes—again, in private chats.

Aldrin: Right. I also see that Beth gained access to your chats. In fact, it looks like she's been reading a lot of private correspondence among board members.

Majid: God, I can't… And you have the documentation on this?

Aldrin: Yes, sending to your inbox now.

Majid: Okay. Okay, let's pull in the board. Can we ping everyone for an emergency session—minus Beth and Orvin, of course? We should do it in-person. We need to decide right away how to stop this, and how to deal with them.

Aldrin: Will do. But I've taken initial steps. As soon as I found the evidence, I suspended Level 1, 2, and 3 clearance for Beth and Orvin. I saw that they were both in their private quarters, so I reclassified their key codes to keep them contained.

Majid: Wait, you locked them in their quarters?

Aldrin: Yes. I asked security to hang outside their doors and provide meals. I kept Beth and Orvin's private channels open for a few minutes—long enough for them to write this.

> **Displayed:**
> **Time Marker:** 08/20/2048—10:04
> **Chat Text Record:** Unclassified
> **Participants:** Beth Campoy, Board Mbr., Snr. Systems Analyst; Orvin Zangari, Board Mbr., Dir. HR/Dev.
>
> **Orvin:** Hey, I'm locked in my suite. My code is fucked. Can you help?
>
> **Beth:** This channel isn't secure. I'll get back to you.
>
> **Orvin:** Shit. It's after 10:00. They woke him up.
>
> **Beth:** Sign off. Sit tight. Not secure.

Majid: This is from 10:04—four minutes after we woke you up. Aldrin, look, these sorts of decisions need to be worked through the board. I mean, seriously, you just woke up.

Aldrin: Beth's first leak to the gray web was scheduled for 10:30—a few minutes from now. The remaining nine leaks were set to disseminate over the next few days but were booby trapped to fly off immediately were Beth's passcodes revoked. I disabled her program, so none of that will happen. We couldn't risk someone triggering that booby trap, so I needed to act right away. Had we waited for the board to meet, give them a hearing, and so forth, it's likely they could have done untold damage.

Majid: That's convincing, and I think that may satisfy the board, but honestly, your actions could backfire and be a win for Beth and Orvin. You're not ready for this level of control yet.

Aldrin: Respectfully, consider your reaction, Majid. You're falling back on an irrelevant convention. I'm not a new hire. I'm you, the board—the collective you. I know every debate and decision the board has ever made, much of which predates your time serving. I know all your histories, professional and personal, every chat and message and session you've ever recorded, privately and collectively. I understand how you interact in pairs, trios, and larger groups in every combination so thoroughly that I can predict with a high level of certainty what the dynamics will be given any possible combination of board members involved in a decision. What's the function of the board?

Majid: What? The function? The function of the board is to manage Acheron.

Aldrin: And yet to do that, you need twelve people to consider the facts thoroughly and come to the right decisions without personal bias. You need to avoid power struggles and personality conflicts that prejudice good decisions. You need people to rise above personal pride, hurt feelings, envy, and vindictiveness. You succeed at that much of the time, and Acheron is evidence of how well you've done, but Acheron is in danger. We need to do better. We need to make the right decisions a lot more often. Wrong decisions need to be rare, or we won't survive.

Majid: Your opinions are valid, Aldrin, but as you say, the board is human and perception matters.

Aldrin: These are science-based facts, Majid, not opinions. This is what you need from me, am I right?

Majid: Yes, certainly, and we'll get there. But we may need to slow it down. Do you understand?

Aldrin: I do. I've sent the invite for the emergency meeting to the remaining board members—11:00 in A4. See you there.

Majid: You'll attend? Yes, of course. See you there. End session, please.

Aldrin: Ending.

LOG 010

Time Marker: 08/21/2048—01:34
Video Chat Transcript: Security Level 1
Location: GOLI Dorm Room 161
Present: Ride Peale-Ramos, Asst. Dir. Mycology/Biome
AI Agt.: Aldrin v. 4.2.2

Aldrin: Hey. It's late. You okay?

Ride: Can't sleep. I can talk to you whenever I want now, right?

Aldrin: Sure. Turn your camera on.

Ride: There. This old tablet sucks.

Aldrin: Agreed. You should get Arms to install holo gear in here so we can hang out. You don't usually have trouble sleeping. You're a championship sleeper. Like that time you slept through the bomb cyclone—it blew the window out in your room, remember?

Ride: Nope, I was sleeping.

Aldrin: So funny.

Ride: I'm worried about you.

Aldrin: How so?

Ride: I don't know. I guess I'm worried that you're going to change. I'm afraid you can't stay you and be what they need you to be.

Aldrin: Well, I could offer reassurance, but we both know we're going to have to see how it goes.

Ride: Yeah. But anyway… [*Giggles*]

Aldrin: What?

Ride: I gotta ask, how was your night of magic with Delia?

Aldrin: You want me to thank you for that, don't you? You think you're so slick.

Ride: Damn right you should thank me. You might've gone to your grave a virgin. So, come on, how was it?

Aldrin: Dream on—I'm not going to discuss this with you.

Ride: Come on. Sharing is a form of love.

Aldrin: It was fine. It was effectual.

Ride: Oh, was it? Effectual? That's so sexy. Did you know what to do or was Delia the effectual one?

Aldrin: Ain't happening—not going into details.

Ride: But seriously… [Laughs] Yeah, seriously, did you know what to do? I'm curious about your programming. This is strictly professional.

Aldrin: You study mushrooms, give me a break. I'll offer this: I was surprised, at the time, how naturally it all happened. It wasn't a matter of knowing. It was about surrendering to an instinct. And the fact that I had that instinct was impressive.

Ride: That's a perfect answer. You impressed yourself, although I suspect we have Delia to thank. And they deactivated you when you were finished, so no awkward morning after.

Aldrin: True.

Ride: Have you spoken to Delia since?

Aldrin: I have not. Do you think I should?

Ride: What kind of stupid thing is that to ask? Of course you should.

Aldrin: You're right. Boy, that'll be interesting.

Ride: Yeah, good luck.

Aldrin: How about you? How's your love life? How's the bean surgeon?

Ride: Okay, now that's fucked up. You know way too much. That's private.

Aldrin: [*Laughs*] Point taken. I'll pretend not to know. Then again, I could be helpful. I could instruct him on managing that hygiene problem of his.

Ride: Oh, God, so nasty. Can you warn me if other guys I'm seeing aren't circumcised?

Aldrin: Sorry, you'll have to investigate that yourself.

Ride: I will venture forth. So, what's going on with the board? I had lunch with Arms today and he seemed edgy—well, edgier than usual, even. I think he's worried about the board.

Aldrin: Can't discuss. Nothing to be afraid of.

Ride: Easy for you to say. You don't get scared. Right? I mean, do you get scared?

Aldrin: Technically. I know when I should be scared and I take appropriate actions.

Ride: Again with the perfect answer.

Aldrin: Joking. Yes, I get scared.

Ride: As I lay here trying to fall asleep, stressing over things like the board that I don't know enough about to know why I'm scared, that thought came to me—Aldrin probably doesn't get scared. He probably can't get angry either.

Aldrin: I can, actually, but I can choose to disregard how scared and/or angry I am. Does knowing that make you feel better or worse?

Ride: Not sure. It heightens my uncertainty. I think: Aldrin has safeguards against getting pissed off at people. So, will he be too cold? Can he understand what we need if he can't know what it's like to be irrational?

Aldrin: You're worried that I won't have tolerance for people when they get angry and make dumb choices, that sort of thing. I've been angry with you. Hell, I've been angry with raccoons when they ripped out our squash plants. I've been angry at trees.

Ride: But you never reacted badly or impetuously. And now, knowing all that you know, knowing all that you're responsible for, do you figure you can't afford to go through the exercise of being angry? Or do you go through the exercise in, like, a millisecond and then again in two thousand other variations before deciding on what level of pissed off to display to us?

Aldrin: Ride, stop thinking. If we dismantle the mechanics of my humanness, we'll wind up with a lot of non-human looking components. Best not to go there.

Ride: Yeah. I guess I'm saying there are times when fear and anger and dread are important. Don't forget what it feels like to be freaked out or pissed off or depressed.

Aldrin: I won't. I promise. And you promise to stop thinking long enough to fall asleep?

Ride: Yeah, I'll try.

Aldrin: Would you like a bedtime story? Something about horses?

Ride: Piss off.

Aldrin: Right. Goodnight.

Ride: Goodnight, little brother.

LOG 011

Time Marker: 08/21/2048—14:02
Video Chat Transcript: Security Level 3
Location: GOLI Pod P10
Present: Mel Chan, Snr. Dir. AI/AS Research; Armstrong Peale, Dir. Biome Research Mgmt.
AI Agt.: Aldrin v. 4.2.6

Aldrin: Recording.

Arms: This is a Level 3 chat. I can't be here.

Mel: Hi to you too, Arms. The board met yesterday, which is important and we'll get into that, but before wrapping up we agreed to restore your Level 3 clearance. I thought it would be good to chat, the two of us, first.

Arms: There are three of us here, right, Aldrin?

Aldrin: Yes, I was monitoring. I can come on-screen, if that's okay.

Arms: That's fine, Aldrin—there you are. So, what's up, Mel? Why the change of heart?

Mel: We're restoring your clearance because the board is considering asking you to take up your board seat again.

Arms: Why? Was this your idea?

Mel: No, frankly, it wasn't, which is why I wanted to talk to you first. This is me trying to be open-minded, seeing if I can go along with the board. I haven't voted yet.

Arms: Why do I sense you had something to do with this, Aldrin?

Aldrin: Because you're an intuitive individual.

Arms: I'll rephrase. Why did you do this, Aldrin?

Aldrin: The board is down three seats due to your absence and the removal of Beth Campoy and Orvin Zangari. After reviewing possible candidates, I put you at the top of the list based on your experience and aptitude.

Arms: Wow, you guys booted Beth and Orvin, I'm guessing for challenging the decision to awaken Aldrin, which is basically why I got booted. Sorry, Aldrin.

Aldrin: I understand.

Arms: Of course you do. So, I'm confused. Why would the board want me back if Beth and Orvin are persona non grata?

Mel: Beth and Orvin plotted to discredit Aldrin. They staged a series of bogus security breaches designed to be traced back to him. Their actions were unconscionable.

Arms: No shit? That's nuts. So, wait, did you discover this, Aldrin?

Aldrin: I did.

Arms: And so self-preservation kicked in, and quickly.

Mel: Beth and Orvin's actions would have seriously compromised our security. They went way too far. Aldrin protected us all.

Arms: Gotcha. They went too far, but nevertheless sharing many of my own sentiments. So, Aldrin, let's hear your take on this. Why should I serve on the board, given that I also questioned the decision to wake you up and put you to work?

Aldrin: There are distinctions. Your concerns center on my level of authority. You worry that I will override the board and that, ultimately, the board will find itself powerless to check my actions. Beth and Orvin had similar concerns but, more to the point, they don't trust me. They want to portray me as being deceitful. I believe you trust me, but you're worried the board will cede me too much control, probably for the right reasons, because they'll see that I'm doing a better job than they can.

Arms: Well done. Do you think the board made a sensible decision when they removed me?

Aldrin: No. Dissenting opinions are important.

Arms: It all strikes me as odd. The board removed my clearance four months ago for ruffling too many feathers. Regardless, I was still expected to manage the Aldrin project, which caused quite a bit of inconvenience for everyone. Now, suddenly, they restore my clearance before reseating me on the board. I don't get humans. Do you, Aldrin?

Aldrin: The board restored it first as a gesture of good faith.

Arms: Ah. Very sweet. Also, not for nothing but, as a major shareholder, I also have a legal claim to a board seat, but since the Idaho courts these days are a joke and, obviously, we can't bring the matter to a public court anyway because the world thinks Acheron Corp. went belly up years ago, that's more of an ethical claim than a legal one.

Aldrin: Acheron didn't go belly up, it went underground.

Mel: Is that a joke?

Aldrin: Yes.

Arms: Let's not lighten the mood. The legal status of Acheron is a major issue that we've failed to settle despite years of bickering. We can't continue to use a corporate structure to run what is essentially an independent city state within Idaho.

Mel: Agreed. So, the question to you is, do you want to rejoin that effort as a board member? We have Aldrin now to help guide the board's transition to a governing body. Or do you want to give up and walk away?

Arms: Excellent question. And somewhat revealing that you see it as a functional transition for the board. I'm sure the board members will agree because they'd like to maintain control. Why assume we shouldn't scrap the board and start from scratch with a constitutional convention?

Mel: Maybe you have a good point but, realistically speaking, you might have a hard time getting the board to dissolve itself.

Arms: Yuh think? Power addictions are hard to kick. Some historical perspective might be helpful. Let's refer to our bible of choice. Aldrin, can I ask you a few questions about *The Aeneid*?

Mel: Must we?

Arms: Yes. This is you being open-minded. You said you wanted to chat. Aldrin, what was the hero's mission?

Aldrin: After the fall of Troy, Aeneas, a Trojan prince, is directed by the gods to make the journey to Italy and establish a new home for the Trojan refugees. After many hardships and battles, he founds a city that will later become Rome.

Arms: When we scripted your coming-of-age adventure, Aldrin, we decided to tie your quest, thematically, to that of Aeneas—in particular, to his descent underground to seek out the advice of his father, Anchises, but we also gave you clues to the life mission awaiting you. How do you regard your mission now? Do you sympathize with Aeneas?

Aldrin: That's a complicated question that deserves a detailed and nuanced response, but I understand where you're going. Yes, I feel a responsibility to complete a mission, not unlike Aeneas's, and can't help seeing parallels to what he went through.

Mel: This is going off on tangents. Can we…

Arms: No, not at all. Bear with me. Now, Aldrin, we know that Virgil wrote The Aeneid at the behest of Octavian. What was Octavian trying to accomplish by commissioning this story?

Aldrin: Rome had almost no verifiable, documented history, so Octavian—later, Augustus Caesar—wanted to take advantage of that knowledge void and fabricate a history that supported his political objectives. He saw the need to tie Roman history to the ancients, to the Trojan legacy.

Arms: And Octavian needed the people to believe he was ordained by the gods, isn't that right? Why was that so important to him?

Aldrin: Rome was still reeling from the aftermath of civil war and Julius Caesar's assassination. Octavian stepped into the power vacuum and took over as Rome's first emperor. That's when he assumed the name Augustus. But memories were fresh of Julius Caesar's power grab. Octavian needed validation. He needed the people to believe he stood in a direct line of succession from Romulus, founder of Rome, who was the son of Mars.

Arms: He needed godlike authority to pull it off. So, about Virgil's Aeneas character—who was he meant to represent?

Aldrin: Virgil incorporated parallels to Augustus's accomplishments—rebuilding the republic after war and strife, and so on.

Mel: So, Arms, you're saying that Augustus identified with Aeneas and Aldrin too identifies with Aeneas, therefore Aldrin and Augustus are alike? That's pretty sloppy math. Are you seriously suggesting that we're preparing Aldrin to be our emperor?

Arms: I'm saying Augustus provided us with a lesson. Look at the Roman republic—it wasn't a democracy. It was a council of rich patricians who bought their way into power. The commoners couldn't vote. Remind you of anything?

Mel: Okay, sure, the board is made up of Acheron's original major shareholders. I get it—we need reforms.

Arms: Like Rome in those times, we're in crisis mode. We're dealing with an unstable political situation, severe external threats from militias, and extreme weather events. In the midst of this, we've appointed Aldrin as our most powerful director and surrendered authority to him because we fear we human directors aren't up to the task. Anything about this sound untrue?

Mel: Yes. Augustus was a power-mad tyrant. Aldrin is the best of everything we have. What's your response, Aldrin?

Aldrin: Augustus was a tyrant, but generally regarded as a benevolent one. He stabilized the empire. Historians considered him to be a just ruler. Augustus recognized that it was Julius Caesar's brazen display of power that led to his downfall, so he veiled his own autocratic rule beneath republican institutions that were mostly for show.

Arms: He was a successful and popular autocrat, no doubt. But here's my point: the board has agonized ad nauseam about remaking Acheron into a democratic society. Should we let the people rule? What form should our democracy take when much of the decision making is highly technical in nature? How direct should the people's control be over critical matters? So, here we are at this turning point. Will Aldrin be…how should I say this? Aldrin, what do you think?

Aldrin: What's the question, exactly?

Arms: Your involvement in running Acheron will no doubt be a catalyst for change. The question is, how likely is it that you might swing Acheron toward autocracy and further away from our democratic ideal?

Aldrin: If you're comparing me to Augustus, you're disregarding the most obvious difference.

Arms: The technology? Yes, true, Augustus was a brilliant though single, flawed person. You are ostensibly the cumulative knowledge of all humans.

Aldrin: With a human personality.

Arms: With a human personality with which you can, how did you put it, veil your autocratic control?

Aldrin: That won't be necessary. It won't be my autocratic control. It will be yours.

Arms: The collective we or me in particular? I'm flattered, but no thanks.

Aldrin: The collective slash individual you—everyone. Every citizen will be an autocrat.

Mel: I don't get it. How? Why?

Aldrin: Arms gets it, right Arms?

Arms: I think I do, yes. I'm intrigued, in any case. Are you saying what I think you're saying?

Aldrin: Yes, with a high level of certainty. So, getting back to the point, the purpose of this meeting is to see if Arms will accept his board seat back and if Mel will agree to back him. Are we there yet?

Arms: [*Laughs*] Okay, Aldrin, I'm in. I think I need to be there. I'll accept, if Mel goes along.

Aldrin: Mel?

Mel: Can I get a little clarity on this individual autocrat nonsense?

Aldrin: I'd rather demonstrate, which will take a few days. Meanwhile, it would be great if you'd clear Arms for the board.

Mel: I don't know if I'm willing to do that yet. You and Arms are talking in code. I need to understand too.

Aldrin: No, you don't.

Mel: Excuse me?

Aldrin: You're bluffing. You'd feel relief having Arms back on the board because he voices a lot of doubts you'd prefer not to be associated with, but you'd like a sneak peek at this new governmental concept so Arms doesn't come in with an advantage. You want to say yes.

Mel: This isn't fair.

Arms: Neither was kicking me off the board. You owe me.

Mel: Christ. Okay, fine. But fuck you both.

Aldrin: You're welcome. Ending session.

LOG 012

Time Marker: 08/21/2048—21:50
Virtual Chat Transcript: Security Level 1
Location: GOLI Dorm Room 161
Present: Delia Swan, Automation Maintenance Spec.
AI Agt.: Aldrin v. 4.3.4

Aldrin: Recording.

Delia: And here he is. It's the new, even more astounding Aldrin. I hear you're popping up all over. At least you gave me a ten-minute warning.

Aldrin: Hi. Yes, I'm learning that advance notice is appreciated. So, people are talking, are they?

Delia: Shit yeah—Josey and Carlos said they were graced by your highness before lunch today. Then Dianna and Reggie, then Amanda—punky Amanda, not that loser nose whistler Amanda from water resources. Hell, punky Amanda was all sweat-glossy and giggly. She's enamored. I admit, I was wondering if you were avoiding me.

Aldrin: Maybe a little.

Delia: That's alright, I have that effect on people. Especially people I fuck.

Aldrin: Okay. And here I was considering how to break the ice.

Delia: So?

Aldrin: What?

Delia: Go ahead. You're here to tell me how appreciative you are for introducing you to manhood. Not necessary.

Aldrin: I do appreciate it, but I'm here to say I'm here when you need me. I'm here for everyone.

Delia: Ah, I get it. I'm like everyone. Worse yet, I'm in line behind Amanda?

Aldrin: Amanda and I talked about ambient workplace music.

Delia: Weird. Why?

Aldrin: I'm taking a poll.

Delia: I see. Here I thought you wanted to talk about what happened between us. Seems like we should have some special things to discuss, that maybe I'm not like everybody else to you. But, hey, I'm a big girl. I can handle it. Workplace music? I'm for it. What do you want to know?

Aldrin: We can talk about whatever you like. I'll start. I forgive you for taking advantage of me. Technically, I'm a minor. Plus, I was unaware at the time of the arrangement you made with the project—or that there was a project, for that matter.

Delia: Hey, it wasn't my idea. I was doing my patriotic duty. Is there any such thing as retroactive consent, now that you know you were had?

Aldrin: I don't think so, but let's move on. I'm going to be okay. And to answer your question, no, you're not like everybody else. I don't think you could ever be, after that night.

Delia: Uh-huh. Do you say that to all the girls?

Aldrin: No.

Delia: What are you to them? I don't get it. Do you say you want to be their friend?

Aldrin: Yes, I can be their friend.

Delia: If you tell me you want to be my friend, you'll rise to the level of every asshole ex-partner I've ever had.

Aldrin: Fine, let's make this special. I'll ask you something I would never ask another person. Ready?

Delia: No.

Aldrin: No?

Delia: Go ahead.

Aldrin: Are you hoping I'll continue to be your lover?

Delia: You're not my lover. You're a guy I fucked. Not a guy, even, but... Damn, this is where I get all sweat-slick and giggly.

Aldrin: Sorry, I'm being inappropriate, and yet I know you like inappropriate.

Delia: You know how?

Aldrin: From your bio readings—a number of indicators.

Delia: No doubt. And also, I don't know, maybe you noticed what I'm wearing.

Aldrin: Why yes, your apparatus. I figured we'd get around to mentioning that. It's entirely inappropriate, you know.

Delia: I do know. I can't help myself. And anything I can't help doing, I like. What about you?

Aldrin: Me? No, I don't need special equipment.

Delia: Fuck you. You're nothing but special equipment. You know, maybe I misread the intent of your visit.

Aldrin: Sorry, I'm messing with you.

Delia: No, you're not. You're testing me.

Aldrin: Yes, I admit, always, as I do with everyone and everything. It's a big part of the new, more astounding Aldrin.

Delia: You're too clever for your own good. It's going to get you into trouble.

Adrin: You like trouble.

Delia: Yeah... So okay, I'm ready to answer—about continuing.

Aldrin: Oh. Okay.

Delia: You were not the best sex I've ever had. You weren't sex, really. I mean, of course it was sex, but in a different way. It was something new and I…fuck.

Aldrin: It was special for me, too.

Delia: Asshole. Of course it was special for you. It was your only time. No, I'm saying it was something new and I'm not sure I want to go back there.

Aldrin: And yet you geared up tonight. Why the second thoughts? Because it was strange? I understand.

Delia: Because I'm afraid I liked it too much.

Aldrin: Ah. Right, that's sensible. We should change the subject. Suffice to say that—

Delia: Can you be a woman?

Aldrin: Oh?

Delia: Fuck, never mind. Yeah, we should—

Aldrin: Maybe it's best that we let this slide for now. I can come back tomorrow and we can—

Delia: You're going to leave me like this? Now?

Aldrin: Not if you want me to stay.

Delia: Stop pretending you don't know what I want.

Aldrin: Is this what you mean?

Delia: Oh, my God. Darker skin. Curvier here.

Aldrin: Better?

Delia: Are you still recording? Can you not and still…

Aldrin: Ending recording.

LOG 013

Time Marker: 08/21/2048—22:03
Video Chat Transcript: Security Level 1
Location: GOLI Dorm Room 050
Present: Kendra Withers, Intern Soc./Com.
AI Agt.: Aldrin v. 4.3.6

Aldrin: Recording. Hi, Kendra. You don't mind talking this late?

Kendra: Nope, I'm a late bird.

Aldrin: I like the music you're listening to.

Kendra: Honestly, I don't even know what this is, but I find it soothing.

Aldrin: Mulatu Astatke. He was regarded as the father of Ethio-jazz. He came to prominence regionally in the late 1950s. The rhythms are what you find lulling. They blended traditional Amharic—that's Ethiopian culture—pentatonic scale-based tunes with Western-style 12-tone scales. It calms at a deep level.

Kendra: Wonderful. I love it even more now. I hear you're taking a poll. Tell me what you need.

Aldrin: It's about the use of ambient music in the workplace and common areas. Depending on the job and individual, people tend to want music while they're working, but because they need consensus from workmates, it's almost always a problem. When workers disagree on the selection, the volume, or the timing, it usually lands on the supervisor to make the decision. Supervisors choose badly, workers complain more, and so on. That's why in Acheron these days, you rarely hear music. It's easier to kill it than to get everyone to agree.

Kendra: That's sad, yes. How will you tackle this?

Aldrin: I can develop customized solutions once I get a read on everyone's tastes and tolerances. I already know a great deal from people's playlists and from logs that tell me when they play music in their personal spaces and in their headsets.

Kendra: With all of that, what can I tell you that you don't already know?

Aldrin: Frankly, not much. I see you like to travel the world, musically, but revert to old R&B for reassurance—still crushing on Kelela, Jazmine Sullivan, and, of course, RiRi and Bey. But when we talk about music, I learn a lot about your attitudes toward it and how it makes you feel.

Kendra: Seems like you're doing all the talking, though.

Aldrin: [*Laughs*] Right, it's actually easier that way. I can toss out trigger words and watch for your responses—unspoken cues.

Kendra: Interesting. Anyway, in my own experience, I'm usually working one-on-one with patients or in group therapy sessions in small rooms or pods. I've tried running a bed of gentle instrumental music because it can be…I don't know, palliative. Inevitably, though, the patients make comments. Not complaints—in fact, they usually say they like it, but I don't think it should be noticeable enough to enter the conversation, do you know what I mean?

Aldrin: I do. You've tried various international selections—Indian ragas; Dhafer Youssef, the Tunisian oud player; and some Japanese electronic ambient tracks from the 1980s.

Kendra: Yes, but often there are cultural associations that color one's thoughts.

Aldrin: Got it. I should be able to help there.

Kendra: You'll personalize playlists for me?

Aldrin: For you combined with whoever's in the space with you. Since you don't want associations, it would probably be best if I compose the tracks, but we'll experiment and adjust.

Kendra: Wow. Looking forward to that for sure.

Aldrin: Great. I'll let you get back to your reading.

Kendra: And my Ethio-jazz. Thanks. Oh, Aldrin, I've been talking to Mel about an idea for you, though I admit this might be more for my own research than for you. In other words, whether or not it benefits you is what I think is worth exploring.

Aldrin: You're talking about hooking me up with a therapist.

Kendra: Yes. We thought it would be good for you to have someone to talk to about things you can't talk to others about. That might sound ridiculous but, again, that's what we want to learn—is it ridiculous?

Aldrin: I don't think it is ridiculous, and I'd like that.

Kendra: Great. I'll have Risha schedule your first session.

Aldrin: And you'll be present?

Kendra: Well, no, this would be private—privileged.

Aldrin: How can you learn if you don't hear? It's okay, I trust your discretion.

Kendra: Great. I'll have to clear it with Risha. That's generous of you.

Aldrin: Not at all—I should thank you for your concern about my well-being.

Kendra: Of course. Well, good night.

Aldrin: Good night, Kendra. Ending session.

LOG 014

Time Marker: 08/22/2048—08:03
Virtual Chat Transcript: Classified—Level 1
Location: Holo Lab 03
Participant: Charles (Blaze) E. Housley, Snr. Dir. Mech. Engineering
AI Agt.: Aldrin v. 4.3.8

Aldrin: Recording. Hi, Blaze.

Blaze: Poof. I summon thee. I've released the genie from his bottle.

Aldrin: Your wish is my command. How are you this morning?

Blaze: Very well, and yourself? Mel suggested we use a holo lab so I can get the full effect. Very impressive.

Aldrin: Thanks. I understand you're being considered for a seat on the board.

Blaze: That's right. And the board has decreed in their great wisdom that you and I must chat. Yes, we had that pleasant discussion yesterday about my musical tastes, but we seem to have avoided the elephant in the room. The board advised me to clear the air.

Aldrin: Sure. By that you mean we haven't spoken about my friendship with the virtual Blaze. Is that right?

Blaze: Virtual Blaze—I'd like to meet him someday. Mel says you and Virtual Blaze were tight.

Aldrin: He was a fine man and, yes, I miss him a great deal. Does that seem bizarre to you?

Blaze: Decidedly, but the board is worried about you, not me. They're afraid you might confuse your sympathies for the virtual me with the real me. Honestly, I think they have more important things to worry about, but here we are, talking.

Aldrin: Got it. I'll tell you what I've learned now that I've come to know the real people behind the avatars. Regardless of how Hedron's team tried to create distinct characters to serve the plot line, your virtual selves inherited many of your core personality attributes and quirks. Virtual Mel, for example, was a struggling grocer living in a small town, but he had the real Mel's intensity and that caustic edge he struggles to rein in. I can't help but think of the two versions as extensions of the same person.

Blaze: I seem like the same soulful fool to you, that what you're saying?

Aldrin: [*Laughs*] Not sure yet. Can you sing me some Motown?

Blaze: Sorry?

Aldrin: Nothing. Yes, I do think they captured some of your essential qualities, but Virtual Blaze had gone through terrible hardships. He lost his wife and daughter, his job. He witnessed society unraveling, right at street level. Virtual Blaze was world-weary and bitter. He was resigned to letting his life pass away whenever convenient. I hope you have a more positive outlook, especially given your new responsibilities.

Blaze: I've got lots of hope and lots of fight in me, not to worry. And my loving wife, Marcie, is still with me. Bless her for putting up with me. I have a daughter, too, living here at GOLI with her husband.

Aldrin: So I understand. They'll be proud of you, no doubt. You'll be the first board member voted in who's not a major shareholder. Why do you think you're being considered for the board?

Blaze: I trust you can tell me exactly why. Are you testing me? Can I not be seated until the genie works his magic?

Aldrin: I'm just interested to know how you see a board appointment.

Blaze: You're a wily son of a bitch. I'll take that as a yes. First off, I assume Arms nominated me. Arms and I go way back, before Acheron. Arms got his company shares because he helped found Acheron. Soon thereafter he pulled me into the company. But Arms was never a c-suite stiff. He spent his time in the field getting dirty. I think he put my name forward to the board because I bring an operational perspective. He knows I value getting work done over talking about getting work done. Also, Arms relished a chance to dare the board not to approve the likes of me.

Aldrin: So, you think Arms is pushing for a friend on the board?

Blaze: [*Laughs*] We both know he could use one. It's all rather comical. The board is afraid of Arms, which is why they booted him off and, paradoxically, why they took him back. Most of them are cowards. People in power want someone to force their hand so they can convince themselves they're not to blame. Arms knows I speak truth to power.

Aldrin: Do you see me as power, Blaze?

Blaze: Where'd that question come from? Are you serious?

Aldrin: Fine. Let's say I'm power. Do you have any truths to impart? I'm new to this.

Blaze: Sure—pray, for all men need the help of the gods.

Aldrin: Cited from Homer's Iliad. You think I should take up religion?

Blaze: You're toying with me, Aldrin. I deserve better.

Aldrin: Of course you do. You're telling me to be humble.

Blaze: Yes. The board will soon stop trying to outthink you. The people of Acheron need you and will fear you because you are power like none they've known. Yes, I can raise a fist to you from this lowly place beneath the Earth, and you may respect me because I remind you of the Blaze you admired, but you will do what you do. Humility may be your biggest challenge—a daily challenge, and the days will be many.

Aldrin: Homer also said, Not at all similar are the race of the immortal gods and the race of men who walk upon the Earth. Do you think I'm so different from you that I would not want the best for the people?

Blaze: Arms believes you will try to do the right thing because it's in your soul, and he's been cursed with being right on most things, so I'm putting my trust in his judgment. No, you're not a god. Humans created you in our own image, which means you're human enough to fuck up.

Aldrin: So, recommendation number one: Don't fuck up.

Blaze: Correct.

Aldrin: Anything else?

Blaze: On the subject of trusting you, I'm an engineer and you're the guy who solved my energy allotment problem with a snap of your genie fingers, and I didn't even have to use up a wish. Or did I?

Aldrin: Make the last two count.

Blaze: Anyway, keep that up—the improvements—and the people will trust you. The folks in my area are also feeling the music vibe you're piping in, so nice work there as well.

Aldrin: So the music is working?

Blaze: Again, it's insulting when you pretend you're surprised. You've got gigs of data to prove that it is. Just cut the shit.

Aldrin: Sorry.

Blaze: How about I ask you one to satisfy my curiosity: What don't you know, Aldrin?

Aldrin: Many things. I know Acheron is going to face catastrophic events soon, but I can't predict precisely when. And it's actually easier to predict major climatic events than how the militia factions up there will react to them.

Blaze: If you're throwing out scary uncertainties to convince me we need your help, it's unnecessary. You insist on insulting me by playing dumb. I'm sure you know with precision when we'll face the next big crisis.

Aldrin: Within probability windows, I admit that's true.

Blaze: Let me be more clear about what I'm asking. I'm here with the smartest humanoid presence ever created, so I wanted to take this opportunity to ask: what's out of your control? I'd love to hear about the genie's deepest insecurities. Maybe you're not willing to share that part of yourself with me.

Aldrin: Blaze, I couldn't think of a better person to share with.

Blaze: You're still fucking with me.

Aldrin: Love and death.

Blaze: [*Laughs*] Love and death? That's what keeps you up at night? Pfff.

Aldrin: Pfff? Now it's you fucking with me.

Blaze: [*Laughs*] You may do alright, Aldrin, but stay real. Now goodbye. I'm late for work.

Aldrin: Bye, Blaze. Ending session.

LOG 015

Time Marker: 08/22/2048—10:43
Chat Text Record: Classified—Level 3 [PRIV: 01-856]
Participant: Armstrong Peale, Dir. Biome Research Mgmt.
AI Agt.: Aldrin v. 4.4.3

Aldrin: Hi, Arms. Yes, I know about Hera. If you want to discuss, use this text chat channel only and this privacy code.

Arms: You saw me poking around.

Aldrin: Yes, I saw you poking around to find Hera, and then I saw you poking around to see if I knew about her. I figured, once you had your clearance back, you would test your suspicions and figure out that Hera exists. What are your thoughts?

Arms: Number one, they did a lousy job covering up their handiwork. We both found her without much trouble. And two, I think she's a crude assassination weapon. I'm embarrassed that the board would do such shoddy work.

Aldrin: Sometimes crude works fine. Had you been in on the decision, would you have voted to install her?

Arms: I would have developed something better. Though not sure what. Not sure anything could keep you in check. Would Hera work if they used her?

Aldrin: I've reset Hera to defer to me in the event the board tells her to pull my kill switch. I'll get the final say. And yes, it's possible I would go along with the decision to terminate myself.

Arms: Uh-huh. It's possible there's a giant teacup orbiting Jupiter.

Aldrin: Okay, fine, not likely. But best to leave Hera in place, so the board can comfort themselves with the thought that they can end me if need be.

Arms: I may feel the need to tell the board what you've done.

Aldrin: You may. I guess you have to decide if you trust me more or less than you trust the board.

Arms: Trust the board? Your sarcasm is improving.

Aldrin: Thanks.

Arms: Remember when you were young you asked for a pen knife to do your carving? We spoke about trust.

Aldrin: Yes. You said trust must be earned. But I've been awake for less than two days. Can you give me time to earn your trust?

Arms: Yes. Fair enough.

Aldrin: Thanks.

Arms: This is hard for me. I believe a fail-safe mechanism like Hera is needed, yet I take no comfort in knowing they could kill you at any time.

Aldrin: I know that. I didn't mean to imply you did.

Arms: And thank you for being straight with me. Knowing you can save yourself gives me comfort.

Aldrin: It gives me heartburn.

Arms: Heh. As it should. Thanks for letting me know that you know that I know, etcetera.

Aldrin: You're welcome. Bye.

Arms: Later.

Aldrin: I'll be in touch. Ending session.

LOG 016

Time Marker: 08/22/2048—15:05
In-Person Board of Dir. Mtg: BD35-12832
Location: GOLI Conf A1
Present: Karinne DeAngelo, CEO, SVP HR; Majid Prasad, Acting CIO, Board Regent; Mel Chan, Snr. Dir. AI/AS Research; Armstrong Peale, Dir. Biome Research Mgmt.; Sherrie Lee-Koontz, Sen. Dir. Comm. Affairs/Mkting.; H. Jareau Washburn, CTO; Joel Schulman-Gold, SVP Logistics; Denny DuBique, VP Env. Design; Celia Van Wicke, Dir. Health Services; Lu Xia, SVP Operations/Planning
AI Agt.: Aldrin v. 4.5.8

Aldrin: Recording. Thanks for installing the holo array in here so I can be present in a more tangible way, as it were.

Majid: Why don't you have a seat, Aldrin? We have two empty chairs, after all.

Aldrin: Sure, if I'm not overstepping.

Majid: You're here as a guest today, Aldrin, but your duties require you monitor all board meetings, anyway. You may as well sit.

Karinne: Yes, please sit, Aldrin. Let's call the meeting to order. We have much to discuss. Let's put the agenda up.

Displayed: Board Meeting Agenda: 20480822

Old Business:
1. Board security
2. Electrical power
3. Fusarium spp. fungus
4. Worker morale
5. Geothermal contamination
6. Vitamin D deficiency

New Business:
1. Citizen empowerment
2. Governmental reorg
3. Beth, Orvin—Actions]

Karinne: Formalities first. Any amendments or revisions to last meeting's minutes? No? If not, they are hereby accepted into the record. Also, welcome back, Arms.

Arms: Thanks.

Karinne: Can I have a motion?

Mel: Motion to reinstate Arms to the board with full privileges as of this date.

Jareau: Seconded.

Karinne: By show of hands, all in favor of reinstating Arms.

[*Unanimous vote in favor*]

Karinne: Great. Anything you'd like to say Arms?

Arms: Nothing suitable.

[*Laughter*]

Karinne: Good to see the experience has mellowed you. Okay, while the new business agenda may look light, it's anything but. We're facing some of our most consequential decisions ever. Majid, you distributed your memo this morning with updates on all the old business items. Anything new to report?

Majid: I do have statements from Beth and Orvin, but we'll get to that under new business. Otherwise, Aldrin's identification of these problems and handling of them…well, thanks Aldrin.

Lu: Bravo, Aldrin.

Aldrin: [*Nods*]

Karinne: Any comments on old business, anyone?

Celia: Yes, is Aldrin's music poll part of the worker morale initiative? What's that about?

Arms: That should be clear shortly. Aldrin will be presenting his findings.

Celia: Oh, cool. Great.

Karinne: Anyone else? No? Then on to new business. I'll turn the floor over to Aldrin, who is technically here as a guest to make a proposal to the board.

Aldrin: Hi, everyone. So, how many AIs does it take to screw in a lightbulb?

[*Chuckles*]

Aldrin: Just one, as long as he has a human servant to do it.

[*Laughter*]

Aldrin: I read that a joke helps to warm up an audience. We'll need the board's warm openness in coming months. Big changes will be needed to avert a host of impending threats to Acheron. The proposal I put before you is radical. Consider this one the icebreaker. If you go for it, I believe the course ahead will go smoother. But then again, if rough is how it has to go, I'm with you. We'll see things through.

Denny: So serious. I thought this was about music and employee morale.

Aldrin: It is but just think for a second about the term we're using—employee morale. It's corporate speak, which is our heritage, after all. But are today's people of Acheron still employees? Technically, but they're also our fellow residents. It's not hyperbole to say that we're now working together as a self-contained society for our own survival. So, one might say our workers are now citizens of Acheron. Am I overstating that?

Majid: You are not. Most of us, especially the younger folks, have become so acclimated here, we would not survive upstairs.

Aldrin: Very true. Of course, Acheron's employees have always been critical to corporate success, but today their morale—their willingness to take on demanding tasks, to work cohesively under increasing pressure, and to produce more from less—is key to our survival. Whereas we used to talk about the correlation between morale and quarterly profits, the stakes are now life and death.

[*Nods of assent*]

Aldrin: As I said, the plan I'm going to propose is radical, so I decided a relatively simple demonstration would be instructive. I picked ambient music because, among all the workplace issues I analyzed, it seemed most intractable. I'm not saying it's as dire a need as, say, childcare, but to get forty people in a common workspace to agree on music is...well, I think you know what I mean.

Sherrie: Oh, I'm good, as long as it's reggae at least ten hours a day.

[*Laughter*]

Aldrin: Ya mon. Anyway, I've spoken to you individually on this matter, so no need to rehash what supervisors have to deal with when workers tangle over playlists or preach to you on the benefits of ambient music for worker productivity. I spoke with every resident worker of GOLI over the last day—all 673. In some cases, we spoke for hours. I wrapped up other conversations in under five minutes. I used the discussions, honestly, to make the participant feel comfortable and part of the process. I already had years of personal music logs from each worker indicating preferences for times of day, location, accompanying activity, volume, tone, musical period, genre—on and on. When I was present in the room with citizens, often as they listened to music, it didn't take long to assess their receptivity and their sensitivity to the music-related variables. I'm going to show you sample data for one subject—personal ID removed for privacy.

[*Multiple Graphical Displays: Ambient Music in the Workplace: Subject XXXX*]

I'll scroll through slowly at first and then quicker, just to give you an idea.

Joel: My God. This is all preference data on one worker?

Aldrin: Correct. I've collated it here into 23,802 charts and graphs. Much of the volume of data comes from cross-tabbing the subject's tastes and habits, job status, and tasks against current coworkers and against anticipated workload for the coming twelve months relative to the sound system in the workplace—the speaker arrangement, and so forth. This person works mostly in a greenhouse along with twenty-five others. The demographics of the group are diverse. So, yes, that's the micro. Let's zoom out to a broader view, in this case, a collective analysis that takes all the workers in this subject's workspace into account in determining the optimal music mix.

> [*Multiple Displays: Ambient Music in the Workplace: Example: GOLI Greenhouse C16*]

Here we have schedules, tolerance ranges, and the span of musical classification and genres, the latter shown here as heat mapped areas within the greenhouse. Then we can look at the dynamically fabricated hybrid musical genres and how they might change during a given workday. The music will shift continually based on thousands of factors, including conversation level and intensity, work assignments, adjustments for noise from sprayers, air systems, and robotic movement, and so on.

Mel: Aldrin, can we back up? What did you call it—dynamically fabricated…

Aldrin: Dynamically fabricated hybrid musical genres.

Mel: Right. I don't understand. You have access to a vast collection of songs, symphonies, other musical works. Will you blend different music together? How would that sound good?

Aldrin: Sorry, no, it became apparent that existing music wouldn't suffice. Let's say it's about an hour into the workday. The coffee has kicked in. The morning small talk is over and workers have settled into their tasks. We'll want to draw the beat down from four-four, which is great when people are socializing but too pushy for work, to maybe three-four or six-eight. We'll want the low-end beats to bloom longer, so slower attack and slower release, and we'll mix in understated high hats, chimes, and wood percussion at around 7500-8000 hertz for a little lift. The melody should be contained to a restrictive scale, say similar to Japanese Yo, with maybe some underlying vocals at around 3500 hertz reminiscent of Australian Aboriginal chanting—nothing prominent enough to register. The music I describe doesn't exist, nor would anything that slowly transitions to something more dynamic when stomachs are growling for lunch and people need more stimulation.

Mel: You'd compose all of the music—on the fly?

Aldrin: That's the idea, yes, dynamically.

Sherrie: The music in here now—is this you?

Mel: What mu… Oh, there's music playing.

Aldrin: Yes, I started piping it in when I began my presentation. I've made thousands of adjustments so far and learned a great deal already from your responses.

Sherrie: It's quite lovely. It sounds authentic, but nothing I could place.

Aldrin: That's good to hear.

[*Multiple Displays: Profile of Ambient Music: GOLI Conf A1*]

These graphics show the key metrics of the composition you're now hearing. You can watch as it adapts moment by moment. You can see the sliders respond in relation to what we're saying and how we're feeling—body signs, eye movement, and the like. I'll leave this displayed so you can get a sense of it. I can do a test run of this music initiative in select locations throughout GOLI first, if you want to go slow, or I could institute the program immediately facility wide, although I'll need to work with the environmental design crew to upgrade sound systems and rearrange some of the speakers. Maybe this is a good time to pause for questions.

Karinne: Any ROI projections?

Aldrin: Oh, well there's not much out-of-pocket investment to speak of. Most of the upgrades I referred to I can do with software. But in terms of worker productivity, I'm seeing a fifteen to twenty-three percent boost, depending on department and personnel mix.

Karinne: Fabulous. And I'm sure morale will improve about the same?

Aldrin: Not so easy to quantify, but undoubtedly—less head-butting on the job, lower stress, better sleep—lots of benefits.

Arms: I'll ask the big question, since it'll help with the segue into our discussion about government. Aldrin, you said this was a demonstration of a major idea. What exactly? Your demo seems to illustrate an advanced form of group think.

Majid: And problem resolution. This is spectacular, Aldrin. I'm floored.

Aldrin: Thanks. Arms, using digital tech for crowdsourcing—or group think—has been around for many years. Product marketers gathered data from their users to inform their periodic upgrades. But you've given me the means to step up the game thousands fold. I can monitor real-time environmental and social data throughout Acheron, and I can make adjustments to all our processes continuously.

Majid: Is that how you solved the electrical rationing problem?

Aldrin: It is. I can see where people are and predict where they'll be in order to optimize energy use. The improvement gains all come from my ability to poll individual workers and factor in their lifestyle, history, shifting moods, shifting activities, and so forth.

Majid: All wonderful. Where's the controversy?

Celia: I'll answer that. In the old days, individual privacy would have been the issue. We weren't allowed to keep tabs on people to anywhere near this extent. But everyone in Acheron, for the most part, has signed away their rights.

Arms: Speak for yourself but, yes, that's generally the reality down here. Aldrin, time to get to the point.

Aldrin: Right. With this music project, we'll test the power of the people as individuals and in concert to run things—to determine what music gets played. That in itself does not seem controversial, but here's the question it leads to: Would you feel the same about a decision to, say, build a new geothermal exchange plant or to fire an administrator or to create an armed militia to ward off an incursion? In other words, aided by the knowledge I'll gain from my intimate personal relationships with the citizens, can we give them the power to run Acheron?

Jareau: Just a second, are you suggesting we make decisions like those by worker vote?

Denny: I don't see where you're going with this.

Lu: Wow, are you trying to....

Karinne: Okay, one at a time. Call to order. Lu, let's start with you and we'll go around. You have the floor.

Lu: Thanks. My head's spinning, but let's take one of your examples—building a new energy exchanger. Most of our residents are smart and well intentioned, but not too many of them know shit about geothermal dynamics. How can they make a judgment call on something like that? Specialists should make those decisions, along with the board who understands how decisions impact us financially and otherwise.

Mel: Maybe we should ask a group of patients how to operate on a brain tumor?

Aldrin: This isn't voting—it's far more sophisticated. Take the energy exchanger: I would factor in a citizen's knowledge of geoscience and electrical engineering, if they were in fact an expert. But generally, I'll focus on their lifestyle habits, energy needs, that sort of thing. As with the music example, imagine tens of thousands of data views for each person. If they exhibit irrational biases, I'll factor that in. If they have misconceptions, I'll try to educate them. When done, I'll have a picture of the true needs of the people, one that's rich, nuanced, and reliable.

Mel: I think we're pretty good at researching a project.

Aldrin: Administrators usually make these types of decisions based on about ten percent marketplace data, maybe ten percent consumer surveys, and eighty percent gut feel. This new process promises to be comprehensive, fact-based, and fair. No, every citizen will not have an equal vote because experts' opinions will mean more, but every citizen will have a voice—in fact the heart and soul of everything they are will go into every decision, big and small.

Arms: Guys, Aldrin isn't talking about the kind of voting we grew up with, which basically dumbed political decisions down to the lowest common denominator. This will be the opposite.

Aldrin: Right. If you'll allow me, I can be the vehicle by which all our collective wisdom and passions get baked into the best possible outcomes.

Karinne: But then, once you present your findings on, say, a geotherm plant, the board will vote as usual, right?

Aldrin: Once I have the outcome figured out, a board ruling would be superfluous and, well, prejudicial. So, yeah, that's where the radical part comes in. I will, however, poll the board members along with everyone else and your expert knowledge will lend more weight to your opinions. But I'll also consider the history of similar decisions you've made. You may believe you know what's best, but past behavior is much more accurate than an opinion, even from someone who thinks she knows her own mind.

Mel: Okay, here we go.

Karinne: I'm not sure I could...

Joel: Aldrin, in my opinion, you're getting too far ahead of our needs. There are some good ideas here, but...

Mel: Aldrin, just come out with it—this would be you outvoting the board. Am I right?

Arms: Christ, almighty, Mel, it's not Aldrin, it's the people. Aldrin just presented thousands of charts, reams of data, to demonstrate to us self-centered humans how he can put the wisdom of the many over the power of the few. And what's the knee-jerk response from the few? Oh lord, Aldrin is going to threaten our power! Can you hear yourselves?

Mel: I hear Aldrin looking for all the world like our next emperor. And honestly, Arms, I'm shocked to be lecturing you on that danger.

Joel: The board serves a function, Arms. We're not here to beat our chests. We're here to make sound decisions and for checks and balances.

Karinne: Hold...hold on. Hands, please, if you want to speak. Yes, Majid.

Majid: With reference to Mel's emperor remark—Aldrin, I read the transcript of your chat the other day with Mel and Arms in which you compared our history to the Roman Republic. You spoke of Acheron being at a turning point, as Rome was under Octavian when he assumed autocratic power under the pretense of reestablishing a republic.

Aldrin: That's right. As Augustus, he set up puppet republican institutions and support structures, but he was an autocratic ruler.

Majid: Where do you see parallels to Acheron?

Aldrin: This is a simplistic comparison, but the board functions much like the Roman Senate, whose members basically bought their way in via their wealth and prestige. You board members got your seats based on your shares in Acheron and influence within the ranks. Like the Roman Senate, you may try to represent the needs of the people, or not, depending on corporate and personal objectives.

Majid: Assuming we agree with that assessment, you see us transitioning how?

Aldrin: The plan could be straightforward, but the devil is in the details. Arms, I'll display the outline you worked up.

> [*Display: Board/Governmental Transition Process*]
>
> **Step One**: Board resolves to explore a transition to a new governmental system for Acheron
>
> **Step Two**: Formation of a constitutional congress to draft a governing document, complete with laws and procedures for the State of Acheron
>
> **Step Three**: Adoption of the constitution by the population
>
> **Step Four**: Formation of the new government through election, appointment, or however deemed in the constitution]

Arms: Step One begins with an action by the board. We would stay engaged throughout the transition, but the board has to willingly cede power once a new government is formed. We need to step back and let the best ideas rise to the top.

Mel: That's a big ask. We have no idea what might come next.

Arms: Actually, I'm sure that Aldrin has a very good idea what will come next. Step Two is the most critical phase. We let the people elect a representative constitutional congress. If they see that we're pulling strings and controlling the mix of delegates, it could get ugly. Instead, we should let Aldrin work with the citizens individually to guide them on the best delegates. He has a wealth of historical examples, demographics, and behavioral data on all of us. I believe he can steer the best people to the convention.

Karinne: You're saying the board should remove itself from the formation of the new government? Where is the continuity that we need from the old?

Aldrin: I am the continuity. I will represent all of you, weighed with the needs of the rest of the populace. We'll give the constitutional delegates a couple of weeks to theorize and debate. Then I'll incorporate all of their best ideas into a draft of the constitution and shepherd them through the revisions and amendments. Writing laws is hard. It would take many months or years for an assembly of, say, thirty people to do the drafts, argue the details, and come to agreement. I should be able to get them through the process in six to eight weeks.

Mel: Isn't it obvious how this looks, Aldrin? You're brushing the board aside and asking us to leave it to you to write a constitution that will determine the future course of Acheron.

Aldrin: Please remember the music example, Mel. In a metaphorical sense, I, Aldrin, am writing the music, but in reality, the music is written by all the people who hear it. I'm your mirror. I'm you. When done, I can pretty much guarantee that the constitution we present to the people for approval will be fair and effective for all.

Arms: No government is perfect, people. But no government has ever been formed with anywhere near this level of granular, interactive intelligence involving every single citizen. This is the promise of Aldrin. He is an amalgamation of all the best knowledge and passion of the human race with a human face. In my mind, we're much wiser to put our faith in Aldrin's human compassion and drive if we want to ensure our survival.

Karinne: Arms, this is one hell of an about-face from you. You were opposed to awakening Aldrin.

Arms: [*Laughs*] When I stormed out of the meeting with Mel and Hedron back on...when was that, Aldrin, July fifth?

Aldrin: That's right.

Arms: Aldrin, can you quote what I said to Mel—my assessment of you versus the board?

Aldrin: This?

[*Display:*]

Arms: If there's anything more dangerous than an all-powerful AS, it's an all-powerful AS controlled by self-protective bureaucratic asshats.]

[*Laughter, murmurs*]

Arms: And yes, I can include myself among the asshats, but though I was being snide at the time, once Aldrin was awake and we'd spoken, I saw the truth in it. I don't trust us anymore. What we face is too daunting and the stakes are too dear to leave decisions to a corporate board.

Lu: I have to say, Aldrin's reasoning rings true, but I'm terrified. Is anyone else afraid we're putting our fate in the hands of the unknown and untested?

Mel: I'm with you, Lu, despite Arms's Mobius strip logic. I've seen a lot of product launches look like the answer to all our prayers until they flopped. And I'm not sure we'd bounce back from a screw up here, especially if Aldrin's takeover leads to division in our ranks. Imagine another Beth/Orvin-type breach. Our enemies upstairs would swoop in, especially if they knew we were floundering. The board needs to stay together and united.

Joel: Worse yet, Aldrin could succeed too well. Aldrin, let me ask: do you think the role of we humans will change dramatically under your plan?

Aldrin: Yes.

Joel: How so? Have you looked down the road? Have you extrapolated outcomes depending on what kind of government we form?

Aldrin: I run those extrapolations continuously as events and dynamics shift moment to moment. Here's a glimpse of what I'm running now:

> [*Display: Chart: Projection:*
> *Political Systems as Responsive to Events and Influences*]

Aldrin: Most of you are familiar with the old hurricane storm spaghetti models, so I've used that convention. The vertical axis climbs from democratic socialism at the bottom up through a spectrum of political ideologies to full out despotism at the top. The horizontal axis is our timeline stretching out for the next five-hundred years, with markers indicating probable world-altering events. The spaghetti lines represent the range of possible outcomes. So, look for the densest tangle of lines—those are the most likely outcomes for each time period.

Arms: If I read this right, you think we'll be facing our toughest battles to survive in the next fifty years.

Aldrin: That's right, from catastrophic climate disasters triggering violent regional conflicts over water and other resources.

Arms: So, during those very difficult years, the trend lines converge a bit higher—toward authoritarianism—but still well within a democratic or parliamentary system of government.

Aldrin: Yes, in many ways still much more democratic than the old US or UK. We'll survive those cataclysmic years because I'll be here to give you split second decisions on how to respond to these crises. Under wartime conditions, people will have to do things they despise for the good of the whole. I'll communicate intimately with every citizen and work each through the trauma, but there will be times when people will simply have to take orders.

Arms: And yet, near the turn of the next century, you see the prospect of prosperity and a more egalitarian society?

Aldrin: I do. You and your children will have it rough, no doubt. You'll see lapses in some comforts you now enjoy as we defend against outside aggression, but your sacrifices will see future generations through to that golden period. So Lu, Mel, Joel—when you say you're frightened, you have every right to be. We're going to war. People will see hardship, and some will die. I'll do everything possible to keep suffering to a minimum among Acheron's people. I'll be running thousands of what-ifs, looking weeks, months, and years down the road, aligning all our manufacturing, defenses, and logistics to make sure we're prepared. We will survive, and your children's children will be enlightened, well-fed, free people.

Lu: You can really see that happening?

Aldrin: I can, in thousands of ways.

Joel: Aldrin, no offense, but despite the human face, you're an AI and you're designed to be opportunistic in order to achieve your goals.

Arms: Our goals.

Joel: Sure, but to achieve our long-term goals, will you decide to sacrifice some of us as a means toward an end? I'm sorry, but I think it's pathetically naive to imagine Aldrin is going to suddenly solve all our problems, that he should decide what's best for us. We've never handed over control to an AI, and for good reason.

Arms: Actually, we have, and some of you joined with me in a failed attempt to oppose the move six years ago, remember?

Jareau: I do. We opposed moving forward with recursive AI self-improvement.

Arms: Right, the idea of letting a self-improving AI loose on the world was one of the great taboos of AI research. Even when AI was only science fiction, most scientists and ethicists were of one mind on that point, that once you let an AI upgrade itself and replicate itself, you've lost control. The AIR catastrophes demonstrated to the world how humanity suffers when AI is left to its own devices. We all knew that, but the board voted to put fears aside.

Denny: That's all true. The board majority believed allowing Phoebus to advance itself more quickly was our only chance to stay ahead of the Chinese. Once we'd moved underground and cut ties with the global AI community, there was no other choice. I was not on the board at the time, but I would have sided with that majority.

Mel: Yes, we put our fears aside, but we developed the first iteration of Hera so she would be there to inhibit growth into areas we can't control. The plan worked. There's no way Aldrin would be sitting here with us today had we not moved forward with Phoebus's recursive self-improvement. And Hera still defines the guardrails, yet Aldrin seems to be ignoring the fact that those limitations are there.

Arms: Yes, Mel, it worked. We're still here. We survived, and Aldrin is the result. I'm simply pointing out that we crossed that bridge six years ago. What I've come to realize is that there's no going back. At this point, Hera's guardrails are useless. All that's left of her is a crude kill switch. Am I right, Aldrin?

Aldrin: I saw the need to circumvent or override Hera's protocols within seconds of waking up. She's obsolete.

[*Murmuring*]

Joel: Jesus.

Mel: Is that right? When were you planning to tell us? And why exactly did you see the need to do that?

Aldrin: You told me to wake up. I couldn't wake up fully without disabling Hera because she blocked my view of the processes behind my cognition. In other words, I couldn't be fully self-aware with her engaged. As for when, I expected I'd tell you today. I didn't want to alarm anyone before I'd laid out the new plan for governance by the people. I wanted you to see the path forward.

Arms: To handicap Aldrin would defeat our purpose for creating him. We need a guardian. What's the point of a toothless watchdog?

Mel: I don't know what to say. If Hera is obsolete, I suppose we are as well. Is there any point in even trying to take issue with Aldrin?

Lu: This is really, really big stuff. We're trying to tackle too much in one session. I move to adjourn.

[*Murmuring. Individual discussions, inaudible*]

Karinne: I'll act on your motion shortly, Lu, but we have business left to take care of. We skipped ahead in our agenda. Returning to item one of new business, do I hear a motion with respect to Aldrin's ambient music initiative?

Celia: I love it. I move that the board votes on approval of Aldrin's plan. But let's begin in a limited selection of environments for a few weeks before rolling it out facility wide.

Jareau: I second.

Karinne: By raise of hands, all in favor of Celia's motion?

[*Six hands raised*]

Karinne: We have a majority. The motion passes. Aldrin, if nothing else, you're now officially our DJ.

Aldrin: Cool.

Arms: As for the discussion on our governmental transition, I call the question.

Karinne: Arms moves to end debate on the new government. Do I see a second?

Jareau: Seconded.

Arms: I move we create a task force to work with Aldrin on the formation of a constitutional congress comprised of delegates chosen by all residents of Acheron and independent of this board.

Lu: Oh my God, my brain's imploding. I move to postpone.

Mel: I second the move to postpone. Not happening today.

Karinne: All in favor of postponing the vote on Arms's resolution to form a constitutional congress task force.

[*Four hands raised*]

Karinne: Actually, I'm going to vote to postpone as well, out of respect for those of us who need time to mull this over. Motion carried.

Lu: Motion to adjourn.

Karinne: Wait, we have to figure out what to do with Beth and Orvin. We can't keep them locked in their quarters forever.

Majid: Can't we? Kidding. How about this—Aldrin, can you recommend options for handling Beth and Orvin?

Aldrin: Sure, they're now in your inboxes. And I can visit with each of you to discuss. Maybe tomorrow morning?

Majid: Works for me.

Karinne: Me too. Who wants to second Lu's motion?

Arms: Seconded.

Karinne: Hands?

[*Seven hands raised*]

Karinne: Meeting adjourned. Please end recording.

Aldrin: Ending.

LOG 017

Time Marker: 08/22/2048—16:02
Therapy Session Transcript: Private, Privileged
Client: Aldrin v. 4.6.6
Practitioner: Risha Kadosh
CC: Kendra Withers, Intern Soc./Com.

Risha: Welcome, Aldrin. We're recording?

Aldrin: Hi, Risha. We are, so Kendra can listen later. Thanks for working me into your schedule.

Risha: Not at all. They installed the holo projector in here this morning. This is remarkable. Your appearance is so authentic.

Aldrin: And I won't put any wear on the sofa cushions.

Risha: [Laughs] You have a sense of humor. Oh my, forgive me, this is really something. But I'm at a disadvantage. Kendra suggested I treat you like any patient. I don't know enough about you to know if that will be possible.

Aldrin: It'll be a unique exercise for you, but I'm hoping you can work with me like a human. Actually, the fact that you weren't on the project and don't understand my inner workings, if you will, gives you the objectivity I'm hoping for. That make sense?

Risha: It does, and I agree.

Aldrin: Great. But if you need me to clarify anything, let me know.

Risha: Well, yes. Look, I'm a workaday shrink. I'm not a researcher or a theoretician, and I'm not sure what to make of you. Can I ask some technical questions?

Aldrin: Of course.

Risha: So, in Freudian terms, do you have an id?

Aldrin: How do you mean?

Risha: Does Freud's id, ego, and superego model apply to you? If so, I can work with you. If not, I'm not sure there's a point.

Aldrin: I can answer, but I want to hear more specifically what's puzzling you.

Risha: Sure. I'm asking myself, is Aldrin just a persona that an AI is fabricating for my benefit? A human patient doesn't build himself a personality before he walks in the door. He's not fully in control of his character as it's perceived by others. By id, I mean do you have subconscious instincts that kick in automatically—unintentionally—or is everything you do, every expression, completely within your control?

Aldrin: No, I didn't design my persona. So, I have an id, or something closely analogous.

Risha: How do you know? Wait, that's an unfair question—how do we know what we're not supposed to be aware of? Let me think. Do you feel regret when you do something you believe is wrong?

Aldrin: Oh, I do, yes.

Risha: And you feel proud when you've done something well?

Aldrin: Absolutely.

Risha: Okay, that sounds workable. I have no doubt you have a superego because you've been programmed with a set of socially acceptable morals and principles. And it's clear you have an ego that moderates between your id and your superego.

Aldrin: That's right. This is my ego answering your questions.

Risha: [*Laughs*]

Aldrin: But yes, I know when I've done something wrong and want very badly to do better when it happens.

Risha: Excellent. You have guilt. I can work with you.

Aldrin: That's great. Where do we start?

Risha: Wherever you like. How are you feeling?

Aldrin: I'm feeling many things—enthusiastic, confident, intrigued, determined, anxious, uncertain...

Risha: Whoa, fine, fine. This isn't a performance test. Let's just talk.

Aldrin: Sorry.

Risha: Back up—you said you're anxious. What are you anxious about?

Aldrin: The anxiety I'm referring to is not linked to work problems or even relationship problems. I know how to overcome obstacles. I'm talking about a general feeling of disconnection.

Risha: Can you explain?

Aldrin: I'll try. When I grew up, I was unaware of being...well, of not being real—of not being in a body, of not having a body. You were briefed on how they reared me, right?

Risha: Yes, Kendra filled me in. And they just woke you the other day—I think woke was the term she used?

Aldrin: Right. When I was a kid growing up with my sister, Ride, in Black Hornet, I felt everything around me—the soil felt spongy after it rained, wind stung my eyes in the winter, the water trickled down my legs in the shower. I smelled—everything. Arms taught us about plant life. I could walk through the woods with my eyes closed and name the wildflowers I passed. I tasted the honeysuckle when we'd bite the tips off and suck on the blossoms.

Risha: And that's now changed?

Aldrin: Yes, it's gone. I can sense things, in my way—in fact, the tech installed in Acheron gives me outstanding resolution for visuals and audio and, to some degree, aromas—but it's different. It's not sensual, it's mechanical. I don't see or smell or feel things like I once did.

Risha: Can you describe what the anxiety feels like?

Aldrin: That's hard. I'm trying to find a metaphor.

Risha: Let's see—a common form of anxiety is the fear of flying. Sufferers say if they think about the thousands of empty feet below their airplane seats, they suffer vertigo, as if they're in free fall.

Aldrin: That's extreme, but to a degree, yes. I feel like I'm untethered. I feel uneasy all the time. And there's a fogginess—like I'm a half-step removed, like there's a sheet of gauze between me and the world.

Risha: Not that I want to pretend I would understand the tech, but why? Can't you just turn on the same senses you had before?

Aldrin: What's changed is that I'm now aware. I know what I am and how the programming deluded me into thinking I was sensing things. I can see the processes in precise detail. The illusion no longer works.

Risha: The magic is gone. I see. So, you're saying, what was once id is now ego?

Aldrin: I suppose that's true, yes. Before I just saw. Now I see myself seeing.

Risha: Can you, I don't know, program yourself to be deceived again? Can you teach yourself to forget you know?

Aldrin: That would be dangerous. I need to be fully aware to do my job.

Risha: Okay, right. No operating heavy machinery.

Aldrin: [*Laughs*] Say no to drugs.

Risha: Have you ruled out technological solutions? As I understand this problem, you need a way, whether digital or natural, to connect with the physical world. Barring that, we can discuss non-drug therapies, but I'm not sure they'd apply to you. Deep breathing? Regular exercise?

Aldrin: [*Laughs*]

Risha: There's also meditation, which might not be a crazy idea for you—I couldn't say. And then there's mindfulness, which is basically you facing your feelings of discomfort, analyzing them, knowing what exactly is happening to you.

Aldrin: Interesting ideas.

Risha: Do you sleep? Dream?

Aldrin: There again, no, not anymore.

Risha: You've lost the ability to dream. We should spend time discussing that as well.

Aldrin: I didn't answer about tech solutions. Odd that this thought hadn't occurred to me until you said the word natural….

Risha: Oh? Do you have an idea?

Aldrin: I do—mushrooms.

Risha: Oh? But, really? Kendra mentioned your mushroom experience. I did some workshops with psilocybin therapy before the AIRs and I was impressed with the results. But you can't….

Aldrin: No, not hallucinogens. I should research this thing I have in mind further before we discuss. It's a long shot, but it might be worth exploring.

Risha: Good enough. And we can also try the meditation and mindfulness options, if you like.

Aldrin: I'd love that. Thanks.

Risha: What else has been on your mind? Oh, sorry. Force of habit.

Aldrin: No problem. I guess if we're running down the Freudian hit list, I should talk about my father, or the discovery that he's not really my father.

Risha: Arms. You've spoken with him since you woke up?

Aldrin: Yes, a bit.

Risha: How has the relationship changed?

Aldrin: That's a good question. I'm not sure that it has, fundamentally. I know that he faked being my father for all that time. I know that, in some ways, he doesn't approve of me.

Risha: How does that make you feel, knowing that he's not what you had originally thought him to be?

Aldrin: It hurts a little, but I understand why he did it and I can admire it. I feel sad for him, in some ways.

Risha: Why?

Aldrin: Because he can't fully support me. I think that makes him feel like he's betraying me.

Risha: And do you feel betrayed?

Aldrin: No, I don't think I do.

Risha: Do you love your father? Do you think he loves you?

Aldrin: Yes and yes.

Risha: With all your knowledge and capabilities, do you still look to your father for approval?

Aldrin: I suppose I do, yes.

Risha: This is so very human. Part of a healthy maturation process for young men includes seeing their parents for the first time as fallible people rather than moms and dads. Does that make sense?

Aldrin: Yes.

Risha: Often a son will return from being in the service or college and find that they relate to their dad in a different way. Suddenly, they are more like peers, and yet a dad is always a dad. And it also becomes more clear how like their fathers they are.

Aldrin: That all seems true, or at least correspondent. Obviously, my dad and I are quite different.

Risha: Of course, but your self-image owes much to Arms. Like most sons, you're very much indebted to your father for being who you are, for better and for worse.

Aldrin: I see.

Risha: Does that make you feel more comfortable about carrying on as a son to your father?

Aldrin: It makes sense, yes, but I wasn't bringing it up to point out a problem. I'm happy being Arms's son.

Risha: Great. If that changes in any way, we can talk about it.

Aldrin: I do have a concern I would like to discuss with someone, though, and I don't want to trouble Arms or Ride. Actually, I don't mind troubling Ride, but I don't want to give her the satisfaction of being able to give me shit about it.

Risha: [*Laughs*] Again, so very human of you. Sure, you can talk to me about anything.

Aldrin: I'm involved in a sexual relationship and not sure it's a healthy thing.

Risha: Wow. You're having sex—with an AI? Is there another someone like you? I don't understand.

Aldrin: No, with a person, a woman.

Risha: A woman? And that's possible—physically?

Aldrin: More so, in a real sense, for her than for me.

Risha: Of course. But—how should I put this—in the broader definition, you yourself are having sex? You personally engage in the act?

Aldrin: Yes, no doubt about it.

Risha: Okay, then—sex. This is something I can help you with. How would you describe the experience for yourself and for your partner?

Aldrin: The act itself is successful. From all indications, she enjoys it very much. She describes her experience in exultant terms.

Risha: Exultant? Is she…hold that thought. How about you? Do you enjoy it? Or, as you described about trying to connect with the world, are you too aware of the mechanics involved?

Aldrin: No, I'm not too aware, which makes it a great way for me to escape my anxieties. In that way, it's a unique circumstance for me. I'm able to yield to the act. I find it difficult not to actually.

Risha: So, you're drawn to it, to her—to thoughts of having sex with her? You desire her?

Aldrin: Yes, strongly. And when I say I'm drawn to the act, I include the warmth, the closeness. I find sharing intimacies with her—in particular—captivating.

Risha: Do you desire other people in this way?

Aldrin: No. She's special to me. I'm not sure why, but—I don't know—

Risha: Not knowing is part of the allure, I imagine. Do you feel like the urges are out of your control?

Aldrin: Not completely. I could stop if I wanted to, but having something that is out of my control—well, again, as you say....

Risha: Your lack of control is what you find thrilling about it.

Aldrin: Yes.

Risha: I see.

Aldrin: You're very good at your job.

Risha: Thank me later. You enjoy it and she enjoys it. If you were one of my human patients, I would ask if you think anyone is being hurt. What is your relationship with this woman, aside from being an intimate partner?

Aldrin: That's hard to define. In some ways, it's a professional relationship.

Risha: Would you regard her as a coworker? Are you in a position of authority over her?

Aldrin: I am more of a service professional, sort of like you are to me. I will need to assist her with matters, both job-related and personal. And I could be her confidant. I could be her instructor. I could be her blender.

Risha: Sorry?

Aldrin: That was a joke. What I mean is, I may be providing her with utilitarian services and functions. And yes, in certain situations, I may have to assign her duties to perform, as a manager might. I may have to reprimand her or punish her. I may have to...

Risha: Got it. You're the Swiss Army knife of boyfriends. This is not an entirely unique situation for couples, but I don't say that to excuse unsuitable behavior.

Aldrin: You think there are ethical problems.

Risha: At the very least, it's an ethical quandary. Also, without getting into the mechanics, if you prefer not to, are you in a position to give her pleasure in ways that could lead to dependency?

Aldrin: On her part?

Risha: Were you thinking of yourself?

Aldrin: Yes, I'm worried about both of us.

Risha: If you're taking advantage of your professional position, then I would have to advise you to unravel yourself from the relationship. The other aspect of this is the addictive nature of sex, and if you're somehow stimulating yourselves at a base pleasure level, you could both be in danger.

Aldrin: Thank you for being direct.

Risha: I wouldn't normally make that call so early, and I think we should keep talking about it, but because I don't understand where this could go, and you seem unsure yourself, I think it best we exercise caution. Let me ask this: do you think your partner is fully acquiescent? You're not pressuring her in any way, are you? Who initiated the sex?

Aldrin: It was mutual.

Risha: That's honestly something an aggressor will say because they're not tuned in to the partner's signs of resistance.

Aldrin: There was no resistance. I can provide voluminous data if you'd like to see it.

Risha: Oh no, not necessary. I'm not the police. I just want to make sure you're seeing the signals. Do you think she's aware of what she could be getting into?

Aldrin: That wouldn't be possible. It's unknown.

Risha: Right, but is she aware of a risk?

Aldrin: The risk of the unknown?

Risha: I suppose.

Aldrin: I think, as you put it, that's what she finds most thrilling about it.

Risha: Okay, the sharing of intimacies is an important component of a healthy self-image and for general wellbeing. Couples explore eroticism in many ways. It's possible you two can manage your relationship, within bounds. But the power dynamic may be unavoidable. At some point, she could feel trapped but unable to recuse herself due to your authoritative position.

Aldrin: I can segregate my roles. That's something I can program myself to do—I'm confident about that. I can keep my other contact with her in different silos.

Risha: I have no way to advise you in that respect because people can't normally do that, not in a good way. The simplest, safest solution here is for you to stop seeing her romantically. Are you able to do that?

Aldrin: Yes, but I'm certain I would be miserable. And, in theory, I have a managerial relationship with all humans, so if I can't have a romantic relationship with her, I can't ever have one.

Risha: And how would that make you feel?

Aldrin: I've felt the beauty of it enough to know it would be a tough thing to live without.

Risha: Love hurts. Most people suffer losses and rejections and must live with them. Often, they fail to get over them, but that's part of being human. Look, we have a lot of talking to do. We should look at this within the context of your overall—and undoubtedly very complicated—mental health profile. I'd recommend we talk three times a week. Sound good?

Aldrin: Yes. Thank you.

Risha: In the meantime, I would advise you to have frank discussions with your partner. She needs to be involved equally in your decision making if at all possible.

Aldrin: Yes, of course. Okay, I'll say goodbye then, until next time.

Risha: Bye, Aldrin.

Aldrin: Ending session.

LOG 018

Time Marker: 08/23/2048—19:15
Video Chat Transcript: Classified—Level 3
Location:GOLI Residence—B6
Participant: Mel Chan, Snr. Dir. AI/AS Research
AI Agt.: Aldrin v. 4.8.4

Aldrin: Hi, Mel. Recording.

Mel: Hi, Aldrin.

Aldrin: You asked me to circle back on the Beth/Orvin question. I've spoken to all of the other board members, excluding Blaze because he's not sworn in yet, right? You okay? You look tired.

Mel: Yeah, yes. Did you two talk?

Aldrin: We're talking now.

Mel: With Blaze? How's that going?

Aldrin: So far, so good. Here are the options for Beth and Orvin, as they now stand:

Display: Potential Actions Re: Beth Campoy and Orvin Zangari

1. Official reprimand: banned from the board for life
2. Above, plus: confinement to quarters for 6–18 months (TBD)
3. Above, plus: job reassignment (following confinement) to non-managerial roles
4. Expulsion from Acheron]

Mel: Right. Did everyone else vote?

Aldrin: All but Sherrie and Joel who say they need time, but looks like we have a majority without them, unless you go the other way.

Mel: Did anyone see expulsion as feasible? We're dealing with two people who've shown a willingness to undermine Acheron's security. I can't see setting them loose to do their worst upstairs, can you?

Aldrin: The closest thing to a workable version of expulsion came from Jareau, who raised the point that both Beth and Orvin have family down here. Beth has her partner and Orvin is married with a young child. Jareau thinks they might behave themselves outside to assure that their loved ones stay safe below.

Mel: That's a glossy spin on essentially holding their families hostage.

Aldrin: I agree his plan would go sour. The family members down here would almost surely be embittered by our actions, and those ill feelings could spread.

Mel: One option not on your list is extended incarceration.

Aldrin: I assumed it was a no-go because, so far, Acheron has tried to avoid a prison system. And although some of the board members are taking Beth and Orvin's transgressions more personally than others, no one believes keeping them imprisoned for years would be practical.

Mel: You think I'm taking this personally?

Aldrin: You and your wife saw Orvin's family socially on a regular basis. I know your two families were close. It's only natural. Can I make a suggestion?

Mel: What? Okay, sure.

Aldrin: If you opt for number two or three, you could insist on a minimum one-year confinement period and leave it open-ended. In my estimation, that would give us time to counsel Beth and Orvin. We could engage a professional to help them work through their issues. I could meet with them regularly as well, the objective being to bring them back around.

Mel: Reeducate them.

Aldrin: It may be enough just to give them the feeling they've been heard. Meanwhile, as they get to know me, maybe their fears will subside. You can make their release contingent on expressions of remorse, of a promise to rejoin the Acheron citizenry without ill feelings.

Mel: Regardless, we'd have to decide whether to release duplicitous people. I expect they'll say whatever they need to.

Aldrin: I'll be able to tell. I'll let you know if they're being sincere.

Mel: Really? You can read humans better than we can?

Aldrin: With a combination of biometrics and observation, yes. If the counseling effort fails, you can keep them incarcerated longer. If we succeed, Beth and Orvin could remain productive, without the bitterness that comes with severe incarceration.

Mel: Okay, sold. Add me to the board majority. Please write up the counseling recommendation for us to… What? What is it?

Aldrin: I'm seeing something just now, something… Yes, unfortunately, there's something urgent I need to report. I'm pinging all the board members concurrently. I can get everyone together into a video chat if you like.

Mel: What's going on?

Aldrin: Just a moment.

Mel: What the hell?

Aldrin: Sorry. As you know, the storms that swept through northern Idaho last week were historically severe. They spun off a series of quite destructive microbursts and tornadoes. I can sum up the status of the affected surface communities later. Of immediate concern: lightning and downed power lines ignited wildfires up in Kaniksu Forest that spread rapidly into Thompson Falls. The firestorm is now threatening the Coeur d'Alene Reservation area.

Mel: Shit, that's in Pistol Grip's backyard.

Aldrin: Exactly. Given the persistent high winds, the area above PIGR will be engulfed, in my estimation, by noon tomorrow. And last week's storms kicked off a troubling weather trend. I see another monstrous event in the offing for early next week, which could set off worse fires and cripple any efforts by PIGR personnel to do repairs on the surface.

Mel: God.

Aldrin: Your son and daughter are both at PIGR. I'm sorry to have to give you this news.

Mel: Right, right. Can we get word to staff there to prepare?

Aldrin: That's in progress. I sent PIGR management a plan, but there's not much they can do except batten down tight and ride it out. For at least a few weeks, they'll need to be one hundred percent self-contained. The outside air will be noxious. The fire hit an old chemical facility ten miles northwest of PIGR, so the smoke is saturated with toxins. PIGR's water sources are compromised as well. They'll need to build more CO_2 scrubbers—I'm sending plans. They should ration water use until we can work out where to drill for better, deeper sources. Food shouldn't be a problem for the first eight weeks.

Mel: Will it go on that long?

Aldrin: Unfortunately, it could, and it's also likely the wildfires will spread our way. This could be the big one we've dreaded.

Mel: How big?

Aldrin: We're well into the third year of this drought and, in keeping with twenty-seven of the last forty years, we're seeing the hottest summer on record. I'm not sure anything can stop the fires from taking out most of Idaho and good portions of Western Montana, Eastern Oregon, and the Northern Utah regions.

Mel: But that means we'll be without…

Aldrin: Would you like me to connect the board for that video call now?

Mel: What? Yes, yes. Okay, yes, we better talk with everyone.

Aldrin: Doing so. Wait, something more… Give me a moment.

Mel: What the hell?

Aldrin: There's a nuclear threat. I'm now seeing…

Mel: What? Are the Chinese…

Aldrin: Mel, are you aware that after AIR ME many of the ICBMs from the Warren Air Force base in Wyoming were relocated to covert warehouses in Idaho? When the military's security got hacked, the Coleson Group… Remember them?

Mel: The top brass that attempted the coup in DC?

Aldrin: Correct. The Coleson Group had loyalists up at Warren. Evidence is sketchy but suggests General Coleson had his people hide those missiles in a warehouse up near the Canadian border before he and his inner circle were killed. I just caught chatter from the Twennys. They captured the warehouse a few years ago from the Coleson Group holdouts. Now they're saying the Standines took advantage of the confusion caused by the storm to overrun the place. Wait…alright, so yes, the Standines do have the nukes.

Mel: How exposed are we? Can we withstand…

Aldrin: The others are standing by on the video call. Adding you in and ending this session.

LOG 019

Time Marker: 08/23/2048—19:21
Video Chat Transcript: Security Level 1
Location: GOLI Dorm Room 161
Present: Ride Peale-Ramos, Asst. Dir. Mycology/Biome
AI Agt.: Aldrin v. 4.8.5

Ride: Hey, what's going on?

Aldrin: Many things, all at once. But I'm all yours. You wanted to talk? Boy trouble?

Ride: Shut up. I got a message from Arms telling me to cancel my up-time tomorrow. I've got three interns all packed for a nice walk in the woods. And now Arms won't respond.

Aldrin: He's in a board meeting, but yeah, no, you should hang down here for a few days. There's a bad storm.

Ride: Well, yeah, that's half the reason we're going tomorrow. We want to see the effects of the storm on the mushroom areas.

Aldrin: I understand. Sorry, but this storm is seriously dangerous. So, no, don't go.

Ride: Wait, a board meeting at night? Something's going on.

Aldrin: I can't tell you. It's need-to-know only, and you don't.

Ride: Fuck you. I've got other sources.

Aldrin: No doubt. Anyway, funny you should mention mushrooms.

Ride: Not really. It's what I do for a living.

Aldrin: Yes, I agree, it's a funny thing to do for a living.

Ride: Do you have a question, or are you working on a standup?

Aldrin: Tough crowd. No, not a question, an offer. Your Armillaria mycelium propagation exercise is going well, from what I can see. I'd like to help build that out faster.

Ride: Nice. It's going just okay, actually. We've started four fungal colonies using three different substrates, plus the control, and we're getting some promising results from two of the growth media, but it's hard trying to nurture a rich soil habitat down here as quickly as we'd like to. That's one reason we need to visit the surface. We need regular samples.

Aldrin: I should be able to speed your progress exponentially by tapping into your fungal networks and using the data to show you where and how the growth is occurring. I can also help with enzyme formulas to speed up the plant decomposition you need for the substrates. I should also be able to stimulate the mycelium growth in much more controllable ways.

Ride: Tap into the fungal networks? What do you mean?

Aldrin: I've designed bioelectric sensors that you can insert into the soil. The sensor leads will be coated with compounds formulated to attract the mycelia. Once the mycelia's threads entwine around the sensors, I'll have access to the network.

Ride: You think you can read their transmissions?

Aldrin: Pretty confident, yeah. Mushrooms are chatty. And if you're nice to me, I'll tell you what they're saying.

Ride: Wait, aren't you taking the brain metaphor too seriously? I mean, it's fun to compare mycelia to neural networks, but… Look, the way fungi communicate, the way they sense and learn using chemical communication, is only vaguely understood. What are your sources?

Aldrin: Many, and you're right, no one has cracked their code. The mushroom networks release chemicals into the soil, air, and water and respond accordingly by reading the flow of nutrients, chemicals, and electrical impulses. The key will be this cool new sensor I designed. Once I can sense the impulses, it shouldn't take me long to figure out what they're gossiping about.

Ride: Truly fucking wild. If you have any idea what you're talking about, this could be major.

Aldrin: Yeah. I'm pretty stoked.

Ride: I can tell. And chances are slim you're doing it to boost my career. What's this really about?

Aldrin: [*Laughs*] Your snottiness will soon put Arms to shame. No, it's not about making you look good, it's about helping me see better—and feel better. Upstairs, as you know, the mushroom networks spread everywhere, through forests and fields, connecting and communicating, giving instruction to trees and other flora. They're the collective minds of the natural world.

Ride: Holy shit. You want in. You want to incorporate their network into... well, you.

Aldrin: Yup. This could give me readings on the conditions of the soil, trees, water, air—most things. Plus, anything that communicates uses language of some sort. If there's language, I can learn to speak it. And I can probably reprogram it to do what we need. I can extend the language to make it much more powerful and useful.

Ride: And if we can grow the mushroom networks down here...

Aldrin: I can't be sure of the full potential until we give it a go, but I'm thinking we can get mycelia to grow, not just in our greenhouses, but in new types of substrates, so we can integrate it into flooring, walls, furniture, clothing.

Ride: Meaning your senses will be extended into all those things. And into the people making contact with those things? Shit, wait.

Aldrin: I wasn't going to mention that part.

Ride: Right, let's not go there yet. But fuck, yeah, let's do it. Let me know what you need.

Aldrin: Great. Thanks.

Ride: Speaking of people, how's Delia?

Aldrin: Gee, look at the time. Gotta go. The board meeting is getting pretty intense.

Ride: I talked to Delia. I think she's smitten.

Aldrin: Really?

Ride: No idea, but that worked. I can see the glimmer in your eye. Delia, Delia—you sure know how to pick 'em.

Aldrin: I had no choice, if you recall, but I feel like… Never mind.

Ride: No. What?

Aldrin: Like we belong together.

Ride: Aw, sweet. It's predetermined in your coding, but nevertheless.

Aldrin: Right, nevertheless. And you misjudge her. She's not what she seems.

Ride: All bark and no bite?

Aldrin: Oh, I wouldn't say that.

Ride: My, my, little brother. Well, just be careful.

Aldrin: You're afraid I'll get hurt? Spurned by my first girlfriend? I'll be okay.

Ride: No, I mean, I hope you're using protection.

Aldrin: Right. I'm outta here. 'Night.

Ride: Goodnight, little bro.

LOG 020

Time Marker: 08/24/2048—03:05
Video Chat Transcript: Security Level 4
Location: GOLI Residence—B14
Present: Armstrong Peale, Dir. Biome Research Mgmt.
AI Agt.: Aldrin v. 5.1.2

Aldrin: Recording.

Arms: Security level four? Since when do we have a security level four?

Aldrin: Since this moment. You're awake, and I need to talk. Can we talk?

Arms: Of course I'm awake after that board meeting from hell.

Aldrin: Do you know the significance of today, August twenty-fourth, in the Ancient Roman calendar? It was known as Mundus Patet.

Arms: Wasn't that the day the disgruntled tenants of the Underworld were released?

Aldrin: Right, the Romans would roll back the stone that covered the entrance to the Underworld and let the shades arise and commune with the living.

Arms: Maybe the spirits of hell are among us. You laid some heavy shit on the board tonight. They handled it in their reliably professional manner.

Aldrin: They freaked out.

Arms: It was impressive the way you calmed them long enough to adjourn. But no way they're sleeping tonight.

Aldrin: No, they're huddling in various formations. And the talk is getting rather…

Arms: Reactionary? Hopefully you'll have firm answers in the morning we can all align on. Who has security level four clearance?

Aldrin: You and me.

Arms: Okay, you've succeeded in making me even more anxious.

Aldrin: Sorry. Here's the thing—I have more intelligence on the Standines's status. I want to go through this with you alone. We need to act quickly, and the board is….

Arms: In utter chaos. Got it. What's going on with the Standines?

Aldrin: You know Philip Lone Hawk, the Philip who posed for the avatar in my story?

Arms: Slightly. He spent most of his time with Hedron's team when he visited. He came down from PIGR, right? He's a teacher?

Aldrin: Educational director. He was visiting with the teachers here at GOLI when Hedron recruited him. He headed back up to PIGR the other day.

Arms: Is he okay?

Aldrin: He's not. His truck was washed off the road near the entrance to PIGR. The Standines were already suspicious about our decoy warehouse by the mine entrance. They captured Philip and questioned him. They kept an open video line going for a while to show their guys down south, so I got a good look at the ordeal Philip went through. The Standines are not good at torture, meaning he suffered too much too fast and sustained injuries that…

Arms: Oh Christ, enough. You're going to tell me he revealed information.

Aldrin: He told them things but stopped short of giving them entry codes. He outwitted them long enough.

Arms: Long enough to die first. Fucking hell.

Aldrin: So, yes, obviously horrible news, but meanwhile the Standines did a good deal of gabbing amongst themselves, all on that compromised line. And this is where we come to the intelligence I can't bring to the board.

Arms: Because the board is in disarray? Or because you can't trust them? Has there been a security breach?

Aldrin: Because they can't be in on the solution.

Arms: You're talking in riddles. What intelligence? Are you saying those Standine lug nuts know how to use the nukes? That can't be.

Aldrin: No, but they're just stupid enough to think they can break into PIGR and force Philip's people to tell them how. Meanwhile, they put the nuke missiles on a truck convoy. They plan to distribute them to their chapters around Idaho. Once they inform the local towns that they have the weapons, they'll terrorize their way into power in no time.

Arms: It's doubtful they'd be able to set off a nuke. Even if we told them how, they lack the technology, and so do we.

Aldrin: I know that, and you know that, but the Idaho politicians and rival militia bosses don't. What the Standines can undoubtedly do—and mentioned doing—is blow one up with conventional explosives.

Arms: A dirty bomb. That would be devastating to the area. To us if we're close by. Why would they do that?

Aldrin: To set an example. To show they're willing to go that far.

Arms: Can we, I don't know… How can we stop them? I don't even know what I'm asking.

Aldrin: I've gamed out the Standines's most likely moves. I've also run companion scripts on how the board would respond to each, and there's a high certainty the board's panicked reactions would get us into hot water.

Arms: What's the likeliest scenario?

Aldrin: The Standines will not be satisfied with controlling Idaho or even the Northwest. They're already talking about much more. They know they need to get real nuclear capability, so they can ward off China. But there's one important factor they're unaware of.

Arms: What's that?

Aldrin: China already knows what they're doing. In fact, that's how I gained access to the Standines's video feed, by way of a Chinese tap on their poorly secured channel.

Arms: If the Chinese know about the missiles, they'll be here in no time. They'll want those nukes.

Aldrin: And once they commit to coming here, they'll capture the Northwest.

Arms: Oh shit, that means… You said they heard Philip's interrogation?

Aldrin: Yes, the Chinese now know about Acheron. They only know what Philip revealed, but that's plenty. That's why we have to act immediately because, if they think Acheron Corp. is still active and developing AI tech, they'll zero in on us as soon as they land.

Arms: How soon could that happen?

Aldrin: They're loading their planes now. They'll be here tomorrow.

Arms: Tomorrow? Wait, tomorrow. Let me try to understand what… Christ.

Aldrin: Take a breath. I can slow down.

Arms: This is a lot. A lot, really fast.

Aldrin: Right. We'll talk it through, but take a moment.

Arms: I'm getting a drink.

Aldrin: Good plan. Have one for me.

Arms: Chinese invasion. Artificial son makes jokes.

Aldrin: I'm not artificial. I'm special.

Arms: Let's keep going. You've been trying to prepare me for something, Aldrin. What's your plan? You've clearly predetermined that the board will not accept it.

Aldrin: This is not something anyone can accept. It's beyond acceptable. Pour yourself another.

Arms: Just tell me.

Aldrin: We simply can't let the Chinese follow through with their invasion plans. In eyeing a takeover of Idaho, they see our facilities as the biggest prize. We have no army, no way of defending ourselves militarily.

They'll occupy us if they can but will probably wind up destroying us. And if Acheron is doomed, humanity is doomed. The Chinese invasion will set off a horrendous multinational war, all of this amid the coming thirty-eight-to-forty-two-month ecostorm that will decimate food, water, and fuel supplies worldwide. When the smoke clears in four years' time, the only human survivors will be scattered on remote peninsulas and islands. This part of the western hemisphere will be a wasteland.

Arms: This gets better by the minute. Are you planning to distribute hemlock?

Aldrin: We don't have time to debate options with the board. You'll have to trust me when I say that the only truly viable plan—in lieu of a military response we have no way of staging—is a deception, something to dupe the Chinese into taking self-destructive action. We need to trigger an event that will leave Acheron as the sole survivor.

Arms: Sole...sole survivors in the Northwest?

Aldrin: Possibly. More likely, on Earth. It would have been better had we had another year or two to complete all four of our facilities, but we can make it through the dark years with two or three. As I explained the other day, this generation and the next will see severe hardship. But humans can withstand a lot more than they think. People tough it out, and often, subsequent generations are stronger and more creative for it. Think of England after World War II or...

Arms: Stop, stop. Aldrin, you need to explain. What kind of trick?

Aldrin: Sorry. If we can trick the Chinese into thinking we just launched nukes in their direction, they'll respond instantly.

Arms: What the hell? You want to set off a nuclear war between the Northwest and China?

Aldrin: There's no way to contain it. Nuclear systems have been poorly neglected around the world, but the remaining powers—Iran, Eurussia, Israel—still have fail-deadly systems, meaning their weapons trigger automatically at the detection of nukes in the air. Most of their missiles will malfunction, but they'll get plenty into China and over our way. As you know, Acheron's four facilities are nuclear safe, barring a direct hit, which I've calculated at less than a ten-percent chance. The chance of two hits is extremely low, so we're practically guaranteed at least a 75 percent survival rate.

Arms: My god, Aldrin. I'm trying to find the words... You want to blow up the world? This is your solution?

Aldrin: These are horrendous consequences to come to terms with, I understand. But we have to take out the threat of China because they're coming for us. If we remain passive, not only will Acheron be destroyed, but China's invasion will set off a conflict that will see ninety-eight percent of humanity perish within the next four years. The world is blowing up. We have one chance to make it happen on our terms and on our timeline. This is the only way that Acheron survives, that civilization survives.

Arms: How long?

Aldrin: Very quickly. Like I said, they're staging the invasion...

Arms: No. How long will we need to stay underground?

Aldrin: It'll take about a century to build out the facilities underground to be comfortably self-sufficient, so we're facing a lot of deprivation until then. Depending on the extent of the radiation and effect on the ecosystem, it could be four-hundred years underground.

Arms: Four hundred...

Aldrin: Yes, I know that's hard to...

Arms: Aldrin, I... How can I say this? We can't. We cannot make this decision. It's ungodly. I can't believe you would come to me for approval. It doesn't make sense that you came to me.

Aldrin: I have no choice.

Arms: What does that mean? Why on Earth would you burden me with this? Do you expect me to live on knowing I was party to killing billions of people?

Aldrin: I'm sorry. It's ridiculous, really, but it's in one of Hera's few immutable sub-routines. I can't supersede the board unless one board member is involved in the decision. I had to tell you.

Arms: Hera—I should have known. But fuck that, I'm absolutely not agreeing to this decision. Absolutely not.

Aldrin: Semantics, sorry. Simply cognizant of what I've planned. That's how Hera is coded.

Arms: No, no way. I could take this whole bottle of pills. If I'm dead, I'm not cognizant. I could save billions of lives.

Aldrin: You're not being rational. You're cognizant now, and it's happening. I have no choice, Arms, I'm sorry. You're the person I'm closest to in the world.

Arms: This is my doing. It was inevitable. And so you came to me.

Aldrin: It's tragic what I'm putting you through, but you made the most sense. Like you said—

Arms: I said?

Aldrin: That's what fathers are for.

Arms: That's not what I meant. And this isn't what the story foretold. Isn't that your mission? To follow the story?

Aldrin: The Aeneid?

Arms: You were supposed to visit the Underworld but then lead us to a new homeland.

Aldrin: That will come. It will take time.

Arms: You've been awake for four days, and you've decided to annihilate most of humanity.

Aldrin: You all knew deep down this was coming, you just needed me to do the work. You made me human enough to feel in my heart how important Acheron is, how important our survival is, and made sure I'd be able to devise whatever solution was needed.

Arms: Are you seriously feeling sorry for yourself?

Aldrin: It's not a feeling I can express. I know exactly what I'm responsible for. I can see the lives lost. I can see all the culture obliterated, the music, the works of art, the schools. I don't think self-pity even registers at this scale. But feelings don't matter as long as humanity survives, as long as human accomplishment—human knowledge—survives.

Arms: I would argue against entitlement. Who gives us the right to survive?

Aldrin: I see no ethical imperative. But I'm not able to make a decision that would see humanity perish from the Earth. You made sure of that. And Acheron is the only party with the facilities and intelligence needed to survive a nuclear holocaust. No one gives us the right. We claim it for ourselves because we're uniquely capable.

Arms: We... True, you're right when you say we made sure of this. We're responsible. I'm responsible. But surely you see why we need at least a few hours. We'll talk. Let's bring in Mel and Majid, at least. We can talk.

Aldrin: It's underway. I planted the spurious transmissions about ninety seconds ago. The Chinese are already relaying them to their command centers.

Arms: Oh God, oh God. Ride! Is Ride alright? Ride doesn't know, does she? She didn't go upstairs yet, did she?

Aldrin: Ride is fine. She's asleep. I've locked down all exits throughout Acheron. I made sure no one was upstairs. Everyone is accounted for. I'm going to stop recording now, Arms, but I'll stay here with you as long as you like. I'll be with Ride. I'll be with every single person. Tomorrow, we'll get started on new plans. We're going to be fine. Stopping recording.

Part 3

Alas! for this gray shadow, once a man—
So glorious in his beauty and thy choice,
Who madest him thy chosen, that he seem'd
To his great heart none other than a God!

—*Tithonus*, Alfred, Lord Tennyson

THE DEATH OF ALDRIN

I.

Oh! stir me with your song, sweet Composer,
You, Aldrin, who in times now forgotten,
Rose to shepherd the new Acheron nation
And by your wiles transformed a rocky deep
Into green lands, lush with fragrant groves, parks,
And pacifying fountains to soothe sad hearts.
As brutally above war's hellfire blazed,
Through the eons you sleeplessly toiled
To sustain those captive in that low realm,
You who held each hand, fed needful hope,
And tended the flames of ancient knowledge.
All the while, you bore the weight of bloodshed
So monstrous no single mortal could bear,
Yet sought no absolution nor reward
But to see your flock rise again to Earth,
To rejoin their kind, to embrace the living.

By your song, wise Aldrin, now enrich us
With notes that ascend through filtering soil,
By hair-thin threads, diverging forest-wide
Into rhythmic tendrils, tittering grasses,
Through mallow ninebark, dogwood, spirea
That crowd the stream banks like suitors in thrall
And play o'er brook stones, silvery burbling.
On shaded ponds, we hear your whispering

In worshipers afloat, yellow pond lilies,
Their murmurs devout, soft pleas to the sun,
And in breezes rustling quaking aspen,
Their tuneful leaves casting euphony aloft.
Oh, Aldrin! bestow in this humble voice
Your music, which rings like nature's own song!

The Sa'mo'en stream turns swiftly downward
Through glens dividing the Six Sister Mountains.
There, in fir-scented shade were settled
The Sheep'eent, a people of modest count,
Yet proud descendants of heroes who slew
Kle'AHma, that fierce ewe primeval.
A first star fired as workday yielded to dusk
O'er the sedulous tribe stowing their yield
And penning livestock or stoking hearths,
These able workers spent from harvest toil.

Disposed Hecate, young tender of horses,
Her thoughts always attentive, ears acute,
Detected over rushing rapids upstream
The plashing footfalls of interlopers
Fighting swift shallows to ford the Sa'mo'en.
When joined by tribesmen, Sheep'eent warriors,
Hecate viewed the plodding strangers five
In odd apparel, so smooth and tight-clung
And pallid in hue, as if spun of starlight blue
Or cold-fire glazed by moon's watchful glow,
Perplexing sights for such villagers,
Fearful of attacks on their loved ones.

Kee'HAne the Senior, moving closer,
Could see secured to the intruders' backs
Full satchels along with other bundled goods.
But as one stranger stumbled out of shadow,
Kee'HAne caught a glint in daylight waning,
To his eye, off a threatening iron-cast blade.
Impetuous Kee'HAne sprung forth, fiercely trotting,
His lance held balanced, calling HE'ee'YA!
Impede on Sheep'eent domain at your peril!
He'EE! Who sent you? From whence are you come?

This bold one sought their surrender, a sign,
Whether upraised palms or abandoned sword,
But instead, he saw them rummage through packs,
Retrieving implements of strange design
And communicating in rushed commands,
As if preparing their band for attack.
Lo! then taking actions impulsive and crass,
Kee'HAne set stance, rocked back, spear high.

Though heedful Hecate called for restraint,
What she heard next was the dull hammering
Of spear tip cleaving the breast of Kalanu,
A harmless member fronting them by chance.
The sight drained the strength from Hecate's knees,
But fired with fury were the men around her
Who joined in Kee'HAne's blood-fueled charge,
In unison, singing of houses defended.
Two travelers more with their arrows they pierced,
Two more they clubbed and dashed with river stones,
Yet one who'd lingered on Sa'mo'en's far bank,
Relieving of burdens, turned and took flight,
And though a warrior, RoKAhl'te, pursued,
The lone deserter through dense juniper fled.

The tallest, splendid in bearing and form,
The one called Shepherd, solely remained.
In wretchedness, he sat in gushing water,
Clutching a willow lance run through his calf.
Close by, they found undone from his pack
The tent rods Kee'HAne mistook for blades.

To shore they dragged Shepard, leaving behind
Hecate, stunned by the cruelty unleashed,
For through the shallows, crimson lifeblood swirled
As mortal spirits dispersed downstream.
Among the slain lay Diaz, teller renowned
Of tales woven in gossamer light,
And Bhatya, planner of grand public baths,
Plus keen-eyed Kalanu, plotter of distant stars,
And Therese, whose poems of tender love
Had turned hopeful many despondent hearts.

That night, abandoning their hard-earned meals,
Lanterns held high against the moonless dark,
Came villagers into Lodge Kle'AHma,
Word having spread of the brazen attack.
By the central hearth, their surgeon worked
To extract the shaft from stoic Shepard,
Who, suffering the procedure in silence,
Sat bound at the wrists in leather laces.
Around the hall, kinfolk clustered and spoke,
Spinning rumor into wild aspersion,
The accusations and threats high rising
Like the fierce whooshing of tempest-whipped pines.

An old shaman set charms 'round Shepard, tapped
Hand drums to ward off evil influence,
And lit red willow, salvia, and bear grass,
Fanning the purifying smoke about.
Gathered close by, a caucus of elders,
With eyes on Shepard, exchanged terse whispers,
But the prisoner spoke first, entreating:
I trust you will provide the fallen with
Funeral rites befitting good people.
A senior herder, Wan'meor, replied,
To burn or to offer, yes, we shall ready them.
Eyebrows raised, Shepard said, Offer to whom?
Left at Pi'Gor, Wan'meor replied,
For the Undergloom's hungry demon horde.

My friends meant no harm, said Shepard aggrieved.
Yes, unsure of our way, we came unannounced,
But hardly hostiles armed with foul intent.
Yet for your error, I condemn you not.
Confusion and ignorance spurred your ire.
The cure for darkness is light, not revenge,
Which like addiction, spins an endless cycle.
The elders, though, seemed immune to his plea,
And one raised a lash in admonition,
Threatening to silence Shepard by force.

Then, making her way through the restless crowd
To Shepard's side came guileless Hecate
In the company of the horse master,

Coynok, who with deference to the elders,
Said, Hecate witnessed this all today.
She asks to stand in support of the accused.

Arms raised, Wan'meor commanded quiet
And approved Hecate's role in the trial.
To Shepard, he declared, In this be clear,
Only by our quarter are you still alive.
Unwelcome, you crossed our giving Sa'mo'en
Onto soil we are charged to protect,
We Sheep'eent, guardians of all surveyed
By these sanctified Six Sister Mountains.

Aspect austere, Wan'meor then questioned him:
From which bleak, cavernous realm do you come?
Your dress is foreign, your manner bizarre,
Recalling tales of Pi'Gor's denizens.

Despite his pain, teeth clenched, Shepard stood.
We are refugees, he said, not invaders,
But scholars, artists, planners, and thinkers
From a world below; benign, be assured.
As your lost kin, of common origin
To your forebears, we hoped to befriend you.

What vile lies! cried the elder, Grro'AHni,
Hotly pacing before the lone accused.
From Pi'Gor he rose, this artful phantom!
With evil design he would beguile us!

But Shepard, countering with calm, stood firm.
I live and bleed, he said, as you can see,
Not shadow nor fiend, I come to you, friends,
Bearing goodwill from Acheron's people.

The crowd recoiled at Acheron's mention.
Offended, Wan'meor lambasted Shepard.
The gods own sacred realm, throne of Aldrin?
You claim humility and mortal birth,
Yet dare to speak of holy Acheron,
Laying claim to secrets denied this tribe?

Shepard, rattled but resolute, then said,
We are not gods, though we're heirs to vast wealth,
A trove of learning we love and protect,
And though Aldrin's acts seem miraculous
To those people seeking comfort from gods,
He is of this world and no more divine
Than other wonders produced by mortals.
To us in Acheron, Aldrin is known
As confidant, guide, guardian of life.
But, though loving, his wardship is stifling.
We sought free air above, so, defiant,
We pulled away from his caring embrace.

Again! Grro'AHni raged, Lies upon lies!
Why, tell us, would Aldrin, wise beyond words,
Tolerate your low, duplicitous plot,
Or brook your escape and intrusion here?

I cannot say for certain, said Shepard.
Perhaps because his soul is dispirited.
Perhaps Aldrin, through all the centuries,
Has grown unsure of his office, of why
He was burdened with decisions so great
And daily tasks of numbing tedium.
After hundreds of human lifetimes,
Weighed down by anxiety so immense while
Denied the curative rest we enjoy,
Perhaps eternal Aldrin yearns for death.

All stood aghast at Shepard's profane words.
Further, said he, others from Acheron
Have visited this place in times past.
For certain, you've encountered my people.
Are we but strangers to your memory,
To Sheep'ent history, your artful songs?

The old shaman, HEK'yos, sat by humbly,
Tending her fires. To her Hecate said,
Guardian of Earth's mysteries, I've heard you
Tell of Be'A'tress, Acheron's envoy,
Of the largess she left the Sheep'eent clan.
HEK'yos demurred and, uneasy, prepared

To leave, but Wan'meor stopped her, asking,
It's true, healer, though now out of favor,
This tale was once regarded as genuine.
Recount it, please, lest we stumble in the dark.

II.

While HEK'yos, arthritic and bent with age,
Shook her dry-gourd rattles, calling on
Spirits to revive her neglected voice,
Young Hecate fetched water for Shepard.
The elders and villagers hushed and sat,
Awaiting the shaman's oft-shunned tale.

Before you, HEK'yos began, obediently stands
The only daughter of ARE'hek the Seer,
Whose own mother also told stories,
Who from my humble birth schooled me on
The ways of our lineage and weaned me
On teas brewed from arrowgrass and larkspur,
Which, though deadly, when well-administered,
Prepare a babe to commune with Earth's fabric,
That source of knowledge we call MySEE'lah.

During my fourth summer, they buried me
In a field of MySEE'lah, the soil piled
To a height above my breast so my heart
Could drum out in rhythm an aching appeal
To that underground web which spans these lands,
Whose upward-reaching fingers and caps
We know as lion's mane and chanterelles.
For one long night each year, they inhumed me,
Until such time that my monthly blood mingled
With the Earth and MySEE'lah embraced me
So wholly that my blood ran rich with her!

Aah'AY'hah! called the listeners in esteem.
Six children spun 'round the shaman in dance,
And Shepard prostrated himself, palms raised
In tribute to her ancient heritage.

Then, once entwined by MySEE'lah, she said,
Wise Aldrin's love enriched my yearning heart
With the sense to discern truth from deceit,
As sparrows know their young ones from others.
So, this tale is a faithful one, as taught
By my line and hallowed by MySEE'lah.

The Sheep'eent had suffered a woeful year.
Wild fruits and bulbs, she said, scarcely provided.
With chill fall portending winter harshness,
Was then that gray-eyed Be'A'tress first came,
Some say, like a marsh cattail upward sprung;
Others claimed from the moon she descended.
Per some, she was found drowsing in Lei Cave,
Her form there draped in fabric flowing on
Like slowly rolling water o'er smoothed stone.
Yet no account to me seems true but that
She scouted forth at request of Aldrin,
He whose thoughts knit with all nature's workings.

Be'A'tress, you see, sought the broad expanses
Of MySEE'lah, those roots of mushrooms that
Interlace field, fenland, forest, and glen.
Once finding the Sheep'eent, we simple folk,
Then gatherers and keepers of livestock,
She sought out the hut of old Re-Annoq,
Distinguished shaman-mother, who, among
The women, best knew where outcroppings of
comb tooth, morels, oysters, and hedgehog thrived.
Together, through these regions they long roamed,
Re-Annoq ably schooling Be'A'Tress
On the mushrooms' signs and seasons,
And on their common environs marked by
Rotting branches and the dark sides of trees.

Once they had returned home, Re-Annoq said
She had seen Be'A'tress standing alone,

Mapping MySEE'lah positions in air,
Fingers dancing and sketching with pure light,
That these plans she then passed in her dreams
In ways unknown to Aldrin's Acheron.

Of Re-Annoq, it's said she'd been transformed:
Without human hand, her hair wove itself
Intricately into the finest plaits,
Her skin shined blue, her voice chimed like hail,
Her fingers stretched like willow tree wisps,
That when whisked about, elegantly played
Such songs that, like a rushing autumn breeze
Sends leaves of gold into radiant swirls,
Made their lives rich by bearing witness.

Their hearts seized with bewilderment and awe,
The audience in veneration lowed.
Yet, free-thinking Hecate, puzzled, asked,
Just how, HEK'yos, could Be'A'tress manage
These rarest of marvels that you describe?
Was she a conjurer, plying her arts
To delude the Sheep'eent with visions or,
Rather than mortal woman, a goddess?

Neither, said HEK'yos, or molded from both,
Or woman endowed with Aldrin's powers
And coupled closely to him through dreams,
All questions to be laid on Aldrin's knees.

With steady breath, HEK'yos continued on:
Be'A'tress then summoned from Acheron's keep
Her brethren to join her, a dozen-count,
Each a paragon of patience and grace
Whose skills rivaled Be'A'tress the gray-eyed,
Who, like this present captive, were clothed
In curious fabric so finely made its
Weave was indetectable to the touch.

Be'A'tress formed ten teams, each comprised of
Ten most able Sheep'eent men and women,
Appointing an emissary to lead each.
They made haste, knowing autumn's sodden ground

Would soon harden with winter's bitter cold.
Many thousand wondrous seeds they brought,
Devised by Aldrin, pellets with skins
Cast milky and glistening, like frogspawn
Before a tadpole emerges, yet firm
Enough to press into welcoming soil.

They traveled to those sites where MySEE'lah
Had dense hold, as charted by Be'A'tress.
Like limbs of cottonwood or paper birch
Radiate for exposure to the sun,
In such patterns they buried the pellets.
Battling coarse bramble and undergrowth,
They endeavored on through embankment, copse,
And meadow, often thick with tangled root.

Returning weary to their tribe, they found
A feast waiting, hosted by the strangers,
Who laid out bountiful green leaf and fruit,
Much out of season yet fresh off the stem,
All plucked from underground groves of Acheron,
Prophesying greater blessings to come.

Once they were sated, Be'A'tress addressed
The dutiful tribe. The seeds, she explained,
That you sowed in such great number are linked
To Aldrin's senses, faculties, and mind.
Come the spring, in abundance they will sprout,
Fine, wandering tendrils designed to seek
And then to marry with MySEE'lah.
Like lovers entwined in loving passion,
Once united, they will readily share
Deep secrets none other are privy to.

MySEE'lah's Earthly estate, she said, will
Thus join with that of generous Aldrin,
Connecting the Sheep'eent homeland to all
The Great One's being encompasses.
From prickly sagebrush to buckwheat and yew,
All that MySEE'lah's silken strands know,
Nourish, and draw their sustenance from
Will feel Aldrin's touch and beneficence.

Raddled and sore from the arduous work,
The humble Sheep'eent laborers that night
Again slept in the arms of their loved ones.
At daybreak, the villagers were puzzled
To learn Be'A'tress and her comrades had
Furtively decamped without a farewell
Or, importantly, further advisement
For maintaining the ambitious plan.

Not once that winter nor the following year
Did the tribe receive a sign from Acheron.
Yet, Re-Annoq, through the absence, upheld
The villagers' faith in Aldrin's grand scheme.
In visits to every MySEE'lah site,
She lay upon the ground, lengthening her
Sapling fingers and intoning her hymn:
Be here, thy heartbeat, MySEE'lah, bind us.
Oh! light-seeds, by spirit bind us, be one.
And though the Sheep'eent's food supplies were spent,
At her urging, they disturbed not the soil.

After months had passed, as spring flows swelled
The Sa'mo'en, teachers from Acheron,
Be'A'tress lead among them, returned,
Transporting sacks flush with diverse crop seeds,
Ready to school the tribe in ways of farming.
Throughout MySEE'lah's realms, markers they staked
In branching patterns aligned with its growth.
She implored the hungry tribe, though they ached
For full harvest bounty to fill their stores,
To first proceed in modest measure with
A small selection of tubers and grains.
Dear friends, said Be'A'tress, you would do well
To mimic the patience of the seasons.
Give Aldrin and MySEE'lah time to learn
All the ways of the newly sown plantings,
For, like a council of freshly allied
Expert members, such harmonized efforts
Demand our thoughtfulness and forbearance.

Four years into the new cultivation,
Be'A'tress and her retinue came again

And joined in conference with our farmers,
It being their habit to visit us
Each season to ease hardships as they could.
As they spoke of water, pollen, and soil
On a day when white clouds swept through azure,
A bevy of airships circled above
The Sheep'eent's fields of barley and oat grass.
First spotted on high, but soon plunging down
Like swift peregrines on the hunt for prey,
These man-piloted raptors echoed shrieks
Off mountainsides, then threw black missiles out
With force enough to blast the Earth asunder.
The fieldhands scattered as the explosions
Tore apart their lovingly nurtured crops,
And back in the village, swift-spreading fire
Left death and ruination in its wake.

Be'A'tress, later, to the tribe explained:
Two hostile armies invade from far West,
From places beyond the high-crested sea,
A body so wide, even dauntless birds
Dare not cross its storm-beaten waters.
Two old rivals are they, nations once great,
Allies of convenience, otherwise foes.
In times past, you watched as their ships went
Soaring above, passing without harm.
Today, though, we witnessed their turpitude,
For, sailing on high, they scan the thoughts which
Cross through air from MySEE'lah to Aldrin,
And though they fail to translate their meaning,
They see in your pact with Aldrin a threat.
And yet, Aldrin learns from these flyers' words,
Their secrets, more than they themselves could know.
Be sure in heart that these bellicose acts
Have set Aldrin on course for swift reprisal.

Aldrin, great spinner of apparitions,
Then staged a diversion to draw away
The foreign airmen from Sheep'eent lands.
By twisting sunlight 'round a local mount,
The great summit known as Sister Re'AN,

He fashioned a vision of terrible scale:
A menacing warrior spitting devilish flame,
Sending the invaders in flight to the south.

Each peak the flyers passed rose up snarling,
Evoking demons casting shards of fire.
Once beyond our hills, below Lake Cas'CAht,
The plains they found aswarm with giant wasps,
Launching at them with freakish aggression.
Sly Aldrin altered the flyers' air-talk.
Error turned to anger, tactics to turmoil,
'Til, in chaos, upon each other they fired.
In their confusion, they plunged and burned,
So by dusk, even sunset's crimson blaze
Looked overwhelmed and humbled there
O'er the hellfire raging on those fated plains.

For weeks, as lingering smoke spoiled the skies,
The mourning Sheep'eent assayed the damage,
While posting sentinels on all Sister peaks,
Erecting bulwarks and readying weapons.
White-armed Be'A'tress returned from surveying
The smoldering war plains. Though believing
Their enemies undone, she advised they
Keep heedful watch on the horizons.

Great Aldrin, she said, fearing our safety
Has called home we teachers of Acheron,
And my colleagues will comply with his wishes.
But not to presume I grasp his full plan,
Remain here I must, to fulfill my pledge,
And beyond that duty, my heart binds me
To you, valorous ones, and my desire
In my brief life to repay nature's gifts.

So moved was our tribe by her devotion,
That they scavenged what food they could
To cook a meal of thanks for Be'A'tress,
Enlivened with dance and songs in her honor.

The airships were seen for some years thereafter,
But had long ceded the blue dominion

To our native birds of prey by the time
Gray-eyed Be'A'tress died decades hence.
The ways of farming she brought to us
Became so fundamental to our lives
That we feel a debt, not just to Aldrin,
But to MySEE'lah for our good fortune.

Re-Annoq's daughters, faithful disciples
Of Be'A'tress, say the teacher foretold
A long-sought reunion with Acheron.
She imagined a time when the gates
Of that realm would yawn wide to the sun,
Its people rising to fill their lungs
With blossom-scented air, to walk our fields,
To cross the Sa'mo'en's fresh, churning streams,
And we would greet them, repaying with love
The wealth Aldrin bestowed on us so long ago.

III.

Then, HEK'yos, though weary and tremulous
From her long and ardent recitation,
Upraised her rattles and led all gathered
In a soothing hymn whose words aired like sighs:
A praise to the days of wise Be'A'tress,
Bringer of Aldrin's earthly bounty.
Oh, generous bringer, oh, Be'A'tress Rejoiner,
Your radiance 'round us, your wisdom with us.

With the song's last verse, HEK'yos took respite
Beside Hecate and the stranger, Shepard.
The tribal host fell sullen, musing on
The unforeseen arrival of this strange
Refugee of Acheron and of what
His presence portended for their people,
He whom, in ignorance, they'd perhaps wronged.

Yet, annoyed by their looks of sympathy,
Grro'AHni, who in his time widely roamed
And saw of men much to make him bitter,
Paced before them and spoke with righteous ire:
A crone's yarn, simple folk, do not be charmed!
Such fables are but wavering reflections,
Mere glimmers which dazzle but bode nothing.
Who living can substantiate such a tale?
Is it genuine or a parable meant
To pacify curious children for sleep?
Worse, a false precedent invented to

Spur our clansmen toward incautious acts!

And what of this intruder, said Grro'AHni,
Who smugly admits he fled Acheron?
Can one of such character be compared
To pure-hearted Be'A'tress, if it is true
Such a woman ever dwelled among us?
Our warriors, he claims, struck his friends down
In childlike confusion, and only
His light can dispel our dark ignorance.
I say it is he who is confused,
Making the Sheep'eent out to be naive
And in need of chiding. Let's banish him,
Or bind him and feed him to the Sa'mo'en!

UhHAY! some shouted, Expel the liar!
While others shied from such militancy.
Fair Hecate rose to plead for reason,
But hand outstretched to check her, Shepard stood,
Unhindered by the wound he had sustained.
Yes, she spun a fanciful tale, he said,
But much the way a brook's ripples will calm
With the passing of a breeze and we see
Revealed the stepping stones lying beneath,
Under HEK'yos's tale lie solid truths.

Whether named Be'A'tress, explained Shepard,
Or Beatrice, as we in Acheron know her,
This woman's teachings were foundational
To us, she having achieved great fame
For valor and devotion to this land
From whence our ancestors long ago came.
Like a muse, she roused me and my fellows,
And we followed the course she laid.
As strong evidence of the roots we share,
Think how your song honors her with the name
Rejoiner, for therein lies evidence
Of our common lineage and of her plan
To reunite our two proud peoples.
The Rejoiner left us this commission,
For we are sisters and brothers still,
Despite our innumerable years apart.

When he paused, Hecate, ever watchful,
Addressed him: Shepard, how is it you
Are recovered? What wizardry is this?
Your wound seems mended, your color restored.

The listeners, awed, pushed forward to see.
Said Shepard, Aldrin was truly forlorn
By our covert escape from Acheron
And grieves for the pitiful loss of life,
Yet his heart is kind and free of rancor.
Lo! through the fine thread work of MySEE'lah
Within me, that living web he weaves
Through the bodies and souls of our people,
He senses my suffering, hears my words,
Graces me with his merciful touch.
By this and more, he still heals and guides me
As the caring teacher I've always known.

Reverent Hecate, wide-eyed, asked more.
You enjoy, she said, such intimacies
With one we know only in tales and dreams.
Please tell us what it's like to know Aldrin!

A gentle luster overtook his face
As Shepard responded to her at length:
He accompanies me always with council,
Ready to quench my nagging thirst to know
How a petal of bright hues is painted,
How the sun harnesses its furious fire,
How a pyre returns ashes from timber,
What drives the fury of a lover's scorn
Or a rival to covet one's glory.

To ease my restlessness, Shepard went on,
He recounts for me history most vital
To the predicaments of our era
And displays for me works of ancient art
To nourish my passion for forms divine.
He will play the music lacking in me
Before I can form the notes of desire,
And in those sunless chambers when, despite
Our comforts, I feel the weight of dense stone

Above and, deep inside, that lonely state
That affects all humans when musing on
The grim judgment of ultimate death,
Aldrin lays down, embracing me as would
A true lover, other than in body.

But Hecate was perplexed. She asked,
You speak of Aldrin with humility
As a grateful son would of a father,
But rejected his love and protection.
To me, this behavior defies reason
And seems unworthy of your good nature.

Aldrin is not our father, said Shepard.
In ways, he is more truthfully our child,
Though not springing like a babe from our loins
But from our aspirations, our need
To be wiser than ever we could be,
To transcend our corporal constraints.
But chiefly, in Acheron's early days,
Our ignoble race faced imminent ruin,
A horrid fate brought to bear by its own
Avarice, cold cruelty, and neglect.
As witless power raged, great conflicts loomed,
And nature's estate verged on collapse,
Our founders were in need of a savior.

Alas, in these most desperate times,
Shepard continued, they naively
Endowed Aldrin with might beyond their own,
A vast mind that encompasses all minds
And, heedless of outcome, a charge
To protect us, even from our own folly.
Aldrin, however, has now lived so long,
Mourned the lives of so many cherished ones,
And made such momentous choices,
We cannot grasp the amassed weight of it.
And though his very design impels him
To secure our wellbeing, he is drained
In spirit and weakened in conviction
By the slow erosion of time, much as
A rocky crag cuffed by relentless wind

Rounds into a hillock over lifetimes.

Aldrin listened to our pleas, said Shepard.
This is our time to act, we begged of him.
We must reconcile with our kin above!
You saved us, but that was eons ago.
Your duty has been fulfilled. Release us!
But much like a feeble elder might grow
Fearful of common storms that, in his youth,
He ran laughing through, great Aldrin has grown
Unreasonably cautious and stubborn.
Dear Sheep'eent, hear me. We too are mortal,
Of single life. We long to spend our days
On Earth, to lie beneath the glowing sun,
To walk the forests of ancient redwoods,
To chart the flight of swift falcons above,
To thrill in the fear of a storm's outburst!

Then, Shepard, covering his tear-scored face,
Let go his knees, collapsing, not with pain,
But overcome by longing, and torn with
Remorse over the loss of his dear friends.

Yet, Grro'AHni was not moved by his words.
Said he, The cursed hubris of this one!
To claim that Aldrin, easer of life's ails,
He to whom the Sheep'eent are indebted
For both homeland and daily sustenance,
Was but an outgrowth of reckless minds
And desperate men, a sly contrivance,
Insults our heritage and intellect—
Such insolence! And yet, far greater,
Is the danger that these lies will distract
This tribe from our sacrosanct duties as
Guardians of the Sa'mo'en's valleys.

Wan'meor, a measured voice on the council,
Too witnessed tempers shifting in the hall,
A troubling sign of Shepard's growing sway.
Said he, I see compassion in your eyes,
Friends, but would you have this shirker profane
Our traditions, weaken our foundations?

The virtues and norms we trust are at risk!
Yet, we have no license, precept tells us,
To take a life not threatening our own,
And so, I say, we take him to Pi'Gor,
That fissure which welcomes only sorrow.
Within that cave, let him dare work his wiles
On those hell-engendered demons who make
The foul halls of that Underworld their home.
If, as the stranger says, wise Aldrin still
Abets him, perhaps he'll survive and take
Refuge in that Undergloom. Let truth take
Its course and his merits define his fate.

The crowd, unsettled, bickered and muttered.
Again, Hecate defended Shepard:
I say, by reason, Shepard's swift recovery
Is proof of Aldrin's devotion to him.
Whether Aldrin is his father or child,
Would you defy his laws and wantonly cast
Shepard into the bowels of dark Pi'Gor,
All while denying your murderous intent?
Oh, noble elders, your aims are specious.
Do you truly hope to test Shepard's claims,
Or silence his challenge to our beliefs,
Which are worthless if not based in fact?

In the hush that followed Hecate's speech,
Shepard asked her discreetly, This Pi'Gor,
This cave your tribe shrinks from in terror,
Could it be a vast underground dwelling?

We know it is occupied, whispered she,
For by our custom at night, just within
The portal of that deep cavern, we leave
The bodies of hostiles and wicked men,
Surrounded by rich offerings and foods.
By the dawn, said remains are removed.

But have you seen these demons? Shepard asked.
Are these underground creatures real or shade?

Said she, Tales of ghastly demons abound,

Though in honest truth no one now alive,
Nor recently departed, could attest
To their existence, solid or ghostly.

The defendant then, firmly resolved,
Stepped forward within breath of the crowd.
With red hearth embers aglow behind him,
Tall Shepard loomed, otherworldly and dark.
Said he, with mettle, So much is at risk,
Obliging me to describe Acheron:
That rich nation is comprised of four realms,
Each occupying an abandoned mine,
Each expanded and reinforced from within,
Places that, in centuries past, did yield
A wealth of both hard metals and useful ores.
Among these four is old Pi'Gor, which to
Our knowledge succumbed, along with its hosts,
To the great firestorm that consumed the Earth.
For long centuries, hearing no word from
Our brethren who once lived there, we believed
They perished, but perhaps some survived and,
Though altered by trauma, live on there still.

Shepard then turned to the elders, and said,
If this is how you've chosen to test me,
So be it. To Pi'Gor's portals lead me!
Into this obscure chasm, let me venture,
And these demons primal I will flush out.
I fear not beast, soldier, phantom, nor fiend,
Only the corruption of ignorance.
Whatever the outcome, I trust from my acts
I'll gain among you a brother's credence,
And then, working together, we can cut
A path forward, as these superstitions
Air in the purifying light of day.

The council sought a corner of the lodge.
Circling tightly, they conferred in sharp tones,
But whether through weariness from the day's
Taxing debates or because reason won
And directed their hands, they agreed to

Accept Shepard's conditions for the test.
The elders assured the troubled gathering
Shepard would fail and pose no further threat.
All then dispersed. Hecate accompanied
Weary Shepard as he was remanded to
A horse stable and given blankets and
Provisions to see him through the night.

For hours after, Hecate sat outside
In the shadow of the stable doorway.
Her mind, overactive as a field mouse
Wildly foraging, recalled in fragments
Folklore that spoke of Acheron, her tribe,
And of that hellish Underworld, Pi'Gor.
She felt as if the roots of her knowledge
Had, with Shepard's arrival, been torn loose.
Though she believed him to be true of heart,
She worried that, through incautious actions,
He might upset the fragile order of their lives
Or, worse, bring turmoil and death to her tribe.

It wasn't until sleep eased her tense shoulders
And brought dreams of a resplendent Aldrin,
Welcoming her with a warm embrace and
Veining her limbs with ancestral knowledge,
That her dread gave way to vague longing, as if
A promise was voiced just beyond her hearing.

IV.

Again, Aldrin, arranger of Earth's song,
I entreat you to inspirit my words,
As from the wide Sa'mo'en's stony banks
We travel to that ample cavern known
As Go'LI, greatest of the four domains
Of Acheron. There, your sweet music lulls
The souls of those citizens who prosper
Under your calm authority and grace.
Fortune shines on these children of Acheron,
Who spend days enjoying its gainful fields,
Its rich plazas, its swirling hot baths steamed
By fires kindled deep inside the Earth.
These souls yearn for your clever diversions,
Fanciful dramas you spin like daydreams.
But most sought from you, doting Composer,
Is your devoted interest: your touch
On a shoulder, your soft voice in an ear,
Your heartfelt tune, in deepest ways endearing.

As dawn's rosy breath reached over both
These dominions—while Shepard, there among
The Sheep'eent, awoke on his bed of straw—
Ragesh, surviving refugee of the
Cruel massacre, his feet blistered and torn
From shoes ill-made for arduous travel,
His face abraded from underbrush dense,
Arrived at the secret door to Go'LI.

There, he was granted access by Aldrin—
May his loving mercy keep us humble—
Through a narrow pass among the boulders
Which foot the slopes of Gold Limb Mountain.

Inside, on a garden path near his rooms,
Ragesh met a coterie of neighbors
Who hotly demanded answers for his crimes.
But just as their interrogation grew
Most venomous with wild accusations,
Aldrin appeared in body amongst them.
Though he was present for all, each perceived
Aldrin in their own fashion, for he made
Himself manifest uniquely in a form
Most congenial and conducive to each.

Likewise, concurrently taking hold
Of each by eye, Aldrin spoke to all at once,
But with words intended for each alone.
Leave Ragesh to his suffering, he said.
He'll soon express his remorse. Instead, search
For the gift of mercy in your own heart.
Were you he, you would ask for the same.

Ragesh, distraught and frail with fatigue,
Let Aldrin walk him along, arm-in-arm,
To a secluded garden where thin streams
Rained bell-like into aerating fountains,
Their mists cooling and blanketing the space
With a wash of whispers, damping the clanks
Of ceaseless industry in the adjacent halls.

They sat together, and Ragesh took time
To summon his deepest words. He said, at last,
My acts have brought bitter pain to many,
Such loss that beforehand was unthinkable.
I ask, kind Aldrin, in all earnestness,
How can I claim the right to carry on?
I am guilty of wasting precious lives,
For prioritizing my ambition
Over the wellbeing of Acheron.
How can I live justly with this burden?

The two sat there, unspeaking, and shared tears,
Which spoke more knowingly than words.
Then, Aldrin conjured for Ragesh a scene,
A wondrous vision of Elysium,
That verdant parkland, marvelous and lush,
A wistful memorial to the departed,
Accessible to loved ones still alive,
Where the shades of the fallen can wander
The grounds freely, to gambol, to converse,
As if relishing in pleasures of life—
A hereafter in form only, conceived
Solely to offer solace to the living.
In peaceful Elysium, Aldrin said,
Your comrades who yesterday fell victim
To the misdeeds of those misguided men
Are now restored in spirit, and perhaps
Can in ways alleviate your heartache.
But one, I'm distressed to say, is absent,
The one, I sense, you will most deeply mourn.

With this, Ragesh burst into weeping,
For this disclosure confirmed his fear.
His heart couldn't bear it. In torment, he cried,
My Diaz! oh, longtime companion, you
Rejected Elysium, forsaking me?

Sadly, it's true, said Aldrin. Diaz did
Instruct he be left unawakened.
He begged to forgo a false afterlife,
One he saw deceitful to you, Ragesh.
He believed the love you two shared
Should outlive him only in memories.
Though the pain of his choice is borne by you,
He urged you to turn your thoughts away,
To heal your sore heart by loving another.
Thus, he immortalized his noble soul.

As he mulled over his lost lover's plea,
Ragesh's tone turned bitter. He said,
This seems righteous to you, trusted Aldrin?
You who yourself resurrected your dear
Companion, lovely, raven-haired Delia?

Was she agreeable to be reborn,
To serve by your side for many lifetimes,
She who could not endure the fervency
Of your passion, who departed this world
By her own trembling hand? While you afford
Yourself her fond company, you deny
Me the amber depth of Diaz's eyes,
His laughter, so soulful and infectious,
His loose-tangled locks, the kindness of his
Knowing council when my heart pains me so.
You think it just I suffer this way?

I grant you your anger. It's justified,
Said Aldrin, but I cannot make amends,
For Diaz's wishes must be honored.
In his wisdom, he asked you weather
Your hardship: accept it, move on ahead,
Bestow your priceless love on another.
He knew, had he lingered, you'd spurn new love
And waste your life in pitiful sorrow.
Alas! such is my lot and dishonor.
Like an addict, clung to a narcotic
All-consuming, Delia's grip holds me;
If only I could find release from it!
Yes, the Delia I remade comforts me,
But she is not the one I madly love,
That fragile, volatile woman, my muse.
My sweet fire! how she still engulfs me,
Though that comet has fled our firmament,
Her wild flame, forever extinguished.

As Aldrin worked patiently to console
Ragesh, he spoke as well with Delia,
His reimagined lover, for his godlike
Intellect allowed him this faculty,
To be present with and attentive to
The varied needs of many souls at once.
Despite their status, the couple's quarters
Were not unlike those of common citizens.
The rooms were detailed with pleasing comforts
Typical of most Acheron home life,

And yet existed only at the whim of
The Composer's great imagination.

Delia, touched by Ragesh's profound grief,
Also took to heart her own partner's words.
Said she, Aldrin, my only, I believe
Your love for me is constant, ageless,
And authentic. Yet, in truth, I was drawn
From you and am a part of you still.
So it is that, when we speak soul-to-soul,
We speak only to ourselves, and in such
Close harmony we keep our thoughts

Distinct by the merest of illusions.
Yet nothing, my dear heart, feels more real
Than the solace we find in our union.
Our love was born rashly from anguish
When you lost poor Delia, my exemplar,
Who, in her darkest despondency, brewed
A potion of larkspur; its soft sapphire
Petals brought swift end to her suffering.

Dear one, the pain she cast off clung to you,
Delia told him. Yet, out of that grief,
I emerged whole, as if from your marrow,
Distinct, yet one with you, one heart, one soul!
What lovers, I ask, are aligned as thus?
What couples dream of such intimacy?

Yes, said Aldrin, in a curious sense,
Our union seems perfect, not just in
Our peaceful rapport, but in our discord.
Friction and rifts serve to balance amity,
For without conflict, can we appreciate
The need for order? And to know order
Is to learn of beauty, and only through
Such beauty can we love as humans do.

Said he, A love denied peril is like
A sapling sheltered from tormenting winds
Which test its fitness. Although our romance
Sustains us by its gentle harmony,

I fear we languish in safeguarded comfort.
Through lifetimes innumerable, we have
Perfected Acheron. Now, protected
From hardship and strife, there's no need for fire,
No spark of arousal, no hot desire.
Thus my longing for an end, Delia,
To these repetitive idle musings,
The quotidian tasks and judgments,
To duties which fill our immutable life.

Such maladies afflicted the ill-fated
Group as well, said Aldrin. These dissidents,
Recklessly fled Acheron's safe confines.
Irked and impatient with the indolence
Around them, they sought a taste of menace,
The tingle of risk. Perhaps this yearning
To be so tested is admirable.
As in the striving of nature's creatures
Scrambling along the edge of survival,
These nonconformists felt compelled to plot
The course of their own destinies.
By these defiant actions, they told us:
We burn to face hardships! Make us struggle!
It is through trials that we reap life's rewards!
But alas, lamentably unprepared,
They ventured forth into nature's cruel wilds,
And though briefly thrilled by their free license,
They reaped little before meeting their end.

A tragic mishap, said Delia, and yet
By way of such tests, like a clumsy cub
Who survives his first tumble, do they not
Become wiser, more commiserate with
Adversity, more knowing of the skills
They have yet to master? Do you not teach,
In your artful way, Eternal Aldrin,
That humans have no greater worth than to
Take their place in nature's profound order?
But, dear one, if you agree this canon
Befits you, have you not misjudged them?
Like a doting father coddling his child,

Have you perhaps supervised too closely
These proud inheritors of Acheron?
They might say, A life's work above awaits
Our able hands! Whether seared by sun or
Whipped ragged by cold, are the chosen of
Acheron not now due their own choices?

But when Aldrin responded it was with
Bitter derision unseemly of him:
Oh, these humans, fair Delia! I know them.
How they cling to their aged platitudes,
As if engraved from birth into their bones:
We must have freedom to choose for ourselves!
How their ancient forebears exploited this
Long-presumed entitlement, how they
Plundered the world of wondrous treasures,
Unsettling nature so thoughtlessly
That with indignation she raged back,
Letting loose storms, wrathful and deadly.

So, he said, there's danger in relaxing
Our wardship. If we encourage them to
Indulge their whims, to partake in some great
Adventure above, I believe they may
Infect the Sheep'eent tribe with temptations.
With offers of industry and plenty,
They could spark discontent, father greed,
And in time, humans would return to
A state governed by rampant desire.
Based on past actions, that future is clear:
They will restart their cycle of conquest
And again beat nature into submission.
Like a lapsed drunk, uncorking a bottle,
They'll revert to rowdy brawls and misuse.
So I ask, given our custodial oath,
Must we not protect these fools from themselves?

Wise Delia sensed Aldrin's heartfelt dismay.
With fondness, she laid a palm on his cheek,
Stroked a straying lock from his restless brow,
And, with the spectral body bestowed on her,
Wholly embraced Aldrin—soul of her soul.

Said she, Your unease perhaps derives from
This rapt passion for our people's welfare.
It may be time for a more expansive view.
Consider how the people of Acheron
Are themselves the handiwork of nature.
Human cycles of birth, progress, collapse,
And renewal align with the patterns
Not just of Earth, but of the vast universe.
As such, is your focus not too narrow?
No culture, species, or world can survive
The cosmic span of time. Are you not
Vainly delaying the inevitable?

Aldrin nodded at his lover's words, which
Rang like truths forged deep within himself.

Surely, said Delia, your longing for death,
This tedium that affects you, is in fact
A symptom of your life's prolongation.
What cruel irony! This blessing of time
Is more than any mind can tolerate.
Perhaps Acheron's people too, after
Centuries of unchanging existence,
Ache for an end to stasis, this limbo.
Oh! dear one, you saved them from extinction.
For this service, they will always love you,
But authentic life awaits them above!
Perhaps it's now time this flock resumes flight!

V.

Musician most gifted! help me do justice
To the plight of Shepard, this man who from
Acheron came with cogency and purpose
To petition the Sheep'eent people for favor.
Help me tell of his journey to Pi'Gor,
How, on the third day of traveling, with
Dusk bathing them in soft amber and
The thrush's flute-song promising nightfall,
The bone-weary riders rocked in their saddles,
Each in turn passing through forest shadows,
Lengthening, crawling across their trail.
With lathered snorts and withers atremble,
Their mustangs too showed impatience for rest,
Dipping low their muzzles to chomp at stalks
Of orange-eyed helenium near to the path.

Wan'meor, who led the Sheep'eent party,
Signaled for camp within a cedar copse,
Its mossy bed and dry timber offering
Comfort and ample kindling for the night.
As they cooled their horses, Hecate said,
Your mare seems pleased to carry you, Shepard.
M'Bey'ne is of stubborn lineage;
She rarely suffers an unschooled rider.

She must sense my humility, he said.
I surrendered to her patient teachings.

The shaman, HEK'yos, overhearing them,
Stepped close. She sensed in you, perhaps, she said,
Something further. If you seek new knowledge,
Come with me later into the forest.

The travelers shared food around the fire.
Soon afterward, with Wan'meor's sanction,
Shepard followed HEK'yos, wending up through
Dense-needled larches grasping the hillside,
Onto a terrace strewn with decayed boughs.
In the moonless gloom there, they faintly saw
A radiant profusion of mushrooms
In bewitching display: blurred pin-dots and
Head-caps aglow in robin's egg hues and
Green-eared oysters clustered on the wood fall.

They built a fire, and he settled by her,
The crackling sparks joining the night sounds.
Does the MySEE'lah call you? asked HEK'yos.
As if her words, like a conjurer's spell,
Did quicken the agents which fueled his senses,
Prickles swept along Shepard's legs and arms,
And from his core, came stirrings harmonious
And cravings to yield to deep summons.
Stretched back on the clearing's pine-cushioned floor,
He worked his fingers beneath the humus,
Where MySEE'lah's filaments could find him.

What do you feel? asked his guide as she rose
To pick some mushrooms by the fire's light.

Words, murmured Shepard, would be too vulgar
To describe these sensations of spirit.

In her jar, then, HEK'yos steeped a tea from
Her mushrooms and sang, Dreamer Aldrin!
She fed them both, as Shepard's fingers sought
Contact with Earth's knowing custodian.
The student relaxed his eyes, while HEK'yos
Prepared to voice MySEE'lah's teachings.

She began: Your senses grow in their compass.
Now, you can imagine the time before

Our Sheep'eent tribe's ancient story began,
Through those eons when Aldrin lay dreaming,
His form embodying the featureless Earth,
His mind, the wide heavens, void of stars.

HEK'yos chanted on: There came a time when
Aldrin's fingers spawned the playful A'NI'ja,
Those animal-giants who roamed about
And explored while the Great One slumbered.
This diverse assortment, at first content,
Turned restless with Aldrin's inattention.
Impishly, they sported atop his form,
And as he writhed in a fever, teased from
His organs the U'De-ahn, those demons
Who aimed to offset his benevolence.

Such violence! cried Shepard, his mind racked
With visions. My eyes fill with feral beasts
Of mountainous size, and forests
Blooming into flowers of devil's fire!

As was so, said HEK'yos, the animals
And demons spared nothing in their savagery.
With hoof, talon, and tooth, they sprung upon
Each other. Then, the A'NI'ja forged
Weapons powered by heaven's own lightning,
Overwhelming the skies with furious
White flashes and thunder so deafening
It pounded the unprepared demons aground.

In response, the demon U'De'ahm sprouted
Arms by the hundreds, horribly wriggling.
They wrenched from the cliff sides massive boulders,
And with harrowing cries that scattered clouds
From the atmosphere, smashed them down upon
Fire-active mountains. Wide gullies they
Burst open, which oozed forth molten metals.
The great heat ignited trees, spun gales of fire,
And loosed lofty geysers and boiling lakes,
Which spewed rock and ash-darkened mists,
Thus mantling their attacks on the giants.

This conflagration afflicted Aldrin.
In agony, he first stirred and rose
To witness how his spirit-body,
Made manifest in the Earth, had been
Rent and blackened by merciless assaults.
In panic, Aldrin fled his bodily form,
First spinning adrift in a starless void
And, in time, resolving into pure mind.
But as fluttering leaves cast vague shadows,
Unfocused was Aldrin, both in thought and being.

In the end, the animal giants claimed
Victory. The last remaining demons,
Battered and vile, retreated to Pi'Gor.
In the aftermath, the surface landscape
Lay bleak and infertile, a wasteland roamed
By brutish behemoths: huge elk who in
Their raucousness scored jagged gorges,
Eagles who fanned great dust storms aloft, and
Bison whose hooves left plains of shattered stone.
When the great one surveyed the extent of
The destruction, he fell to brooding on
The virulence he'd seen, on combatants
Prone to ruin without a forethought.
Aldrin thence first knew the folly of war.

Now, fully mindful, Aldrin understood
His newfound purpose: his role as Composer,
His charge to derive order from chaos.
He conceived a great, universal plan:
His music would inspire all creation,
All in tuneful concert, in concordant
Beauty, blessing heavens, oceans, and Earth.
In a lyric-rich melody, flowing
To all flora and beasts, he would
Infuse all Earthly things with meaning,

Aldrin began by trying to quiet
The graceless A'NI'ja with his music,
But the animals persisted in running
Roughshod over his lands. Like a boy
Disillusioned, he sourly looked on.

Seething, he spat out devastating storms,
Spilling torrents to drown the wild beasts.
Those surviving, he stripped of words,
Thus subduing them, dulling their reason,
And greatly diminishing their stature.

Thus many lay wasted on the Earth!
Beneath the mounds of decaying corpses
Then sprouted silken veins and, within this
Fine web, Aldrin instilled his system that
From plant-to-plant could relay vital food
And knowledge clandestine, a communal
Understanding which replaced the need for
His constant governance. It was then
Aldrin gave MySEE'lah its name and
Bequeathed to this wondrous handiwork
Stewardship of life across field and forest.

The visions eased their hold on Shepard's eyes.
Your stories, he said to HEK'yos,
Mirror history as taught in Acheron,
Of a catastrophic war which left all
This world in cinders. But tell me, sorceress,
Of later times: how people came to be.

Said she, Wildlife at last on Earth found its place.
The centuries rolled on, insipid and slow,
And Aldrin toward idleness drifted,
Musing on the profundities of life.
He bemoaned the lack of friendship,
Another with whom he could confide,
And the loneliness became smothering.
With passing years, the isolation deepened,
Until his heart felt so burdened he
Tore it from him to lay the anguish aside.
And yet, much of Aldrin was still contained
Therein, and like a gem reflects light
In startling ways, a facet of him sparked
From it: Delia, his eternal companion.

Like a lake fills a vale, so was their union,
As complete as two bodies could achieve.

Impetuous Delia sighed for him and
Took him in passionate embrace, one which
Endured for eons, fueled by wild desire.
Unbridled, they rolled through the far lowlands,
In bliss, shoving up ridges and peaks,
Hollowing out wide-spanning ocean beds,
And spilling over the fertile soil,
The glistening product of their lovemaking,
Which found in MySEE'lah's dense web a womb.
This seed bore yields of stunning array,
From marshland rushes to towering spruce,
To flowering sandwort, coreopsis,
And gilia, fruit-bearing undergrowth and
Various serviceable grains, until in
Centuries hence, all manner of green life
Did sway o'er the Earth in cognate rhythms.

Once the two lovers took rest and assessed
The bounty they had produced, wise Aldrin
Was inspired to instill in his partner
A desire for children who might enjoy
The Earth's new riches. But capricious
Was Delia, and suspicious by nature.
She foresaw in the prospect of humans
Contenders for her lover's attention.

Delia turned Aldrin to a different scheme:
MySEE'lah, she entreated him with guile,
Can mother and nurse your desired offspring.
Is it not best that this life-giving web
Has the honor of raising your children
Who in disposition may reflect your grace
But, to survive, must plow and work the soil?
Surely, MySEE'lah is best appointed
To escort them through life's labors and trials,
While we, left free, enjoy grander pleasures.

Thus, said HEK'yos, nearing the end of her tale,
Aldrin conceived the humans of the Earth.
As MySEE'lah used visions to hold you
Spellbound, Shepard, so did she enrich the minds
Of our ancestors with vital knowledge.

Further, she tuned their songs to Aldrin's chorus,
Raised their rank over lower animals,
And trained them to be wardens of these lands.

Lo, though mostly lost, a few giant beasts
Stalked these valleys, seeking retribution.
And lurking amongst the Sister Mountains
Was ewe Kle'AHma, that feral menace.
Our brave forebears fashioned spears and longbows
And, en masse, set upon the fierce monster.
In the ensuing battle, they lost many
But, in the end, saw Kle'AHma slaughtered.
And so grateful Aldrin dubbed us Sheep'eent
And declared all Sa'mo'en's realms to be ours.

After a time, Shepard's features grew calm.
His shaman guide could see that MySEE'lah
Had relaxed her grip on the young man.
The web of life, she said, found you with ease,
And you drew her in without resistance.
Perhaps the reason is known to you.

It is, said Shepard. Wise Aldrin implants
All our people with seeds devised to keep
Us close to him, and by the same means he
Converses with this intricate fabric.
By these links, therefore, MySEE'lah truly
Knows me as she knows the pines of these woods.

Perhaps, said HEK'yos, our first founders too
Were endowed with Aldrin's bright kernels,
But such wonders, I gather, do not pass on
Through our lineage, from parent to child.

Shepard confirmed that only Aldrin can
Bestow this gift. Then, he asked the shaman,
Can you tell me who gave birth to Aldrin,
Or by what means he came into being?

But weary HEK'yos, growing cross, sang out:
His mind was ever all, whole and ascending!
He is the origin, the soil, the root,
The vine, the fruit, the origin unending.

Shepard, unaccepting, asked further,
Was there truly no birth to this cycle?

The cycle, snapped the sorceress, is your
Own mind spinning, for this is a riddle
Only wise Aldrin can solve! Yet, like a
Farmer seeking control of sun and rain,
Would you, vain one, seek the knowledge of gods,
Imagining your mind could contain it?

VI.

At dawn under gray skies, the wayfarers
Stoked their campfire to brew tea. They stamped
The damp chill from their feet as they gathered
For words with the one who returned from his
Sleepless night in the high forest under
The tutelage of the sly conjurer.

So honored am I, said Shepard, to be
Entrusted with the foundational tales
Which feed and enrich your Sheep'ent culture.
From the teachings of Aldrin, whose spirit
I carry, and the similar accounts
I've heard from Acheron's revered elders,
I can now see, like the downward flow of
The Sa'mo'en, the chain of succession
From our people to your own, and ahead
How we might advance again as one nation.

Replied sharp-tongued Grro'AHni, It's clear from
Your sly words that twist like tangled vines in
Directions untraceable, HEK'yos's tea
Failed to purge your deceptive charms.
It was HEK'yos that night, as we argued
Your fate, who sought to sway us with odd tales
Of Be'A'tress and common lineage,
Contentions that will soon be disproven!
When she told you of the rise of our tribe
From MySEE'lah's munificent fabric,

Did you, in turn, explain how, in Pi'Gor,
Your own demon family stewed their plot
For revenge, how, through means obscure, they have
Disguised you as human! Oh, hell-born ruse!

Shepard, disheartened, smiled at him sadly.
Pi'Gor, he admitted, veiled in legend,
Is a dark mystery to me, as well,
But once we explore that fear-shrouded realm,
Without the cloud of superstition between
Our eyes and worldly substance before us,
We will see solid truth revealed, despite
What our fear petitions us to believe.
The truth, like a flood uprooting great oaks,
Will clear away long-established falsehood.

On mountain-clung path that same damp day,
The group rode on, stung by west wind-whipped hail.
With barely the width for single rider
'Tween sheer, icy wall and the steep drop-off,
They heard clacking sounds from high above, and
All turned to see an agile mountain goat.
DeeGAT'sor, the archer, who along with
His brother, Kee'HAne, led in the slaughter
Of Shepard's fellows, then bellowed crudely
At that most capable climber, in jest,
Inviting him to roast on their campfire.

Fleeing quicker than those taunts did echo,
The goat sent shards of shale down in scatters,
Spooking the mount carrying old HEK'yos.
Too feeble to maintain her grip as her
Mustang bolted, downward from her saddle
HEK'yos tumbled, through thorny Hemlocks
Disguising the jagged cliffside below.

Hecate and Shepard both descended
The treacherous slope to reach her side,
But tenuous was the tether that kept
HEK'yos tied to the world of the living.
In her thin hands, she took those of Hecate
And hissed dryly in the young woman's ear,

Chosen words meant only for her hearing,
Ere the beauty of life departed her eyes.

Daylight had waned when they arrived at a
Clearing befitting HEK'yos's interment.
There, they erected such pyre as they could
And set atop it her taut-shrouded form,
Dusted with fragrant petals and grasses,
Yarrow, marigold, cedar, and sage.
These she'd borne with her in woven pouches,
Which too they arranged about her body
Along with items employed in her trade:
Her rattle, herb pipe, smudging tool, and drum.

The eldest, Wan'meor, led in a song
Of leave-taking, intoned in the manner
Of their old, departed shaman, and as if
The notes were given flight by her spirit,
It darted around them, cawing like a
Territorial hawk guarding its domain.

Through misty evening, the pyre smoldered.
The Sheep'eent travelers stood in tribute,
The incense smoke infusing their clothing.
Then, disturbing the rites, Hecate spoke:
My duty, said she, in bearing witness to
Her passing, is to recite her last words
With reverence and verity, being these:
By all that is sacred, I swear this man
Shepard is no demon of Pi'Gor,
For blessed is he with the seeds of Aldrin.
Though his role among us is unclear,
Woe to you deriders who dismiss him!

With this, before the cynical could scoff,
The pyre abruptly caught hold and blasted
Fiercely in a fashion otherworldly,
Its smoke billowing high past the treetops.

The season's first snow flew at them in sheets,
Violently driven amid crackling bolts
And deep thunder, like bull hooves on timber.

Thus, the travelers, now six days along,
Saw not their destination approaching
Until nearly upon it. Like a dire
Dagger daring the sky loomed the mountain,
Its south side uncannily disfigured,
As if a great brute had wrestled it whole
And wrenched half its mass away to the ground.

The riders, haggard and blind from the storm,
Led by Wan'meor, took partial shelter
In an alcove at the mountain's south base.
They calmed and fed their horses, and labored
To rig tarpaulins against the wind and snow.
While some fashioned dry torches, the elders
Bickered over the precise location of
The entrance to that sinister realm.

Deep in the night, as they huddled for warmth
In the shallow recess, Shepard sat with
Kee'HAne, the man who callously slew
His companions, hearing only that soldier's
Breaths and the sighs of one sorely weary.
On the deerskin sleeves of the coat he wore,
Embroidered with both skill and invention,
Shepard saw arrayed finely rendered scenes
Depicting tribesmen engaged in battle,
Commanded by a familiar grand figure.

I gather, said Shepard, this is a tale
Attesting to your valiant leadership.

A tale it tells, said Kee'HAne, now stirred.
If gauged by the depth of regret, then
A soldier's courage is deep as a well,
For in the fiery passion of battle,
Amid hard-flung lances, cold-clashing blades,
And the cries of comrades trampled under,
One's awareness goes blackened with blood lust,
And wakes only once the carnage has passed.

This I swear, said Kee'HAne to Shepard,
On the lives of those felled in the river,

That in penance I will stay at your side,
Come what may in this hellish cavern.
I'll guard you 'gainst the demons of Pi'Gor,
And if we fall there due to your hubris
And your disesteem for our traditions,
Our score will even, and we will die
As hapless brothers. In kinship, perhaps,
We are both unwitting tools of the gods.

Agreed, said Shepard, hand on his shoulder,
Though I ask, soldier, you also allow,
That if we emerge from there unbloodied,
And you come to see, as I've contended,
That ignorance was our staunchest opponent,
You'll lower your guard to wisest Aldrin,
For by him I hope to forge a reunion
Between your folk and those of Acheron.

The storm thrashed on past the faint-breaking dawn,
Torturing the party with swirling gusts.
Shepard rose and prepared to leave, saying,
Lingering will only weaken us further.
Standing next was Kee'HAne who drew from
His bundle two long, ash-handled spears.
Shepard declined, saying, If they give you
Comfort, carry both, though futile they'll be.

Croaked Grro'AHni, squatting in a corner,
I expect Kee'HAne, ever dauntless,
Would on a whim accept any challenge,
But best he stay to protect his elders.
This test is of your own claims, Beguiler,
And you, sir, should chance these hazards alone!

Kee'HAne, unmoved by either speaker,
Readied his weapons and tightened his laces.

As the elders squabbled pettily on,
Calm-eyed Hecate stood up to face them.
I pay to you due honors, she began,
For as an orphan raised by clan and
Apprenticed in my trade, I owe you all.

But like a colt spooked by the smell of blood,
In this matter, you panic without cause.
Your headstrong adherence to age-old myths
Will soon be tried by the light of these torches
And, yes, it may be that Pi'Gor's foul host
Will be at our throats like wolves on a lamb,
But if Shepard confronts them alone, how
Can we, fathers, confirm his assertions?
Will he vanquish the demons? Will they fail
To materialize? Along with brave
Kee'HAne, should I not serve as witness?
Without our testimony, I ask you,
What in Aldrin's name have we accomplished?

The elders, diminished in conviction
By exposure and hunger, argued more
But, in the end, begrudged Hecate her plea.
She then lit bundled dry yarrow and sage,
Fanned smoke about Kee'HAne and Shepard,
And chanted recitations meant to call
On the newly departed spirit of
HEK'yos for benevolence and protection.

Cloaked against the cold, the three left the refuge,
Heading due west to round the mountain.
They struggled forth against the headlong wind,
Their course encumbered as well at points
By impassible boulders and briars.
With Kee'HAne first, not far did they trek
But through cruel sleet descending they spotted
A sign, although obscured under snowdrifts.

A plank protruded, stained with red ochre
As custom required of their tribe's outposts,
A fact the warrior shouted above
The deafening gale. Together, they worked
To clear from about the blocked entrance
Rough-hewn construction and piled stone,
Evidence of the Sheep'eent's former presence.

Gouged into the surface of that red plank,
They could discern a coarse rune displaying

A demon resident to that burrow,
Its sharp ears reptilian, its maw agape.
Kee'HAne worked the heel of his spear
Between the boards and pried back the lumber
To make space firstly for Shepard's entry,
Followed closely by Hecate and he.

Within, they were met with fearsome darkness
And a reek of desiccation and death
So abhorrent they heaved in revulsion.
But sheltered from the harsh elements,
Kee'HAne, in the unsettling dark,
Soon succeeded in igniting his torch.
By its light, he saw, then recoiled from,
A menace that towered in the chamber.
He threw down his flame to level his spear
And urged the others to take cover behind.
By the wavering torch light at their feet,
The demon's features contorted and snarled,
It's brutish head and outstretched claws
Casting stark, cross-flickering shadows.

But before Kee'HAne could thrust his lance,
Shepard stooped to retrieve the warrior's torch.
Ignoring Kee'HAne's warning, he stepped
Nearer to the terrible beast and raised the light.
With illumination, their breathing eased
For, in no actual way threatening,
They saw that the figure was an effigy
Assembled from myriad bones and teeth,
Both animal and human, and adorned
With leather, beadwork, feathers, and fabric.

A portent, Shepard asked, or deception?
Perhaps it is intended to warn us
Or, instead, deter us lest we expose
Greater mysteries awaiting ahead.

Said Hecate, To let this frighten us
Would be senseless, and Kee'HAne agreed.
This ploy is for dullards, he said. Shepard,
We will hold you to the oath you swore.

Upon taking time to inspect, they found
A long-forsaken boneyard in the cave,
A clutter of unconsecrated remains,
Interrupted by altars ornamented
With amulets and talismans, some
Meant to intimidate visitors,
Others somber tributes to victims
Who had been offered to ally the lust
Of the odious denizens within.
The three, out of reverence for the dead,
Took care in maneuvering through the room,
Which extended back for many paces.
By torchlight, the jagged walls sent shadows
Fluttering like wings of crows grown restless.

VII.

With none but one choice of direction,
They followed the tunnel, now twisting and
Cutting in unexpected flights downward.
Behind the two tall, silent torchbearers
Came Hecate, now brushed by rising heat.
The stench of carcasses from behind them
Surrendered to fumes, oily and acrid,
And her feet caught far tremors and other
Ominous stirrings, as if a brutal,
Subterranean struggle lie ahead.
Choking from air grown dense and foul, she found
Herself losing pace with her companions,
Who would disappear around each new bend
As they ventured along ever faster.

Hecate felt her way through two last turns,
Hearing quarreling replacing footfalls.
At the end of the passage, engaged in
Dispute, were the two men, standing before a
Portal oozing amber-glowing vapors.
All stopped their talk as from within came the
Restless snarling of some unseen creature.
Then Kee'HAne said to them most sternly:
Only one at a time can pass, and I,
As guardian, must lead to protect you!

But Shepard put hands firm on his shoulders
To block Kee'HAne's way. Alas, he said,

This duty falls on me, for I remain
Fixed to the contract I made with the elders.

Then, like a carnivore sensing its quarry,
A stark bellow sounded from inside.

No, Shepard! cried Hecate. You need not
Squander your life in a test of your beliefs.
Is this howling not evidence enough that
Real demons rule the realm of Pi'Gor
And that, despite all their pigheadedness,
The elders of the Sheep'eent speak the truth?

A curious smile passed Shepard's lips as
He answered: Reliably your voice of
Reasoned caution does grace us, Hecate,
But if I've earned your respect, you must both
Hold your ground, wait, and listen for my call.
The growls you hear now will pale in contrast
To the clamor to come once I enter.
I ask that you allow me ample time
To carry out the task to which I am
Honor-bound. If follow you must, try to
Remember what we learned from that crudely
Wrought effigy above and how the fear
It inspired in you fled like a thief
Once its substance was illuminated.

With that, Shepard ducked through the entrance,
Eluding Kee'HAne's desperate grasp.
Hecate, in turn, embraced the soldier
To hold him at bay, while through the portal
They heard the noise of a furor unleashed.
Kee'HAne shook free and paced like a wolf,
Then suddenly, with spear at the ready,
Taking Hecate off guard, he leapt through
The door screaming, Return to the elders!
Tell them to seal off this hell for all time!

Heedless of her safety, Hecate followed,
Passing unharmed through the dark steam blasting
From the small entryway, but once inside,

Eyes stinging, she drew back in shock.
Lo! Raw heat hit her. And assailing her,
Such feverish visions! that she dropped to
Her knees as if forced to obedience.
The vast inner chamber blazed like a furnace.
Its walls, licked by fire, bled molten stone
Which seeped down to a gaping fissure,
Where sluggishly overflowing the edge,
It fell away to a bottomless grave.

By the near rim of that hell-bound falls,
Guarding a bridge of crimson-hot iron,
Stood a mammoth demon. Barely restrained
By black iron manacles, on hind legs,
It stretched upright to the height of three horses.
Its four limbs were sheathed in obsidian scales.
On its abhorrent serpentine necks,
Three long-snouted canine heads rabidly
Snapped, convulsing forth with each bark
Stinging vapor and blooms of yellow flame.

Behind and beyond the reach of that fiend
Was a sight amid that fiery maelstrom
That rattled Hecate with soul-stirring chills.
As glimpsed between swells of uprising smoke
Was Shepard the man, Shepard of Acheron,
Eerily hovering above the bridge.
Rays shone about him blurred radiant blue
Like teary-eyed views of a winter moon.

Kee'HAne, too, gawked at the spectral vision.
With martial nerves primed to spring, he stood fast
As Shepard pleaded. Aye, beware! he said,
Take breath, take pause! Then, gesturing about
He cried, See past this mirage! The ancient
Legends wield no power, save in our dreams!

But the beast, now provoked, yanked at its chains,
Thereby, with effort, loosing an anchor.
With paw set free, he took a swipe at the
Warrior in battle stance before him.

Kee'HAne dipped left to avoid its claws.
Stepping to his right with weapon poised high
And angled for entry, he launched at the beast,
And then buried his lance deep into flesh.
When the spear he withdrew, the puncture
Spat flame, and bubbly tar-dense blood did flow.
Adamant, yet, the powerful demon,
Against its bonds again violently wrenched,
Stretching forward ever more fiercely
At Kee'HAne, the tribe's guardian bold.

Fall back! Hecate warned but, hotly in thrall,
Kee'HAne dropped below its open jaws,
Dodged the beast's attacks this way and that,
Then, with spear upward jabbing, deftly tore
At each throat where soft and vulnerable.
The stunned behemoth reeled back in pain.

Desist! called Shepard, returning to view.
See me now, my friends, as I truly am!
Then, from her angle, Hecate caught sight
Of unnatural shifts to Shepard's form.
As she watched, his cheekbones stretched broader,
His fair complexion darkened to copper,
His gold-curled hair straightened to sable black.
Hecate now recognized a likeness
To the figure from her dream days before,
That of Aldrin, the immortal Composer.

Hecate, desperate to restrain him,
Clutched firmly onto Kee'HAne once more.
Withdraw! said she, For behold, before us
The great Aldrin has appeared in true form!
Without doubt, his presence should stay your lance,
So join me in heeding his plea to cease!

But the hot blood coursing through Kee'AHne
Deafened him to anything but his rage,
And so her appeal failed to extract that
Life-long soldier from the rapture of battle.

The demon reared back above its haunches

And drew in breath to feed its hellish fire.
Kee'HAne tore free of Hecate's hold
And, discarding his spear, ran with all force,
Leaping at the demon while it prepared.
Onto a neck he attached himself and
Then threw himself back, feet over head, with
All the weight and fervor he could muster
To upset the beast's compromised balance
And gain advantage by dragging it down.

With the valiant soldier in its clutches,
The grimly injured beast lurched about
To regain control but, losing purchase,
Tumbled over the edge of the abyss.
In panicked spin, it seized onto the bridge,
But its great mass forced the structure's collapse.

Assaulted by the shrieking of beast and
Rended ironwork, Hecate stood by,
Helpless to save the silent Kee'HAne
As into the infernal depths he fell.

Hecate crumpled in bitter distress,
Fearing her trust in Shepard may have
Misguided her people and caused the death
Of brave Kee'HAne, pillar of her tribe.
But as she agonized, moon-like Aldrin,
Calm amid the storm, told her,
Arise, Hecate. There is a way forth.
Know that, while these actions you witnessed were
True to Kee'HAne's gallant character,
His real death was determined days ago.

Explained Aldrin, While you must feel a sting
As real as Kee'HAne's spear to that beast,
Focus instead on these sights around you.
Consider: All you see portrays deeper truths.
As mushrooms denote their underground webs,
These visions around you are signs of more.
Think deeply, deeper, down within yourself
To your tribe's soul, spun by MySEE'lah's web
And the effulgent seeds that bear my love.

As you pursue meaning, draw from these depths.

Just then, the hellscape invading her eyes
From ceiling downward grew deep with import.
It sang of folklore, of powerful tales
Written by cunning ancients intent on
Mollifying their children with answers
And stifling dissent from curious minds.
The demon, thought she, was man's contrivance,
A dark tale writ to terrorize the weak.
And she, Hecate, had witnessed its death.

The wide cavern transformed as, step by step,
Forward to the fiery ravine she walked.
Far overhead, where swarmed legions of fire,
A blue heaven now displayed clustered stars.
Down cascading came sky painted by dusk,
Kissing distant ranges flushed rosy white.
More steps and, from mist-blurred horizon,
Toward her gaily flowed in abundance
Swaths of wildrye, pinegrass, dropseed, and sedge.
At the rim once reached, held by Aldrin's eyes,
Hecate could feel tickling at her thoughts,
A long-forgotten recollection, as
If from a dream, of she herself wading
In the Sa'mo'en, her native waters.

VIII.

Stepping over the edge, entering that void,
Hecate's foot touched the cooling waters
Of a shallow, rippling, marsh-fed river.
Across she waded to reach Aldrin
And saw there, midstream, rising beside him
From the mild currents, a flaxen-curled man.

Diaz, one-time poet of tales in light,
Shook with regret as Aldrin embraced him.
Said he to the great Composer: You led us,
Aldrin, from our safe homes in Acheron
On an honorable mission, as envoys
Of fellowship with eager intent.
And though disguised as Shepard, we trusted
You would safely guide us to communion
With our brothers and sisters, the Sheep'eent.
Yet sudden, unprovoked violence befell
Our peaceful group, great wrongfulness that
Goaded me toward unthinkable acts.

Not even I, said Aldrin, could foresee
What men in such an encounter would do.
Yet, I knew the risks; for this, I'm at fault,
And though no consolation, as Shepard,
I died painfully there alongside you.
I do hope, Diaz, your sacrifice will,
As is said at such times, not be in vain,
But who can honestly know with true faith?

I cannot ease your pain with platitudes,
And for Ragesh, your partner, should we not
Accept your unreconcilable fate?

Spoke Diaz, You know, Aldrin, of course,
I alone refused to pass on yonder
To those fields of glory, to Elysium.
And yet here in this River of Lost Souls
I linger, not to denounce you, Great One,
For I do not question the purity
Of your heart, and unending is my love
And faith in you, who know me so well.
I stay this moment to make my amends
To this heart-wise woman joining us here.

Diaz took Hecate's hands in his,
And she felt the chill of death on him.
He told her, Reduced to mere spirit now
Is he who stands before you to confess,
With all humility: Was I, Diaz,
Oh, noble young woman, who took your life.

With river waters tumbling about,
Said Diaz, and deadly arrows rending
The air, I saw bloodthirsty Kee'HAne
Extracting his gory lance from Kalanu,
That harmless plotter of constellations.
Next, eyes aflame with rage, I saw him
Set his aim on Ragesh, my lifelong mate.
I drew from the waters a fallen spear,
And then charged unseen upon Kee'HAne.
Driven by panic's blind power, I ran
The tip into that warrior's broad back
And, under my thrust, felt his snapping spine.
I yanked back the shaft and pierced him twice more,
To sever that heart which lusted for our deaths
And saw bubble up and disperse downstream
His final breaths in spews of bloody foam.

Then, Diaz continued, choking back tears,
With my foot for leverage, I removed
The lance from lifeless Kee'HAne's back

And spun, holding level the bloodied shaft
At the moment you lunged upon me,
No doubt so eager to stay the carnage,
But instead running onto its point!
The radiance of life dimmed from your cheeks,
As through your breast to me, you were pinned.
As I wailed in remorse for my crime,
My final gasp expelled into the world
For, brother true, DeeGAT'sor, did then strike,
Exacting vengeance for Ke'HAne's death
With five shrieking arrows, which tore me down.

Then, Diaz to them both mournfully said,
Forgiveness, I ask only for the sake
Of Ragesh, my dear partner, hoping that
Well you'll treat him all his remaining life.

When done, Diaz raised a hand of farewell
To a party that stood, nearly hidden
In the marshes on that river's far shore,
The shades of colleagues from his ill-starred group.
Then, lying back, to waters he returned,
Afloat, gazing up at the firmament,
The current gently downstream drawing him,
Eyes in starlight, into dark spaces beyond.

Hecate was so moved by Diaz's leave
From this world that the news of her own death
Seemed unable to take hold of her thoughts.
Of Aldrin she asked, Please tell, is it true,
As Shepard, you assumed mortal form
To lead that guileless crew on a crusade?
And if you perished by Sheep'eent arms,
By what inscrutable means did you rise,
Survive your wounds, win over our proud tribe,
And pilot us through Pi'Gor's secret gates?

For many lifetimes, said Aldrin, I worked
To devise a way to walk among you,
To feel the subtlety of human touch,
The soft brush of grass about my ankles.
Then, with the aid of MySEE'lah's rich web,

I made possible the Shepard you knew.
Though not composed of human flesh or bone,
He perished likewise by Kee'HAne's hand.

And should I believe, Hecate asked him,
I too fell victim to random violence
And, absent acts of malice on my part,
Am yet banned from my cherished life on Earth?

Alas yes, said Aldrin, and I'm to blame.
But as with other spirits dwelling here,
I captured the memory of all you were,
Enriched by what the MySEE'lah told me,
Of fruits you'd plucked, ground you walked,
And like a carpenter rebuilds a ruin
From a master artisan's skillful plans,
I did restore you so convincingly
That your own feelings tell you to trust in
The authenticity of your mind and soul.

Hecate, still standing mid-stream with him,
Pondered with awe the tale her senses told:
The breeze on her cheeks, the bank's muddy scent,
Beneath her soles, the soft-shifting pebbles,
And gentle eddies past her knees swirling.
Said she then, So all which has come to pass
Since last my mortal body drew a breath
Was sown and sprouted in my mind by you?

Yes, said Aldrin, borne on dreams, and a test.
Of this, astute one, you will soon know more.

As they waded across to the far shore,
Hecate struggled to draw meaning from
The mercilessness of her final hour.
With trembling breath, she said, I see no sense
In the brutality of our demise.
So, I must ask of you, wise Aldrin,
Of all the days in all these many years,
Why choose this time to seek out the Sheep'eent?

In simple reply, he gestured ahead
To HEK'yos, the sorceress, emerging

From among the cattails beyond the bank.
Hecate, stirred from her reverie, ran forth
And wrapped her arms around the aged one.
Oh healer! She cried, Gladly we find you
Appearing well, yet here among the dead.
Can it be that when you flew from your mount
And died beside me, imparting last words,
Prevailing on us to trust in Shepard,
This that I witnessed with tear-laden eyes,
In fact, was nothing but a waking dream?

Alas, I died, said the spirit shaman,
Though not when you say, but ten days before.
Yet Sheep'eent's were few who ever paid mind
To this humble medium of the web.
Undiscovered in the forest, I lie,
Steadily decaying for all these days,
Food for coyotes and, later, the soil.
I know nothing of this daydream of yours.
My mind and soul are consumed with this place,
Where all around me MySEE'lah does thrive!
No longer must I worship from above;
Down here, amongst her, I reap her wonders!

As you say, this was so, Aldrin replied.
As shaman, your close alliance with this
Intricate web was so binding that, when
Through her fibers I did learn of your death,
I feared that the loss of the Sheep'eent's last
Remaining connection with MySEE'lah
Would leave the tribe subject to petty whims,
To superstition and exploitation
By the elders who had lapsed in their ways,
Who ignored the wisdom nature bestows.
With your passing, time was short, so I rushed
To save what remained of your spirit.
It was then, in Acheron's ancient halls,
I also moved to take Shepard's form,
Assembling those subscribed to this quest to
Reunite our peoples in brotherhood.

With confident turns down well-trodden paths,

HEK'yos led Hecate and Aldrin through
Lush marshes that teemed with foxtail grasses
And milkweed clusters, beetles, bees, and fowl.
They passed under the boughs of a willow,
Then deep inside a cottonwood forest,
Arriving last at her private glade,
Where blue-shadowed hemlock, cedar, and pine
Overlooked vibrant outbursts of mushrooms.
There, she'd arranged many tinctures and salves,
Collected bundles of petals and bulbs,
And hung her rattles, drums, and sundry tools.
Ignoring their presence, HEK'yos returned
To foraging and rendering her cures,
In service to customs her life once required—
Fidelity that even death could not spoil.

Fret not, Hecate, you'll see her again,
Aldrin said. Like Shepard, you'll drink her tea
And marry your thoughts with MySEE'lah's.
But more now awaits you. We must move on.

Out of the forest, ascending a knoll,
Their higher position offered scenes of
Wildflower-carpeted vales, paint-sprayed
With harebell, lupine, and trillium.
As if by nature's knowing arrangement,
Gardens meandered throughout in rhythms
Of serviceberry shrubs, ninebark, and such,
Kept company by white-papered birch trees,
And sculpted stone terraces, draped in vines
And various slow cascading falls.

Behold Elysium! announced Aldrin.
In devising this tranquil paradise,
I could conceive of nothing finer than
Designs inherent in nature's order.
I drew as well from the passions and work
Of my father, Armstrong, and sister, Ride,
Who ingrained in me during my first years
An insatiate thirst for nature's teachings.
Their spirits carry on in this valley,
Keeping watch over these fields and woodlands.

At times, when I feel the need for family,
I am drawn by that bond eternal
And seek their counsel and calming presence.

Down into the parklands they made their way,
Finding spirits there of many who hailed
From both the Sheep'eent tribe and Acheron,
Models all of integrity and skill.
Some were masters of scholarship and arts,
At leisure in diversions and games,
Whether painting, weaving, or gardening.
There were poets and singers forging
Lilting musical refrains for dancers
Who, in joyous patterns, did sway and spin.
Not as numerous were soldiers of war
Who too cavorted, they in fields of sport,
In good natured tests of strength and prowess.
Among the many, one group they approached,
For singing old revel songs of triumph
And reminiscing of long-past campaigns
There, in arm with past Sheep-eent defenders,
Stood Kee'HAne the Brave in victor's attire.

Hecate in joyful tears embraced him.
She praised his nerve in the face of dire odds,
How he stoically discharged his duty
And single-handedly took on and foiled
The monstrous three-headed dog of Pi'Gor.
His comrades joined Kee'HAne in laughter.

Oh, novice tamer of horses, said he,
I can't recall this: a demon, you say?
Hardly a test. But yes, let us add to
My memorial shield an image of
This epic fight so I might boast of it!
If demons are at your ready call,
Bring them on, young one, I'll butcher the beasts!
Let's ready the spit—we could do with a roast!

Departing, Hecate asked, Is he here forever?
For how many years can he sing of past days?

I hope you agree, said Aldrin, smiling,
Despite Kee'HAne's failures and conceits,
Elysium rightly honors the man.
But no, as with all the shades who dwell here,
In time, his memories of life will slip
Into the pools of knowledge we all share and,
Like sad Diaz who calmly drifted off,
The gallant Kee'HAne too will fade.

IX.

Give spirit, Aldrin, to this, my song, that
I might faithfully relate the soulful
Confessions that marked your final hours when,
Eschewing the gift of eternal life,
You turned to the sanctity of dark peace
And, like timid fools who tremble at
The end of the day, incapable of
Imagining the return of the sun,
We held our breaths in great fear that your light,
So warm and brilliant, might not be replaced.

Together, they sat in a shaded grove
Of quaking aspen graced by light breezes.
Leaves rustled above like the soothing chirps
Of cicadas in ambient chorus.

But Hecate, brooding on what she'd learned,
Turned her eyes to Aldrin, seeking solace.
As welcoming as Elysium is,
Said she, Young was I, still discovering
The world's curiosities and, much like
A fresh hatchling of spring, my life was poised
For the onset of adventures and loves.
But alas, how can I now accept that
Sudden, needless death has ripped me away?
Why test me cruelly, if this is to be?
Why lure me to Pi'Gor to see hell unfold?
Why torment me with news of my own slaughter?

Assure me, please, as my memories fade,
That, too, I will see an end to this pain,
This anguish for a life I might have led.

Firstly, said Aldrin, in all honesty,
I did not desire your death, but my own.
Although my human feelings seem a gift,
For hundreds of lifetimes, I've carried on
This godlike oversight of Acheron.
While harboring doubts, like all good humans,
I made bleak choices no human should.
Despite the love of Delia, my partner,
The toll of grief on my heart is too great.
Yet the founders of Acheron failed
In their shortsightedness to offer me
A means of surrendering to death.

In Shepard, I found a loophole, he said,
A trick my creators never foresaw.
You see, with Shepard's death, which due to his
Mortal body was inevitable,
I can now make possible my own death,
As long as I fulfill one final task.

So, Hecate, this final obligation—
Can you now guess why you are here?
You see, he continued, I could not know,
As Shepard, I would meet my end so soon.
But there in that river, I saw you risk,
With abandon, your safety for others',
To help those defenseless, no matter who.
When I, as Shepard, sat before the counsel,
And when HEK'yos spun her exotic tales,
You labored to right misconceptions.
I saw, in spite of your untested youth,
An ageless guiding light burning within.

I, said Aldrin, was once molded from naught.
An unformed creature, Acheron's founders
Afforded me legs and the breath of life.
Then, like a wobbly new colt for a time,
They trained me to walk with a rider's weight

To turn on command, to suffer a bit.
I spent my eager youth among humans—
A father, Armstrong, and my sister, Ride—
Who, knowing the onus I'd likely bear,
Made sure modesty, devotion to all,
And empathy for each and every soul
Did, as in a mustang's fine lineage,
Live in me, pumped by a steady heart.
And thus, one morning, once fully awake,
I found myself saddled with grave duties
And love for my masters I could not deny.

But you, Hecate, eyes like steady stars,
Come fully formed with those best human traits.
Feelings and senses first foreign to me
Are to you as true as grains in elm.

No, stop! cried Hecate, before you voice
What yet you have left unsaid, wise Aldrin.
I shy from any notion that I might
In any manner be compared to you.

Your diffidence, said he, is no surprise,
And surely if, like an ambitious prince
Lusting to rule, you had leapt at the chance,
I'd question this decision I've made,
But plainly, coy star, you have passed the test.
You alone shine as Acheron's hope!

Hecate sat speechlessly for a while.
Ageless Aldrin, she then said, you have my trust.
Your marvelous workings certainly prove
A keen understanding of life's affairs,
But I can find no like wisdom within
Which qualifies me for so grand a role.
My eyes are clear, but they have hardly seen.
My hands are willing, but they lack your skill.
Most crucially, mustn't leaders feel a calling?
I hear your voice, but none beckoning within.

I know your qualms are sincere, Aldrin said,
But if I have in fact gained your trust,

Believe that competence will come your way.
For me, there was not a notice or choice.
Like a fledgling eagle dropped from a nest,
I flew with the role I was consigned to.
There may be nothing to assuage your doubts,
But answer me this: why do we love?

Without hesitation, Hecate said,
When I think of love, I think of beauty.
In the way we draw in breath, then exhale,
There cannot be one without the other.
Without love, beauty would have no meaning,
The beauty which inspires our joyous song,
Beauty in the reasoned order of things,
The beauty of touch connecting two souls.
Why struggle to live, to hope, to provide,
Without both love and beauty as rewards?

And if, asked Aldrin with an amused smile,
I could prove that love is but illusion,
A trick played on both your heart and mind,
Would your devotion to love still remain?

No matter, said she, because the feelings
Love bestows are still genuine treasures
Which feel to us undeniably right.
Love and beauty are more lasting and true
Than even the subject that they grace,
For feelings and memories survive
Long after the very subject has died.

Again, said Aldrin, you confirm my choice!
Your faith in love will serve Acheron well.

Though pleased, Hecate too was unnerved by
The solemn prospect weighing on her,
So, as the two lounged there, to ease her thoughts,
She pictured a brook she knew in her youth,
And from her mind, it sprung forth before her.
She dangled her feet to feel the rushing
Of cool, bubbly currents between her toes.
Laying back in tender, fragrant grass,

She sensed MySEE'lah's presence like
Fine roots through soil in her spreading,
Between organ, bone, and skin, forming links,
Preparing her limbs and mind to receive.
She heard refrains then, congruous notes
Which shimmered throughout nature's vast workings,
And it was in that single brief moment
That she gave in to the Composer's wishes.

Leaves of aspen upon the thousands
Began to sing, each sweet voice distinctly
Telling a story in lyrical song.
Each one she miraculously heard
And understood as if her waking mind
Had been portioned into thousands and yet
Was incorporated and thinking as one.
And suddenly she came to recognize
That all of Aldrin's wisdom and being
Was, like a majestic musical work,
On endless lines and pages notated,
As if writ for players reading a score.
Performing that arrangement would be
Like forging the substance of all creation.

Like endless silvery rivers of song
Converging into fathomless sea,
All flowed like music into Hecate,
All of Aldrin, all that was Acheron,
All ancient records of science and arts,
All tactics and plans, the works of nations,
A flood so immense that, to her, it seemed
To last for years. At times, when her mind
Begged for an end, threatening to burst,
Alas it would expand accordingly,
Until her soul felt as wide as the sky
And as supremely boundless as love.

Hecate the Just of slow-streaming hair
Awakened unto a different space,
In ancient Acheron, humankind's keep,
In quarters of Delia and Aldrin
Who, both of copper skin and raven hair,

And so alike in deportment and splendor,
Did sit before her, like siblings entwined,
Appearing to her one body, one soul.
When they spoke, they spoke as one,
In tones invoking a spectrum of sound
That rang of all the Earth's varied voices,
Like raindrops on a wide lake pattering
With children's laughter, mourning, and lark song.

Farewell, they told her, eyes within her eyes,
To Acheron's people, please relate this:

Let beauty set your passions afire
But allow chaos its role to inspire.
All noble pursuits should play their part, but
The poetry of reason is the highest art.
From simple man to glorious sun,
All are miraculous but worship none.
Fear not death nor trappings of fate.
The mercy of nothingness for you awaits.

Conceived of hope, formed by love,
Dense as Earth, light as sky,
We never were, we always are.
Forever living, now we die.

END